THREE DIVERS DEEP

A Donald Youngblood Mystery

THREE DIVERS DEEP

KEITH DONNELLY

HUMMINGBIRD BOOKS
Kingsport, Tennessee

Hummingbird Books
A division of Harrison Mountain Press
Kingsport, TN 37660

Designed by Todd Lape / Lape Designs

Library of Congress Cataloging-in-Publication Data available

ISBN 978-0-9993667-7-6

Printed in the United States of America
by Maple Press, York, Pennsylvania

To Tessa,
Miles behind us, miles to go, love forever

Prologue

The Halloween bachelor party was held at an expensive Upper East Side penthouse apartment owned by the firm of one of the groom's friends. *Who has a bachelor party on Halloween?* Bentley thought. *Well, maybe in some weird way, it's appropriate.*

The party was well under way when Bentley arrived. Twenty of New York's young Turks in the financial world had chipped in sizable sums to make it a party to remember. A handful of beautiful young women circulated. None were wives or girlfriends.

Bentley, Bent for short, planned on staying a reasonable length of time, sufficiently teasing the groom, and then quietly making his exit. Parties were not his thing. He preferred intimate gatherings of eight or fewer. He accepted a beer from the bartender and made the rounds, his dark good looks not lost on the ladies. He deflected a couple of advances, leaving them wondering if he might be gay. He wasn't.

"Looks like you could get lucky tonight, Bent," Garrett said. Garrett was the organizer, the groom's best man.

"Not my style," Bentley said.

Bentley had a gal pal—a friend, not a fiancée, a driven career woman who, two or three times a week, liked to get together for dinner and sex. He liked their arrangement.

"You need to lighten up, Bent," Garrett said. "You're too serious."

Bentley knew Garrett was right. He was serious—serious about making money and the power that came with it. Not much else mattered to him.

"I'm going to say hello to Wells and then slip out," Bentley said, ignoring Garrett's comment. "I'll see you in the office on Monday."

Bentley started to move away when Garrett grabbed his arm. Getting near to Bentley's ear, Garrett said, "Don't leave before the belly dancer does her thing."

"Right, the belly dancer." Bentley had almost forgotten.

"It won't be long," Garrett continued. "She's already here. She's changing in the master bedroom, and she's an eyeful."

"Calm down," Bentley said. "You're gay, remember?"

"Maybe not tonight." Garrett laughed giddily.

Bentley was intrigued. The only time he had ever seen a belly dancer was in the movies, and he couldn't even remember what movie. And if Garrett thought she was hot, well, she must be smoking. *Might be worth sticking around*, he thought. He got another beer and went to harass the groom, Wells Finley.

◆ ◆ ◆ ◆

Fifteen minutes later, a single chair was placed in the middle of the large living area, and the guests either hugged the walls or retreated to the bar. They waited with eager anticipation. Wells was led to the chair and ordered to sit. He had a bewildered look on his face, knowing what was to come would be embarrassing. Then the music started, a haunting, seductive melody that was decidedly Middle Eastern. The faint sound of finger cymbals got louder as they grew nearer.

"Ladies and gentlemen," Garrett announced, "the lovely Lola."

She came dancing out of the hallway and down a step into the sunken living area. Bentley felt a jolt somewhere inside him. She was gorgeous, about five feet six inches of perfect curves, dark, curly hair to her shoulders, olive skin, and flashing, dark eyes. She was maybe twenty-five, possibly thirty. She danced around the chair, belly and hips moving effortlessly to the music, finger cymbals keeping time. She was barefooted, which made her even more seductive. Her outfit reminded Bentley of what Barbara Eden used to wear on the TV show *I Dream of Jeannie*. She had a bright-colored stone in her navel. She twirled a sheer pink scarf in the air and used it to tease Wells.

Wells, a bit of a straight arrow, was beet red. He had a terrified grin on his face, anticipating what would happen next. His hands moved nervously in his lap. He had no idea how to respond to this unexpected circumstance. As the belly dancer moved around the chair, she smiled, enjoying herself and at the same time making eye contact with her audience. Her eyes fell on Bentley and stayed there a beat too long. Bentley's heart raced. Had she singled him out?

The dance lasted about ten minutes. When the belly dancer finished, she bent and kissed Wells softly on the cheek. Then she removed the stone from her belly button and handed it to him.

"Thank you," Wells managed, not knowing what else to say.

"Better not tell the bride where you got that," she teased, playing to the audience. That drew a good laugh.

Garrett stepped forward and said, "Ladies and gentlemen, let's have a big hand for the lovely Lola."

The applause was loud and boisterous. Lola took a deep bow, then ran toward the bedroom. Bentley watched her go and soon excused himself, unable to process his feelings. He was the first to leave.

◆ ◆ ◆ ◆

Bentley waited for her on the street outside the apartment building. He felt embarrassed in doing so, but he was a risk taker, and she had captured his curiosity and his heart with just one look. He had to pursue her. He had on jeans, dress boots, a dark brown mock turtleneck, and a camel hair blazer.

When she came through the revolving door, she spotted him instantly, leaning against a parked car—a limo, no less. She smiled and walked toward him, carrying a brown leather duffel bag. She was wearing jeans, high-heel leather boots, a cream-colored turtleneck, and a brown leather jacket. The boots, jacket, and duffel matched perfectly and looked expensive. The late-October Friday night was in the mid-forties, and she was dressed just warmly enough.

"Trick or treat?" Bentley said.

She laughed. "You tell me."

Treat, I hope, Bentley thought.

"Are you waiting for someone?" she asked.

"You," Bentley said. *She looks spectacular*, he thought.

"How nice."

"Bentley Williams," he said, offering his hand.

She smiled and gently shook his hand. "Lola Madrid."

Her touch was electric. He felt his pulse rate increase. He started to say, *I enjoyed your performance.* Instead, he went for the gold. "Have you had dinner?"

"I have not," she said.

"I know a nice little bistro not far from here," he said. "Would you like to join me? My treat."

"I accept," she said without hesitation.

◆　◆　◆　◆

The bistro was practically empty. They took a table in the corner. Bentley sat with his back to the wall so he could keep an eye on the waiter. Lola set her duffel bag on a chair behind her. They shared a bottle of red wine and explored each other's pasts. At some point, Bentley realized he was sharing more that she was.

"Are you married?" he asked, realizing it was an important question he had failed to consider.

"Certainly not," she said. "I would not be here with you if I were married."

"Sorry," he said. "I thought it was important to ask."

"You probably should have asked before you invited me to dinner."

"You're right," he said.

"I assume you are also not married."

"I am not," Bentley said.

They ordered, ate, and continued exploring each other with questions.

"How did you learn belly dancing?" Bentley asked.

"From my mother," she said. "What do you do for a living?"

Bentley noticed how she answered succinctly but with no embellishment. Her phrasing was unusual, and she had an elusive accent that was there one minute and gone the next. She gave her answer and immediately asked him a question.

"I'm an investment counselor," he said. "Pretty boring stuff."

"Are you good at it?"

"I am," Bentley said. "And I'm lucky."

"A nice combination," Lola said.

"It is," Bentley said.

◆　◆　◆　◆

On the street again outside the restaurant, Bentley said, "I live nearby. Would you like to come to my place for an after-dinner drink? I have Baileys Irish Cream, Frangelico, and amaretto."

"They all sound wonderful," Lola said. "I accept your invitation."

They walked the few blocks to Bentley's apartment building. It was getting late, but the night doorman was still on duty. He nodded to Bentley and said "Mr. Williams" as he held the door for them. The first Christmas after moving in and every Christmas since, Bentley had given the doorman a nice cash gift. The doorman always remembered Bentley's name.

"Thank you, Frederick," Bentley said as they entered.

Inside the elevator, Bentley pressed *PH*, and the elevator raced nonstop to the penthouse. Inside his apartment, Bentley pressed a button to open the draperies to reveal a spectacular view of Central Park and much of the city.

"Amazing view," Lola said, smiling widely.

"What would you like?" Bentley asked.

"You choose."

Bentley poured a generous portion of amaretto for each of them, and they sat on the couch in quiet conversation, admiring the view.

At one point, Bentley asked, "Where are you from?"

"Canada," Lola said. "And you?"

"Long Island," Bentley said.

"So," she said, "we are from two different worlds."

"Seems so."

Their conversation went much as it had earlier, Bentley learned little and Lola a lot. The clock rolled past midnight, and Bentley realized how tired he was.

"How far do you have to go tonight?" he asked.

"Brooklyn," Lola said.

"I have a guest room," Bentley said. "The door has a lock."

Lola smiled. "Would I need a lock?"

"No," Bentley said, "you wouldn't."

"In that case, I think I will stay."

Bentley showed her the guest room and said goodnight. He went to the master bathroom and got ready for bed. Five minutes later, he was under the covers of his king-sized bed, lying on his back, thinking about Lola Madrid. He was hoping she would come through his bedroom door and into his bed—and knowing he would be disappointed in her if she did.

Much later, he rolled over and went to sleep.

Alone.

◆   ◆   ◆   ◆

They spent the weekend together. They walked in Central Park, visited some of the famous sites Lola had never seen, saw an off-Broadway show, and immensely enjoyed each other's company. Saturday night, Lola again stayed in the guest room. Sunday night, after another spectacular day and a fabulous dinner, she took Bentley by the hand to his king-sized bed and showed him a level of lovemaking he never knew existed.

When he reached for her Monday morning, she was gone. He found a note by the coffeemaker in beautiful handwriting that read,

"The weekend was wonderful, I'll call."

She never did.

1

Early morning on the last Saturday in October found me sitting on the lower deck, drinking coffee, and enjoying the start of what promised to be a peaceful, uneventful day. The hint of smoke was in the air, a reminder of a wildfire burning near Knoxville. The day held the promise of a Tennessee Volunteers football game. The Vols were favored in a home SEC contest. Hopefully, they would take care of business.

My cell phone and iPad resided beneath the umbrella that rose from the center of the circular table that also held my covered, half-full coffee mug. The lake was calm, a plane disturbed occasionally by a fish breaking water to enjoy a morning bug snack. The lake house was eerily quiet. Our adopted daughter, Lacy, was off to college at Arizona State, and my wife, Mary, was off to the Saturday-morning flea markets with the county medical examiner, her good friend Wanda Jones. I was alone. Occasionally, this was not a bad thing.

I was checking high-school football scores when my phone rang. Caller ID read, "A. Ben Shoney." Abraham Benjamin Shoney had been my boss when I worked on Wall Street at Maple Financial. He was older than I was but secretive about his age, and I could only guess the gap was ten years or more. Had I wanted to find out, I could have, but I let it go. He called me about once a year and was never consistent about the day or time. Ben's reputation as a financial analyst was as legendary as his success with the ladies. He had been married and divorced three times.

"What are you up to, you old letch?" I answered.

"How the hell are you, Youngblood?" Ben said.

"Never better. How about you. Are you married again?"

"No," he said. "I decided three is enough. I'm going to play the field in my old age."

"How is Nikki Anderson working out?"

"Just great," he said. "Thanks for sending me her résumé."

Nikki Anderson was an attractive financial advisor I had met in Vegas while working the CJK case. I had sent her résumé to Ben, and he eventually hired her. She was probably safe, since Ben had a rule that he and the male staff were forbidden to mess with the female staff. I had a feeling that rule was not always adhered to.

"How is business?"

"Never better," Ben said. "Are you keeping your hand in?"

"Some," I said. "Cherokee Investigations is keeping me busy, but the Street is in my blood. That will probably never change."

"I still can't get over the fact that the best guy I ever had quit and became a famous private investigator."

"I quit so I could go home," I said. "The famous private investigator thing came later."

"Do you miss the city?"

"From time to time, I do." New York was also in my blood. In my mind, there was no place on earth like it.

"Want to come up for a little visit?" Ben asked. "I'll take you to the Four Seasons for lunch, or dinner, if you prefer."

"They still let you in the Four Seasons?"

"Sure they do," he said. "I'm a great tipper."

I knew Ben, and I knew this phone call wasn't about lunch or dinner. "What do you really want, Ben?"

"There is someone I want you to meet."

"And?"

"He's my best guy, and he's distracted right now."

"And?"

"He needs you to find someone."

I was silent while I considered if I wanted to search for another missing person. On two previous occasions, my searches had not turned out well. But Ben had been my mentor and friend, and we had a lot of history.

"Don?" Ben said. "You still with me?"

"Lunch on Monday," I said.

2

Monday morning, I flew into Teterboro Airport on Fleet Industries jet number one. Jim Doak flew the jet, and I enjoyed the luxury of the main cabin, a perk I had enjoyed for a number of years since becoming close friends with team Fleet, headed by Joseph Fleet and his right-hand man, Roy Husky, now president of the company. I had solidified my position with Fleet Industries by agreeing to serve on the board of directors.

When I deplaned, carrying only my briefcase, I was greeted by a familiar face from past adventures. Carlo Vincente's bodyguard, Frankie Pastore, was waiting by the back door of Carlo's limousine, a big smile on his face. Carlo Vincente was a semi-retired New York mob boss I had helped out a couple of times and who felt forever in my debt. From time to time, I took advantage of that. I had called Frankie directly to see if he was available to pick me up. He checked with his boss and called me back. "Mr. Vincente would be only too happy to offer you my services," Frankie had said.

Frankie was a big, burly guy with curly, dark hair, maybe an inch taller than me. He had a pleasant, almost childlike personality, but I knew beneath all that was one tough customer. If you got into a bar fight, you would want Frankie on your side.

"Frankie," I said, extending my hand, "good to see you. How are you?"

Frankie hesitated, then shook hands. In Frankie's world, I was royalty, since I was on a first-name basis with Carlo, and he didn't shake hands with royalty.

"I'm fine, Mr. Youngblood," Frankie said. "It's good to see you, too."

I slid into the backseat, and Frankie shut the door. I noticed the *New York Times*, the *Wall Street Journal*, and *USA Today* on the backseat. Frankie hustled around the front of the limo and took his place behind the wheel.

"Where to, Mr. Youngblood?"

"The Four Seasons," I said.

"The Four Seasons," Frankie said. "Nice."

We were on the move.

"How is Carlo?" I asked.

"Mr. Vincente is fine," Frankie said. "He sends his regards."

"The rest of the family?"

"All fine, except for Regina's father. He's no longer around." Regina Capelli was Carlo's granddaughter. Regina's father had fallen out of favor with the family. I could see why. I had met him once.

"Still above ground?"

Frankie laughed. "He's in L.A., alive and well. Mr. Vincente wouldn't whack the father of his granddaughter."

"Lucky for him," I said.

"It sure is," Frankie said.

"How are the Giants doing?"

"Not that great," Frankie said. "But nobody in their division is very good, so who knows? I see that your Tennessee Vols lost a close one."

Tennessee had dropped an SEC game on Saturday: a close game that ended with a Volunteers on their opponent's two yard line.

"Not pretty," I said. "A loss is a loss no matter how close."

"You got that right," Frankie said.

I had run out of small talk. I picked up the *New York Times*. Frankie noticed. He didn't miss much.

"Tap on the glass if you need anything," he said, sliding the privacy partition closed and leaving me alone with the *Times*.

◆ ◆ ◆ ◆

The Four Seasons opened in 1959 and was arguably still the best restaurant in the city. Everyone who was anyone had dined there: presidents, movie stars, sports legends, and, of course, me. There had been a time when I knew most of the staff. Now, I was just another face in the crowd, someone who probably wandered in by mistake, not realizing this was a meeting ground for important people.

"Sir?" the maître d' asked when I approached him.

"I am joining Ben Shoney," I said.

"You are expected, Mr. Youngblood," he said. "Follow me, please."

Ben had a table in the corner of the Pool Room. He stood as I approached and greeted me with a firm handshake and a slap on the shoulder.

The maître d' pulled out the vacant chair. "Sir," he said.

I sat. "Thank you."

"Thank you, Henry," Ben said.

"Let me know if you require anything else, Mr. Shoney," Henry said. He gave a slight nod and excused himself.

"How much did you tip him to remember my name?"

Ben smiled. "I take good care of Henry. He would never forget the name of one of my guests. You look great, by the way. Married life must suit you."

"It has so far," I said.

"Got a picture of the wife? I'd like to see the woman who got you to the altar."

I removed a picture of Mary and me from my wallet and handed it to him.

He nodded approval. "I'll bet the rest of her looks as good as the face."

"All six feet of her," I said.

Ben laughed, then signaled for our waiter. We ordered drinks.

"Tell me what this is all about," I said.

"It's about Bentley Williams," he said.

"Bentley," I repeated with a smile.

"Yeah, I know, but what can you do?" Ben said. "Not his fault. Anyway, he's my best guy. Almost as good as you were, but not quite. He's been moping around for a while now, still doing the job but not enthusiastically like he normally does. I asked him a couple of time if he's okay, and he said, 'I guess,' but he didn't seem too sure. Then, last week, he came in and asked if I knew a private investigator, and I said I did, and he asked if I could set up a meeting, and I said I would, and here you are. You're meeting him at two-thirty in our conference room."

Our drinks arrived. I looked at my watch. "We'd better order," I said.

◆   ◆   ◆   ◆

I sat in the conference room of Maple Financial high above New York's financial district and gazed at the spectacular view. A brilliant eggshell-blue cloudless sky punctuated a crisp late-autumn New York City day. At that moment, I missed the old days of living in the city and the energy that went with it. Ben had moved his offices into the newly built One World Trade Center, also known as Freedom Tower.

My thoughts were interrupted by the sound of the conference-room door opening. Ben Shoney reappeared, trailed by a younger man, probably in his mid-thirties, undoubtedly Bentley Williams. Bentley was dark haired and slender, taller than me, but not by much.

"Donald Youngblood," Ben said, "meet Bentley Williams."

"An honor," Bentley said, shaking my hand.

"Thank you," I said. "Nice to meet you, too."

"I'll leave you two alone," Ben said.

I sat near the end of the conference-room table. Bentley sat opposite me.

"I appreciate your coming all this way to meet with me," he said. "I could have come to Tennessee."

"Not a problem," I said. "Ben lured me here with the promise of lunch at the Four Seasons. We just came from there."

Bentley smiled. "Not a bad reason to come."

We passed a moment in awkward silence.

"Why don't you tell me why I'm here?" I said.

"Of course."

Bentley told me a story of a weekend with a woman named Lola Madrid, a belly dancer he had met at a bachelor party. He was haunted by her, he said. He could not get Lola out of his mind and was desperate to find her.

"Have you ever made love with someone the very first time and known this was a woman you could spend the rest of your life with?"

I thought back to my first bedroom encounter with Mary, years ago in a high-rise condo overlooking the beach on Singer Island, Florida—a life-changing experience. "I certainly have," I said.

He looked surprised. "What happened?"

"I married her."

"Then you know why I can't let her get away," he said.

"I do."

"Will you help me? I'll pay whatever it costs."

"I'll try," I said. "Tell me everything you remember from the time you met until the time she left."

Bentley talked for an hour as I took notes. Most of it was romance-novel stuff. Not much to go on.

"I'll give this some thought," I said. "I'm sure I'll have lots of questions. In the meantime, put together a list of everyone at the party you knew."

"Everyone?" He looked uncomfortable.

"I won't talk to anyone you don't wish me to talk to," I said.

"Okay. I don't want to hinder your efforts, but at the same time I'll require a certain amount of discretion. It'll be a short list. I didn't know a lot of the people there."

"Discretion is us," I said.

Bentley didn't laugh. I hoped he had a sense of humor in there some-where. He might need it.

3

"How would you have felt if you awakened that morning and found me gone?" Mary asked.

I had arrived back in Mountain Center in time for dinner at our condo in town. A day trip to New York for lunch at the Four Seasons and a new client. *Youngblood, the worldly detective.*

"In a panic," I said.

"Me, too," Mary said, "if I had found you gone."

"Obviously, neither of us was about to leave. Especially me."

"How sweet," Mary said.

We were having a post-dinner round of drinks at the kitchen bar. Mary was a police detective in Mountain Center and the woman who had rescued me from bachelorhood some years ago. We had officially adopted Lacy soon after we married. Mary had been married before and had two grown children, Jimmy and Susan. Mary and Lacy looked like mother and daughter. They were extremely close, and Mary had been suffering from mother withdrawal since Lacy left for ASU. I, on the other hand, was taking full advantage of the empty nest. I did the Groucho Marx thing with my eyebrows, smiled, and took another drink. Mary laughed at my silliness. I took a drink of my Michelob Amber Bock.

"Do you have leads on this new case?"

"Well, there's the bachelor party. I want to interview some of the guys who attended. Bentley doesn't have a picture of Lola, but if she's the knockout he says she is, then at least one of the guys took her picture. I'll talk to whoever put the party together and see if I can track her to an agency that handles belly dancers. I'm betting Lola Madrid was not her real name."

"So you'll have to go back to New York," Mary said.

"I will. I'm not too happy about being roped into a missing person case again, but I feel for the guy."

"When will you leave?"

"Couple of days."

"Maybe I'd better start saying goodbye now." She smiled. It was a smile I knew all too well.

"I have a better idea."

"Really? What could be better than you and me making love?"

"You and I making love in New York," I said.

"Big Bob is not going to like that."

Big Bob Wilson was the chief of police in Mountain Center and my best friend from high school. He was also Mary's boss and whined like a begging dog whenever Mary tried to take time off.

"I'll take care of Big Bob," I said. "You start getting in the mood to paint the town."

4

I parked my Pathfinder in my usual spot behind the Hamilton Building, which housed my second-floor office, then walked down the alley to the back entrance of the Mountain Center Diner. The overcast sky seemed to have sucked most of the color out of the cold morning, and the brisk wind was a reminder that winter was approaching. I felt like Dorothy stepping into Oz when I left the cold, gray alley for the warm, colorful, teeming diner. A table in the back was permanently reserved for me by the owner, Doris Black, a cherub-like mid-fifties whirling dervish who moved through the diner dispensing coffee and goodwill. She spotted me in an instant and graced me with a steaming mug of coffee and a couple of preowned newspapers.

"Gonna have company?" Doris asked.

"Big Bob," I said. "He should be here soon."

I was reading an article on Clay Carr, a freshman running back at the University of Tennessee, when the hum of the diner got noticeably lower. I knew the big man had arrived. I looked up as he headed for my table. He tossed his cowboy hat on an empty chair and sat. As soon as it was apparent that no arrests were going to be made, the hum returned to normal.

"Thanks for the invite," Big Bob said. "What's the occasion?"

"Breakfast."

"Uh-huh," Big Bob smirked. He knew me too well.

Doris arrived with more coffee and took our orders. We talked sports until the food arrived and then local politics until we finished.

"Who do you think are going to be the presidential nominees?" Big Bob said.

"Too early to tell. The Republicans have as many people running as horses in the Kentucky Derby."

Big Bob laughed. It was a hearty, deep rumble not unlike distant thunder. "Maybe we should take 'em all up to Churchill Downs, put 'em in the starting gate, and let 'em run. The first five across the line get to stay in the race."

"That I'd paid to see," I said. "But I'm not sure any of them could finish."

Doris appeared, freshened our coffee, and whirled away.

"I want to take Mary to New York for a few days," I said.

"How many is a few?" Big Bob asked.

I paused as if considering his question. We both knew he was going to say yes no matter what my answer was. He had no leverage.

"More than three, less than eight."

He blew out a lungful of air. "This is what happens when I have a detective with a rich husband. She does what she damn well pleases."

"Not true," I said. "If you said no, she wouldn't go."

I saw him relax a little.

"Well, you know I'm not going to say no," Big Bob said. "Mary is the best I've got, and whatever she wants within reason she's going to get." He took a long drink of coffee. "Keep that to yourself," he added.

◆   ◆   ◆   ◆

I was in the office before Gretchen arrived. Gretchen was my Girl Friday—and every other day of the week, for that matter. Of course, I did not refer to her that way. I would do that only if I wanted my head bashed in. Gretchen's official title was office manager. She ran things. She had become the star of the show, and I made guest appearances when it suited me. I liked it that way, and I think she did, too. Gretchen would come in and tell me what I had to do that day. Occasionally, I would tell her what to do. I wasn't sure who was boss, and I didn't care. It worked.

As usual, Gretchen gave me a list of things I needed to do. I nodded in all the right places.

"Anything for me?" Gretchen asked.

"No," I said. "Just do your usual magic."

She smiled. *It never hurts to stroke the troops.*

"By the way, I'm going to New York tomorrow with Mary. We'll be back in a few days. I'll keep you posted."

"So noted," Gretchen said as she got up to return to her desk in the outer office.

◆   ◆   ◆   ◆

Later that morning, I phoned a number I hadn't called for a while. It was a number known to only a few.

Carlo Vincente answered after the third ring. "Mr. Youngblood," Carlo said in his unmistakable gravelly voice. "So good to hear from you."

Caller ID leaves no secrets.

"I wanted to thank you for letting Frankie chauffeur me around on Monday," I said.

"Not a problem. Anytime."

"Well, speaking of that, is he free tomorrow?"

Carlo laughed. "Certainly. What time?"

"I'll let him know for sure," I said, "but probably around ten in the morning."

"Good, good," he said. "And how are things in Tennessee? Are you still investigating?"

"I am."

"The family?"

"Wife and daughter both are fine," I said. "Our daughter is at Arizona State in her freshman year. Time slows for no one."

"How true," Carlo said.

"How is your family?"

"All okay," Carlo said. "Regina is still at Silverthorn and finishing her degree online. That place has been a godsend, and you are responsible."

A few years ago, I had encouraged Carlo's granddaughter, Regina, to go to Silverthorn to get help with her gambling addiction. She not only responded well to treatment but ended up an important part of the staff, headed by my good friend and confidant, Sister Sarah Agnes Woods.

"Perhaps God had a hand in that," I said.

Carlo chuckled. "Yes, perhaps He did."

5

"**I** can see why you whine about flying commercial," Mary said. "This is so nice."

We had just departed Tri-Cities Airport on Fleet Industries jet number one with Jim Doak at the controls, heading back to the Big Apple. Mary had been on jet number one on two other occasions, neither that relaxing. She had recently flown with Lacy and me to Arizona, accompanied by Lacy's boyfriend, Biker McBride, and his parents to visit Arizona

State—a hectic trip, to say the least. The other time was a flight to Las Vegas while I lay in a coma in a hospital there. I doubt that, in her state of mind, she had enjoyed the Las Vegas flight. Now, it was just the two of us, and Mary was soaking in the experience.

"I don't whine," I said.

"Okay," Mary said. "Bitch and moan."

"Guilty. I admit I'm spoiled."

"I would be, too."

Jim Doak's voice came over the intercom. "Looks like smooth sailing all the way to Teterboro. You can move around the cabin at will."

Mary unfastened her seatbelt. "I'm going to do some exploring," she said as she headed to the back of the Learjet's cabin.

◆ ◆ ◆ ◆

Frankie dropped us at the Marriott Marquis, where a well-placed fifty got us a suite high above Broadway. I tipped the bellhop a twenty, and he implored me to call him for anything. He almost bowed as he shut the door on the way out.

"Fast and loose with your money today, Mr. Youngblood," Mary said.

"It's New York City," I said. "If you want to go first class, you have to be fast and loose."

"How much did you bring?"

"Enough," I said. "Want some?"

"What do I have to do to earn it?"

"Not a thing."

"Well, that's no fun," Mary said.

◆ ◆ ◆ ◆

After lunch, we took a taxi downtown to Ben Shoney's office building. We were escorted from the reception area of Maple Financial through a maze of partitions and desks to Ben's office. More than a few eyes were on my statuesque blond wife. Ben stood in his doorway watching us approach. He was smiling widely.

"Ben Shoney," I said, "this is my wife, Mary."

"A pleasure to meet you, Mary," Ben said.

"Likewise," Mary said.

"Please come in and sit down," Ben said.

We sat in front of his desk and exchanged small talk. Then Ben picked up his phone, punched in a couple of numbers, and waited. "Bentley, Mr. Youngblood will meet you in the conference room."

Much to Ben's delight, I left Mary in his office and headed out.

◆   ◆   ◆   ◆

Bentley sat across from me, the long mahogany table dividing us. He seemed relaxed, his briefcase set to one side. I flipped open my notebook like those ace reporters in the movies and made a show of looking at the notes I had taken during our last meeting.

"I want to get into more detail about your mystery woman."

"Sure," he said.

"How tall?"

"Around five-six, I'd say."

"Weight?"

"I'm not good at guessing weight," Bentley said. "She was perfect, not fat but not thin either."

"Any distinguishing marks, scars, or tattoos?"

"She has a tattoo on the small of her back," he said. "A pentagram. One word at the end of each tip."

"Spirit, earth, air, water, and fire?"

"Yes," he said. "How did you know that?"

"I watched a show about pentagrams on one of the cable channels with my daughter a few years ago. The pentagram is an interesting and controversial symbol. Is Lola's pentagram in a circle?"

"Yes," he said.

"It can mean many things. Basically, it means the four elements are tied together by the spirit. Is the star pointed up or down?"

"Up," Bentley said. "The word *spirit* is at the tip. Does that mean something?"

"It could mean a lot of things, but the tip pointing up doesn't indicate anything evil. She could be using it simply to perpetuate the mystique of herself as a belly dancer. Did you ask her about it?"

"I did. She said she just liked it because of what it stood for, and then she changed the subject. I didn't press her because I didn't really care."

"Any other tattoos or distinguishing marks?"

"None," Bentley said.

"You're sure?"

"Unless they're on the bottom of her feet. That's about the only thing I didn't get a good look at."

He was bragging. I said nothing. *Professionalism is all.*

"You told me you talked a lot but that you did most of the talking," I said. "Did you ever get a clue where she's from?"

"I've been thinking about that," Bentley said. "She responded to something I said about growing up. She said, 'When I was a young girl growing up on P.E.I.,' something, something. I don't remember the rest of it. I asked her what P.E.I. meant, and she just said, 'Oh, nothing,' and changed the subject. If I'd thought I would never see her again, I would have paid closer attention."

I wrote "P.E.I." in my notebook and added a question mark.

"Could you detect an accent?"

"I'm not sure," he said. "Maybe, but certainly not foreign, and certainly not anywhere in the five boroughs. I was so caught up in her that half the time I barely heard what she was saying."

"Any odd phrasing you might remember?" I said. "You know, like *roundabout* instead of *traffic circle* or *car park* instead of *parking lot*?"

Bentley frowned, concentrating, trying to remember. Then he slowly shook his head. "I can't think of a thing."

"Anything that she wore that might be a clue where she's from? Rings, a watch, necklace, clothes?"

"Some nice costume jewelry, good clothes that looked expensive, but I don't know women's clothing that well. I commented on the jewelry, and she was quick to point out it wasn't real."

"Did anyone talk to her at the party?"

"I'm sure Garrett did," Bentley said. "Garrett Day was the groom's best man. He organized the party. He probably hired her, but I'm not positive."

"You didn't ask?"

"No," he said. "I didn't want anyone to know I had fallen for a belly dancer."

"And now?"

"And now I've told you," he said. "Ben said you know how to keep your mouth shut."

I was running out of questions. "Anything else?"

"Only that I'm obsessed with finding her," Bentley said. "No. I've thought long and hard, and unless I zoned out there is nothing else."

"You got that list of names I asked for?"

"On my computer," he said. "Do you really have to talk to all of them?"

"Not if you don't want me to," I said. "But I'll have to talk to Garrett. He might have the only possible lead to finding her."

I handed him a card. He took a long look at it.

"The woman you walked in with," he said. "Your wife?"

"Yes."

Bentley nodded. "So you should understand."

I said nothing.

He reached into his briefcase, pulled out a DVD, and handed it to me.

"Garrett gave this to me. Lola's dance at the bachelor party. He made it for the groom, but the groom didn't want his wife to know what went on at the party, so Garrett gave it to me. Garrett swears there are no other copies. I can't look at it anymore."

Curious, I thought. I took maybe ten seconds to think about that.

"Garrett's gay?"

Bentley smiled for the first time since I had met him. "You're good," he said.

"Best reason I could think of for him not to keep a copy."

He stood and offered his hand across the table. "I'll send you Garrett's address and phone number. I'll give him a heads-up on what's going on."

"I'll talk with him as soon as possible," I said.

"Anything else I can do?"

I briefly thought about it. "When you get time, sketch the tattoo on Lola's back. Do it in color if you can."

He paused, conflicted by my request. "I'm ashamed to tell you this," he said.

"You have a picture of the tattoo," I said.

"I do. She was asleep in the nude, lying on her stomach, and I took it with my cell phone."

"I'll need to see it," I said.

"I have it on my home computer. I downloaded it and then deleted it from my phone. I'll email you a file."

"Got any head shots?"

Bentley smiled. "A couple. She doesn't like having her picture taken."

"Be sure to include them," I said.

He nodded. We walked toward the conference-room entrance.

"Thanks for helping me," he said.

"I haven't done anything yet."

"I have a feeling you will," Bentley said.

◆　◆　◆　◆

As I went back to Ben's office to retrieve Mary, I heard her laughing. Ben always managed to make women laugh—part of his disarming charm.

"Time to go," I said without preamble.

Ben stood. "I have offered to take Mary to lunch tomorrow while you do your investigating. It would greatly enhance my reputation to have such a beautiful woman on my arm."

"The Four Seasons, I hope."

"Certainly," Ben said.

"It's up to Mary," I said.

"I'd be delighted," Mary said.

"Where are you staying?"

"The Marriott Marquis," Mary said.

"I'll pick you up out front in a limo at eleven-thirty," Ben said.

◆　◆　◆　◆

Late that afternoon before dinner, I watched the DVD. Then I watched it again. The dance took about ten minutes. Most of the time, Lola Madrid was facing the camera. Every now and then, she whirled and showed her fantastic backside. When she did, I could not see the tattoo. I could understand Bentley's obsession. Lola Madrid was something else—dark hair, expressive eyes, beautiful features, seductive smile, perfectly proportioned body.

Mary looked over my shoulder the second time I watched. "I assume you're taking this case."

"Not much choice," I said. "Ben asked for my help. I cannot say no."

We watched Lola's seductive dance.

"She is gorgeous," Mary admitted. "How many times are you going to watch this?"

"Couple of hundred."

"In your dreams," Mary said.

"Maybe I could get you one of those little outfits."

Mary laughed, the sexy, throaty laugh I knew so well. "Why don't you just forget about the outfit," she said, unbuttoning her blouse, "and go for the gold?"

"Why don't I?" I said.

6

The next morning after a late breakfast, I went online to search for belly dancers. Mary was in the bathroom making herself gorgeous for her lunch at the Four Seasons with Ben.

She came out and twirled. "How do I look?"

She wore a long black wool skirt with a black cashmere sweater, black boots, and a handmade silver belt she had purchased in Arizona when we took Lacy to visit Arizona State. A sliver chain adorned her neck.

"Better than Lola Madrid," I said.

"You sweet talker."

"That's me," I said. "Private detective sweet talker."

Mary laughed and took one last approving look in the mirror. "See you later," she said.

"Enjoy," I said, returning to my laptop.

I heard the door shut as I stared in amazement at the list of belly dancers in New York City. I began opening websites. Most were for individual dancers. They were professional and well done. I went from site to site, looking without success for Lola Madrid. I Googled "Lola Madrid; belly dancer" and did not get a hit. A few websites offered more than one dancer. I started making phone calls. They generally went like the initial one:

"Empire State Entertainment."

"I'm looking for a particular belly dancer named Lola Madrid," I said.

"I've never heard of Lola Madrid," the female voice said, "but I can assure you we have many beautiful and talented dancers."

"I'm sure you do," I said. "I may call back." *Or not*, I thought after hanging up.

I quit making belly dancer calls around noon and called Garrett Day. We made an appointment to meet at five o'clock in the View bar on the forty-eighth floor of the hotel. Then I changed into shorts, sneakers, and a T-shirt and headed for the Marquis' fabulous exercise room.

◆ ◆ ◆ ◆

The View is supposedly New York's only revolving lounge. I'm told it takes approximately an hour to make its 360. I had never timed it. If I didn't pay attention, I would never have known I was moving. Back in the day, I had visited the View often and was known on sight by the staff, whom I tipped generously to be remembered. I slipped a twenty to the attractive greeter and was seated in a prime location with a spectacular view.

The lounge was sparsely populated. I did not see anyone matching the description of Garrett Day, so I ordered and sipped on a Blue Point Toasted Lager. I didn't have to wait long. A slender, good-looking blond fellow smiled at me as he made his way to my table. Mary says all the best-looking guys are gay. I, of course, am the exception.

"Mr. Youngblood?"

"Garrett," I said as we shook hands. Garrett had a firm grip. "Call me Don."

"Certainly," he said. "Great table."

"I never get tired of this view."

"Neither do I," Garrett said.

The city was dark by four-thirty in the winter, and the lights that illuminated that darkness gave it a magical aura.

The waitress appeared to take Garrett's order.

"What are you drinking?" he asked.

I told him.

"I'll have one of those," Garrett said, pointing to my beer. "So you want to know about Lola Madrid."

"Yes," I said.

"You want to locate her."

"Yes," I repeated.

"For Bentley."

I said nothing.

"I know all about it," Garrett said. "I gather Bentley is desperate to find her."

"How do you know?"

"After her dance, Bentley left in a hurry. I didn't think much about it because Bentley's not real social, and he was there just to make an appearance. After Miss Madrid changed out of her outfit, I escorted her down and watched as she left the building. I saw her talking to Bentley. It was as if she expected him to be there. I can't say how I knew that. Then they walked away together, and I went back to the party. I'm guessing he spent the weekend with her because I tried to call a few times and didn't get an answer. He is desperate, isn't he?"

"You'll have to ask him," I said.

Garrett laughed. "Fat chance. Bentley doesn't share his personal life."

"How did you come to hire Lola Madrid?" I asked.

"About a month before the bachelor party, someone handed me a flyer on the street. It was an advertisement for a belly dancer, Lola Madrid. The flyer was a four-color piece on good stock and was well done. So an idea popped into my head: a belly dancer at the bachelor party. Miss Madrid looked spectacular, and I thought, *Why not? She'll be a big hit.* I mean, I'm gay but I'd still consider sleeping with her."

He said he was gay like I would say I'm right-handed. If he was looking for a reaction from me, he didn't get one. This, after all, was New York.

"Anyway, I called the number on the flyer, found out her rate, and booked her."

"How much?"

"Five hundred dollars."

"Not cheap."

"Well within our budget, and she was available," Garrett said. "Besides, in the city, five hundred dollars is like fifty dollars anywhere else."

"Who answered the phone when you made the booking?"

"She did," Garrett said. "Very professional voice with just the hint of an accent."

"How did you pay?"

"Cash."

"Did you tip her?"

"One hundred dollars."

Garrett's beer arrived, and we saluted each other and took a drink.

"What was your impression of her?"

"She was all woman," Garrett said. "Mature, probably older than she looked. She was professional and socially distant. When she began to dance, it was like she flipped a switch and her personality was unleashed. Then she finished and immediately became herself again."

We drank some more and ordered a second round.

"Anything else?"

"Maybe," he said.

"Tell me."

"I watched her closely as she danced, and I could swear she made eye contact with Bentley more than anyone else."

"Eye contact," I said.

"You know, like you see someone across a crowded room that you don't know and you make eye contact that says, 'I'd like to meet you.' It was brief, but I swear it was there."

I nodded and said nothing. We drank and enjoyed the lights of the city.

"Does Bentley come from a wealthy family?"

"Very," Garrett said. "Millions."

"Is there any way Lola Madrid could have known about the bachelor party before you called her?"

"I don't see how. Bentley and I knew we were going to do something, but we hadn't planned what, when, or where when I first called Miss Madrid."

"First?"

"I initially called to find out her price. Then I talked to Bentley, and he thought it was a great idea, so I called back to book her once we settled on the date."

"Did she ask for a deposit?"

"Yes, one hundred dollars cash. I left it at the reception desk at my office, and she picked it up and left me a receipt."

"Still have the receipt?"

"I tossed it after the party. Didn't see any reason to keep it."

We were quiet again, and then Garrett finished his second beer and looked at his watch.

"Sorry," he said. "I have to run. If I can do anything else, please let me know."

◆   ◆   ◆   ◆

When I got back to our suite, Mary was there.

"How was lunch?"

"Fabulous," Mary said. "We received the royal treatment."

"What did you do after?"

"Well, Ben offered to show me around the city, but I told him that was your job. Then I asked if he wanted to go shopping with me, and he high-tailed it back to the office."

"Don't blame him," I said. "Where'd you go?"

"Saks Fifth Avenue. And I spent a lot of your money."

"Good for you," I said. "Where's the loot?"

"Saks is shipping my purchases back to Mountain Center," Mary said proudly.

"Good thinking."

"Let's go have dinner," Mary said. "I'm starved."

"After lunch at the Four Seasons?"

"Well, I practiced restraint at lunch, and I did do a lot of shopping and a lot of walking. And it's cold out, and I burned a lot of calories."

"Okay," I said. "I get it. Let's go."

◆   ◆   ◆   ◆

Gallagher's Steakhouse on West Fifty-Second Street is another New York institution, famous for prime steaks and chops for almost ninety years. If a roomful of New Yorkers starts arguing about the best steaks in the city, Gallagher's will certainly be in the discussion. I ordered the ten-ounce filet mignon and Mary the lamb chops. After a leisurely dinner, we returned to the Marquis, and Mary went to bed early and read. She had enjoyed a great day. She loved the city and its energy. She loved everything it had to offer. She was a kid in a candy store. I could relate. The city gets in your blood and stays there no matter where you are. It will always be a part of me.

I went online to check email. I had one from T. Elbert Brown, friend, confidant, and retired Tennessee Bureau of Investigation agent sentenced to a wheelchair by a drug dealer's bullet that should have killed him.

> Where are you? Haven't seen you or Roy for a while.
> Send me details! T.

T. Elbert was a stickler for details. I wrote him and explained that I was on a new case that was probably going to turn out to be nothing. I told him we were staying the weekend so Mary could see some sights, and that I would visit him early next week.

Then I turned my attention to the remainder of my emails, most of which were junk. There was, however, one from Bentley Williams with a file attached. I downloaded the file. The file's name was *Lola*. I opened it. There were about ten JPEGs. I ran a slideshow.

The first picture showed all of Lola Madrid. She was asleep on her stomach, completely naked. She was a sight to see. I ran through the balance of them. More naked Lola on her stomach from different angles. The last was a close-up of the tattoo. The photo was first rate. The details of the tattoo were excellent. The pentagram lay inside a vibrant purple circle with a black background. The upright tip of the pentagram was white, almost glowing against Lola Madrid's dark skin. Above the circle, also in white, was the word *Spirit*. The right tip of the pentagram was yellow with the word *Air*, also in yellow. The left tip was green, *Earth*. The bottom right tip was red, *Fire*. The bottom left tip, blue, *Water*. The circumference of the tattoo appeared to be three to four inches. The craftsmanship was excellent.

I went through the slideshow again. *Thoroughness is all.* Then I shut down my computer and joined Mary in bed. Sometime during the night, Lola Madrid came to me in a dream. She was doing the belly dance I had seen on the DVD. I was just one of the many guys at the bachelor party. She stopped and looked at me. *Don't come looking for me,* she said. *He's dangerous.*

7

Mary and I spent all of Saturday as tourists. I doubled as tour guide. We took the morning Circle Line cruise around Manhattan. I had never done the Circle Line, and it gave me a whole new perspective of New York City. Around lunchtime, we went to the top of the Empire State Building. We spent the afternoon in the Museum of Natural History. We agreed we could have spent days there.

That evening, we had drinks in the View and then went to a Broadway musical, *Wicked*, followed by a late-night dinner at Becco, an upscale Italian restaurant on West Forty-Fifth Street. I sipped a Peroni, an Italian beer, and Mary was well into a glass of full-bodied Italian red recommended by our waiter.

We talked about our day, the places we'd been and the things we'd seen. In the middle of that conversation, our food arrived, chicken parmigiana for Mary and osso buco for me.

"Great day today," Mary said between bites. "*Wicked* was so good."

"It was," I said. My veal shank was dwindling.

Mary smiled. "And the day's not over."

"I was hoping it wasn't."

◆　◆　◆　◆

We lay naked in bed in the dark, floating on a high of good food and drink and great sex.

"God, this day was fabulous," Mary whispered. "I'll remember it forever. But I have to go back tomorrow. It wouldn't be fair to Big Bob not to."

"I understand," I said. "I've already set it up with Jim."

"Are you going to stay?"

"No, I'm going back with you."

I needed to get in the office. I did my best thinking there. Next week was Thanksgiving, and that meant our annual dinner at the Fleet mansion. How many years was it now? I'd lost count.

"Good," Mary said, kissing me. She rolled out of my arms and onto her side, staying close.

I lay beside her, attempting to put together a strategy to find Lola Madrid, but my mind wouldn't focus. I was asleep in minutes, dreaming I was in Oz and looking behind a curtain to see if I could find the Wizard. He was there in the shadows, a dark silhouette dressed all in black. I did not have the impression he was friendly.

8

Early Monday morning, I sat in my office drinking Dunkin' Donuts coffee and going over notes left for me by Gretchen. I replayed my New York trip. Mary and I had flown home Sunday morning and spent Sunday night at our lake house. We would stay at our Mountain Center condo until Friday, then return to the lake house. That was our routine when I was in town. I wondered how full her plate was at work after our New York adventure.

My mind was wandering when I heard the outer office door open and shut. I looked at my watch. Ten o'clock. Gretchen.

Fifteen seconds later, my intercom buzzed. "Look sharp. The boss has arrived."

Always a snappy one-liner to start the week.

"Tell the boss to get coffee and join me for our Monday-morning meeting," I said. I was completely out of smart remarks.

A few minutes later, Gretchen sat in front of my desk with her notepad and pencil at the ready. "Have you read all my notes?" she said.

"Yes."

"Any questions?"

"No," I said. "Looks like you handled things. I sometimes wonder why I bother to come in."

She smiled. "How was your trip?"

"Really good." I gave her the short version.

"Anything you need me to do regarding this Lola Madrid person?"

"There is," I said. "Go online and see if you can find her." I handed her the DVD of Lola's dance and my notes from talking with Bentley. "Read my notes and watch this before you start."

"Anything else?"

"No," I said. "You?"

"Actually, yes. You realize I've been taking on more and more responsibility."

Where is this leading?

"I do," I said. "And you'll get another raise at the first of the year."

"My compensation package is very fair," Gretchen said. "I have no complaints."

"What, then?"

"I have some ideas for expanding our business," she said.

Our business?

It took me only a few seconds to see where this was going. "You want to be a partner."

"I do," Gretchen said. "And you won't be sorry."

"What do you have in mind?"

"A seventy-five, twenty-five split," she said. "You get the seventy-five, of course."

"Of course."

"I'll keep doing what I'm doing, plus work to expand the business. I'll determine how much to bill for each small job or big case. You never get paid enough because you don't need the money. I'll ask for your approval before I do anything significant as far as business expansion. I'll keep the books, and we'll share the profits at the end of the year. I think some of the profits should go into a general fund. We'll discuss that when the time comes."

"You've given this some thought."

"I have," she said.

"You think I'll say yes."

"I do."

"Why?"

"It makes sense, and you don't really care."

"Does Mary know about this?"

Gretchen smiled, which meant if I said no I was going to get pressured by Mary until I said yes. But Gretchen was right. It made sense for many reasons. Especially, if it meant more freedom for me.

"Okay," I said, "let's do it. You take care of the paperwork."

"I will."

"What else?"

"The office next door is available. I want to rent it."

"You want your own office?"

"No, I'm staying put," Gretchen said. "I want to hire a junior investigator. There are a lot of small jobs we could have if we had someone to do them. Rollie says he can keep us busy a few days a week, and I know there would be other opportunities."

Rollie Ogle was a divorce lawyer who had an office at the end of the hall. Over the years, we had become friends. He was a good source for finding out what was going on in Mountain Center.

"Okay, as long as it makes financial sense."

"I'm not in this for fun," Gretchen said. "We're going to make a profit."

"Sounds like you have work to do," I said.

"Maybe I'd better get started."

"Make Lola Madrid your top priority."

"Will do," she said as she disappeared into the outer office.

◆ ◆ ◆ ◆

That night at the kitchen bar in our condo, we ate three-cheese tortellini Alfredo with my infamous Caesar salad and toasted garlic bread with Parmesan cheese. We shared a bottle of Pinot Noir, which meant I drank approximately a third of the bottle and Mary the rest. As usual, Mary recounted her day, which was sometimes funny because of the dumb things criminals did. But today had proven to be boring. I listened because I enjoyed the sound of her voice and had learned it was important to pay attention. There might be a quiz later.

"I have a new partner," I said after Mary finished.

"I'm glad," Mary said. "She deserves it."

"Whose idea was it?"

"Mine, mostly."

"I thought so."

"It'll be fine."

"I'm sure."

Mary took a drink of wine. She had slowed down, savoring the final inch in her glass.

"What are you going to do about finding Lola Madrid?"

"I've got Gretchen doing an internet search. If she comes up empty, I'll ask Scott to run her through the FBI computers."

"Lola Madrid might not be her real name," Mary said.

"Probably not."

"That will make it a hell of a lot tougher."

"Toughness is us," I said.

9

"I found two Lola Madrids on Facebook," Gretchen said in our regular morning meeting. "They both live in Spain, and neither looks anything like the Lola Madrid you're searching for. I couldn't find a Lola Madrid anywhere else."

"Okay," I said. "Thanks for trying. What else?"

"I'm going to sign a one-year lease for the office next door. The building manager has agreed to cut a doorway from our outer office so they connect."

"Will the doorway have a door?"

"It will," Gretchen said.

"Good. Anything else?"

"I'm going to the University of Tennessee tomorrow to interview some students from the Sociology Department who are concentrating on criminology and criminal justice."

"No grass grows under your feet," I said.

"Not likely. I'll be interviewing five students."

"You set this up yesterday?"

"Not exactly." Gretchen smiled. "Just trying to get a head start. I could have canceled if you said no, and I certainly won't hire anyone without your approval."

"Well, good hunting."

◆　◆　◆　◆

Later that morning, I called Scott Glass, college chum and presently special agent in charge of the FBI's Salt Lake City office. After we exchanged the necessary pleasantries about his love life, Scott asked, "What's going on, Blood? This isn't just a social call."

"I need you to run someone through all the databases you have access to."

"I feel honored," Scott said. "You're asking me and not Steely Dave."

David Steele was the deputy director of the FBI, who had once tried and failed to train me as an FBI agent at Quantico. My fault, not his. I didn't play well with others. In the past few years, we had reconnected and I had gained special consultant status, complete with my own ID as a reward for my help on a few of my cases that had intersected with the bureau's. To my surprise, we had become good friends. "Steely Dave" had been his nickname at Quantico.

"I didn't want to bother him with such a menial task," I said. "You, on the other hand, I'm glad to bother."

"I am but your humble servant," Scott said.

"Her name is Lola Madrid. She is maybe thirty to thirty-five years old. I'll send you a picture. She's a real dish."

"That's it? You have nothing else?"

"Nothing."

"What's it about?"

I told him almost all of Bentley's story.

"You're turning into an old softie," Scott said.

"Don't tell anyone. It'll ruin my reputation. Beside, I'm curious why she would spend this supposedly fantastic weekend with him and then just vanish."

"Try not to stumble onto a serial killer or a domestic terrorist group," Scott said. "My plate is full right now."

"I'll do my best."

Although I do seem to have a knack for that, I thought.

◆ ◆ ◆ ◆

That afternoon, I sat in front of my computer looking at the pictures of Lola Madrid. Of course, all I was really interested in was the tattoo, but it didn't hurt to have a good visual of the person I was looking for. A few years back, I had worked another case involving a tattoo and had received some help from a retired master forger by the name of Amos "Teaberry" Smith. I had met Amos on my first big case, and he had become a valuable source of information and was someone I trusted. It had been awhile since we talked. I dialed his international cell phone, wondering if he was still in Italy pursuing *amore*. I hoped it wasn't too late to call.

"*Ciao*," the voice answered.

"*Buon giorno*, Amos," I said. That was about the extent of my Italian, although I did speak fluent Spanish.

"Youngblood, is that you?"

"It is," I said. "I assume you're still in Italy."

"I am," Amos said.

"How's that going?"

"I'm living a dream."

"Glad to hear it. Ever coming back?"

"Unlikely," Amos said. "But I will always be available to you. You are the reason I'm here. I'm forever in your debt."

"You owe me nothing," I said. "But I need a favor."

"Anytime."

"I'll send you a picture of a tattoo and the girl who goes with it," I said. "I need you to take a look at the tattoo and give me your impression. Then I'll tell you a story that's right up your alley, an affair of the heart."

"Sounds intriguing," Amos said. "I look forward to it."

"Same email address?"

"Yes."

"We'll talk tomorrow. Should I call earlier?"

"This time is fine."

"*Arrivederci*, Amos."

"*Arrivederci*, Youngblood."

10

The next morning, I went through the Dunkin' Donuts drive-through, picked up coffee and an assortment of muffins and donuts, and drove to T. Elbert's house on Olivia Drive. He was waiting on his porch underneath the overhead heaters that kept the early-morning chill away on a cold, damp day. Daylight was trying hard to make an appearance but was being restrained by thick cloud cover. As always, I was hoping for snow, and the forecast showed some promise.

"Good to see you," T. Elbert said. Translated, that meant it had been too long since I was last there.

We settled in to drink coffee and eat our carbs. I started with a corn muffin followed by a glazed blueberry cake donut. I wondered how many extra miles I would have to run to break even.

"Tell me about your trip to New York," T. Elbert said.

I spared no details. T. Elbert was interested in the restaurants we visited and the food we consumed.

"Never been to New York," he said.

"We should go sometime."

"Not interested," T. Elbert said. "Just a bunch of damn Yankees."

"Yankees are people, too," I said. "Good and bad and everything in between."

"Of course you'd say that." He laughed. "You practically were one."

I said nothing as I finished my coffee and the last of the donut.

"Tell me about the case you're working."

I told him all of it.

"Lola Madrid is probably not her real name," T. Elbert said.

"Probably not."

"Anything I can do?"

"You can take a crack at finding Lola Madrid on any of the databases you have access to."

"Why not?" T. Elbert said. "I'm not going anywhere."

◆   ◆   ◆   ◆

Scott Glass called before Gretchen arrived.

"You're up early," I said.

"Never went to bed," Scott said. "I worked all night trying to find Lola Madrid. You're right, she's quite a dish."

"Professor, it's not that import . . . ," I started before realizing I'd been had.

"Gotcha," Scott said. "Actually, I put John on it, and he drew a blank, but I didn't make him stay up all night."

John Banks was a computer whiz in Scott's office. If John hadn't found anything, there was nothing to be found.

"John says Lola Madrid might not be her real name," Scott said.

"A lot of that going around," I said. "A stage name, maybe, for lack of a better description."

"Anything else I can do for the great Donald Youngblood?"

"You can bow as you hang up the phone," I said.

◆   ◆   ◆   ◆

I spent the morning catching up on the stock market, marveling the DOW was bouncing around twenty thousand. I had little chance of hitting a home run, so I had to settle for singles and the occasional double. Still, that was better than striking out. For lunch, I ordered potato and cheddar cheese soup from the Mountain Center Diner. Doris threw in a homemade biscuit for good measure. I had a leisurely meal at my desk and played Spider Solitaire.

After stretching lunch as far as I could, I shut down my game, picked up the phone, and dialed Amos Smith.

"It's a beautiful day in the neighborhood," Amos answered.

"Well, be glad you're there and not here," I said. "What did you think of the tattoo?"

"Well . . ." Amos paused. "The tattoo was one thing, the girl was something else. What's her story?"

"Her name is Lola Madrid," I began, and told Amos the story of Bentley Williams and Lola.

"I can see why he would want to find her," Amos said.

"So what's your impression of the tattoo? I'd like to find the artist."

"That won't be easy," Amos said. "It's good work but not original. I found a few pictures of pentagrams online that look a lot like the tattoo on Lola Madrid. There could be some kind of hidden signature that only a master tattoo artist might recognize, but it's hard to tell."

"Anyone you know who I could talk to?"

"I'll have to think about that," Amos said.

"I'll pay for his or her time."

"That would help. How much?"

"Whatever you think is appropriate," I said.

"I'll be in touch, Youngblood," Amos said. "Take care."

11

Most private investigators have trouble making ends meet unless they can establish a client base with repeat business. It's either feast or famine. Most are retired cops who put in their twenty years, took their pensions, and moved on to safer work. Private investigators rarely get shot at or even have to draw their weapons of choice. I was the exception. I was rich and had drawn and used my arsenal on more than one occasion. But I was susceptible to the reality of feast or famine.

The next morning while driving to work, my plate got fuller—loaded, even. My phone beeped a few blocks from my office. The text message was from Howard Cox, father of Megan, grandfather of Cindy. More than four years ago, Cindy Carter had been kidnapped by some low-life scumbags and held for a short time in order to put pressure on Cindy's father, who owed the men's boss considerable money. I had resolved the situation with the help of Amos Smith. I saw the Cox clan at the Mountain Center Country Club from time to time, and they always wanted to stop and chat. The text read, "Donald, I need to see you immediately. Urgent. Come to my office. Acknowledge. Howard."

I pulled into a nearby parking lot and replied, "On my way."

I turned the Pathfinder around and headed out of Mountain Center.

Cox Foods was a cannery a few miles outside town off a two-lane lightly traveled state highway. It bought locally and sold locally and had a reputation of quality that most locals had grown up with and continued to demand. Practically everyone in East Tennessee had eaten Cox's baby peas, sweet corn, and green beans as a child and still did.

I pulled into a visitor's parking space in front of the main office building. The receptionist pointed me to an elevator. "Third floor," she said.

I got on and punched 3. When the elevator door opened, I exited into a small foyer facing Howard Cox's office door. I went through and found another receptionist, who took me through another door to the inner sanctum. Howard was waiting. He was a stocky man, shorter than me by an inch or two, and balding. We shook hands. Megan Cox sat silently on the couch like she was in shock. She had been crying.

"Thanks for coming on such short notice," he said. He looked distraught.

"What's wrong?"

"Listen," he said. He accessed his voice mail and replayed a message on the phone's speaker.

"We have Cindy," the electronic voice began. It sounded like a 45 RPM record played at 33⅓. Like those sinister voices on TV and in the movies. "Withdraw one hundred thousand dollars by ten o'clock today and wait for our call. Small bills, tens and twenties. Nothing sequential. You'll need to involve one other person you can trust. It would be a disaster to call the police. Cooperate and you can have Cindy back today unharmed. Sorry to do this, but I really need the money, and you can afford it."

I listened to it again. *An apology,* I thought. *Now, that's weird.*

"That's it? Nothing else?"

"That's all."

"You're sure they have her?"

"Yes," he said. "They took her from Megan this morning from the parking lot behind her apartment as she was preparing to take Cindy to school. I've complained before that her parking lot is not well lit. They drugged Megan and took Cindy."

I looked at Megan. She was staring out the window.

"Megan," I said.

Nothing.

"Megan!"

She jumped.

"Oh, Mr. Youngblood. They took Cindy," she said. "Will you get her back, please?"

I had done it once before, so I guess to her it was perfectly logical I could do it again. She spoke like a ten-year-old girl who had lost her doll.

I knelt in front of her. "You didn't call the police?"

She stared at me.

"The police, Megan. Did you call the police?"

"No," she said, gaining control. "He told me not to right before he drugged me. He grabbed me from behind, and a voice whispered, 'Do not call the police.' He put something over my face, and then I was out. When I woke up, I called Daddy, and he came and brought me here."

I looked at Howard Cox. "How long?"

"An hour, maybe."

I turned back to Megan. "Were there just two of them?"

"I think so," she said. "One grabbed me, and one grabbed Cindy. I didn't see either one. I heard Cindy make a noise like she was trying to say something. There must have been a hand over her mouth."

I looked at Howard. "What do you want to do?"

"Give them the money and get Cindy back," he said. "The money is peanuts. Why didn't they ask for a million?"

"They want a quick score," I said. "Something reasonable that you can get fast and won't miss all that much. Pretty smart, actually."

"Wait here with Megan," Howard said. "I'm going to the bank."

◆　◆　◆　◆

"We'll get her back," I said to Megan.

"I know you will," Megan said. "That's why I told Daddy to call you." She paused and took a deep breath. "I'm so tired."

"Get some rest," I said. "This will all be over soon."

She lay on the couch and curled up in a fetal position, a little girl again. I took Howard Cox's cashmere topcoat off the coatrack and covered her. Most mothers would have been frantic in her situation. Maybe it was the drugs, or maybe our history had convinced her that Cindy was going to be okay. No matter. She was asleep in minutes.

I sat and thought. I didn't like coincidences. What were the odds that the same little girl could be kidnapped twice before she was eight years old? Next to nothing. But this time was different. This time, it was for ransom. The last time, it had been to get back money some drug dealers felt was owed them. Those men had worked for Rasheed Reed, and Rasheed had made it right in turn for a favor from me. I couldn't see that Rasheed would be connected to this. I wouldn't put it past Cindy's father, but according to Rasheed, Ricky Carter was dead. Still, someone knew Howard Cox could lay hands on a hundred grand fast. Or maybe they just guessed he could. Maybe a disgruntled employee. Maybe someone in Ricky Carter's past or Megan's present. Too many maybes and no real clues.

I was still trying to work it out when Howard Cox returned carrying a suitcase with one hundred thousand dollars inside. He looked at Megan asleep on the couch and said nothing. He went to his phone and lowered the ring volume to the lowest level. We sat and waited in silence for the call.

It came at ten-fifteen. Howard answered on the first ring. Megan seemed not to notice. It was short and not so sweet. Howard held the receiver so we both could hear.

"Check your personal email and reply," the electronic voice said. "Then wait for another call." Then the person behind the voice hung up.

Howard Cox brought up his email as I leaned over his shoulder. Five or six emails down the list was one titled "Instructions." Howard opened and printed it. We read the single page together. The instructions were detailed. One person would drop the money at a specific location right after the second person confirmed that Cindy was alive and well and ready to come home. Driver two should bring binoculars. We were to email the cell-phone numbers of the two drivers and wait for instructions.

"What do you think?" Howard asked softly.

"We cooperate. Too dangerous not to. I think if we do what they say, we'll get Cindy back. They seem smart and organized. They'll take the money and run. We can sort the rest of it out later."

Though Megan appeared to be asleep, I did not want to bring up the subject of Cindy being harmed. I looked back to Howard. "They don't want other complications, if you get my drift."

"I do," he said. "I have binoculars here."

"No need," I said. "I keep binoculars in my SUV. They're part of the private investigator's starter kit."

"I'd say you're way past a starter kit."

Howard replied to the email with our cell-phone numbers. He was driver number one, with the money, and I was driver number two, who would pick up Cindy.

A minute later, the phone buzzed. Howard picked it up before it could make another sound. "Yes?"

We listened. It was the same electronic voice. "Any questions?"

Howard looked at me, and I shook my head.

"None," Howard said.

"Excellent," the voice said. "Do as I say, and you have my word your granddaughter will be returned and you will never hear from me again. Leave now. Driver one goes south. Driver two goes north. You both will soon get a call. Do not call each other." The caller hung up.

"Cindy has seen me enough over the years so she should recognize me," I said.

"Let's go," he said.

12

I followed Howard out of the parking lot and watched as he turned south. I waited a few seconds, then made my way north, doing the speed limit.

A minute later, my phone rang. "Proceed to Center of Angels Cemetery," said a slightly different electronic voice. I guessed each caller had a voice-changing device.

Center of Angels Cemetery was maybe five miles away, and I would have to drive on back roads that only locals used. The day was cold and the sky seemed pregnant, about to deliver on forecasted light snow.

As I neared the cemetery, my cell phone rang again. "Turn into the cemetery and keep right," the same voice said. "Do not hang up. Do you have binoculars?"

"I do."

"Good," the voice said. "I have eyes on you now. Drive to the top of the hill and stop."

I did as instructed. I had a Glock Nine, loaded and ready, in my center console. I hoped I wouldn't need it. I was tired of shooting people.

The cemetery was on a large tract with small hills on both boundaries and a valley in the middle. I was guessing Cindy Carter would be with her abductor on the opposite hill—a hill where I once had a shootout with another bad guy. I stopped the car and got out.

"Take a good look at the opposite hill," the voice said.

I raised the binoculars and scanned the hill, stopping when I saw something I had a hard time processing. Standing beside Cindy Carter, holding her hand, was a clown. They were a half-mile away, maybe a little more. The clown, his face a silly grin, waved. He said something to Cindy. Then Cindy waved. There was something horrific about the scene. I could feel my face getting hot with anger. If I had been holding a high-powered sniper rifle with a scope at that moment, I would have put a bullet right through the center of that happy face.

"You see us?" the electronic voice said.

"Yes."

"Satisfied?"

"Yes."

"I'll send her down as soon as the money is dropped. Hang up."

I disconnected, never taking my binoculars off Cindy. The clown made another call. I waited.

My phone rang. "Do you see her?" Howard Cox asked.

"Yes."

"Does she appear to be okay?"

"Yes."

"Thank God. I'm leaving the money," Howard said. "I'm throwing it out the window now and driving away."

I could hear his car's engine. About thirty seconds later, Cindy Carter started running down the hill, and the clown disappeared into the woods behind her.

"She's free," I said. "I'm on my way to get her. I'll call you back soon."

I jumped in the SUV and followed the road down and around to the spot where Cindy was heading. We arrived at about the same time.

Cindy did not hesitate. She opened the passenger door, got in, urgently fastened her seatbelt, and looked at me. "He told me not to be afraid, that it was just a game," she said.

"And you're the winner," I said.

"That wasn't really a game, was it?" she said, tears streaming down her face.

"In a way, it was." I put my hand on her shoulder. "A weird little game, and it's over. We won."

"That clown was strange. All he did was whisper. I was scared."

"Yes, he was strange, but he's gone, and he's not coming back."

Cindy forced a smile and stopped crying.

I called Howard Cox. "Got her," I said. "She's fine. I'll see you back at the office."

"Thank you, Jesus," he said, and started sobbing just before he broke our connection.

◆   ◆   ◆   ◆

I can describe Big Bob's mood only as agitated. I had called him on my way back to Cox Foods and asked him to meet me there, stressing that it was important. I had also told him to put out a BOLO on a clown.

"Be on the lookout for a clown?" he bellowed.

"Just do it," I had said. "I'll explain later."

He was pacing Howard's office as we explained the events of the morning. Megan and Cindy had gone home with Megan's mother. Those two would need some counseling. We finished our tale, and Big Bob sat on the couch. The leather hissed under the big man's weight.

"Explain to me why you didn't call the police," Big Bob said. He was looking at Howard Cox. Howard looked at me.

"Play the voice mail," I said.

The three of us listened.

"So instead of calling us, you called him," Big Bob said, nodding at me.

Him? This was not going well.

"All that mattered was getting my granddaughter back safe and sound," Howard said, sounding annoyed himself. "If we hurt your feelings, I'm sorry." He didn't sound sorry. He sounded sarcastic.

Big Bob made a noise and turned his glare on me. "What's your excuse?"

"I was hired by Mr. Cox to get his granddaughter back," I said. "I felt police involvement would complicate matters, and we had to move swiftly."

"Swiftly," Big Bob snorted.

Nobody said anything for a while. Big Bob alternated his glare between Howard and me.

"Did either one of you see anything that could help us catch these guys?"

"Nothing," Howard Cox said.

"I saw a clown," I said. "Maybe six feet tall, slender, red nose."

"Great," he said, shaking his head. "We're looking for Bozo the Clown."

I don't think Big Bob found that remotely funny. He got up, headed out of Howard Cox's office, stopped at the door, turned, and looked at us. "We'll need to talk with your daughter and granddaughter as soon as possible," he said to Howard. He turned to me. "I'm going to send Mary to do that interview. I expect you'll have some explaining to do when you get home."

I said nothing. It made sense to send Mary. She was MCPD's best detective, and a woman might get more out of a little girl than a man could.

He fired one final shot in my direction. "The diner, tomorrow morning, eight o'clock. Be there or I'll pull your ears off." He didn't wait for an answer.

We watched the big man go.

"He's pissed," Howard said.

"He'll cool off. We did the right thing."

"I want to hire you to find the men who did this," Howard said.

"Might be a waste of time," I said. "My guess is they are long gone. I'm sure they had an escape plan and executed it as soon as they had the money and released Cindy."

"More than likely. Still, I'd like you to look into it. I don't care what it costs. Take all the time you need."

"I'll give it some thought," I said. "If I come up with any leads, I'll follow them. In the meantime, check and see if any of your employees failed to show up for work today, or if any quit or were fired recently."

"Absent, quit, or fired," he repeated, making notes. "How far back should I go for the quit or fired?"

"A year ought to do it."

I stood up, and we shook hands.

"Thanks for your help," he said. "You were a lifesaver."

I didn't know what to say to that, so I just smiled and left the building.

◆   ◆   ◆   ◆

That night, Mary and I ate takeout lasagna. I made my infamous Caesar salad, and we uncorked an expensive bottle of Bordeaux. Mary had been insisting that, since I could afford it, we treat ourselves to better wine. She was right, of course.

"Let me tell you about my morning," I said. "I'll bet it was more exciting than yours."

"From what I hear, it was," Mary said.

As we ate and drank, Mary listened to how my morning had gone, my side of the story. She had already heard Big Bob's, Megan's, and Cindy's. So I told all of it in as great detail as I could recall.

"What are the odds that one little girl would be kidnapped twice before she's eight years old?" Mary said.

"Pretty far out there. She should be in the *Guinness Book of World Records*."

"And you with her. You rescued her twice."

I started on my second helping of lasagna and Mary on her second glass of wine. The woman had her priorities in order.

"No lecture?" I said.

"None. Wouldn't do any good. Besides, Cindy is safe, and that's all that matters. Big Bob knows that."

"I know he does," I said. "But I'm still going to get a lecture."

"Without a doubt."

"What did you get from Megan and Cindy?"

"Nothing relevant," Mary said. "They were both drugged. Probably ether. Cloth over the face from behind. Never saw a face."

"Except for the clown."

"Except for that. Evidently, Cindy was out the whole time. She kind of remembers the clown carrying her through the woods, but the first thing she really remembers is being on the hill a few minutes before you showed up."

"Did she know it was me?"

"She thought it was you," Mary said. "She recognized the Pathfinder. The clown didn't tell her it was you. He probably didn't know who you were. He just told Cindy you were there to pick her up, and that she should go down the hill to meet you."

"How did she seem?"

"Brave and focused," Mary said. "She's really something. If it bothered her, she's not showing it. I didn't mention kidnapping, and I didn't mention ransom money. We told her someone was just playing a bad joke on her mother and that we wanted to find out who and punish them. I also told her not to mention it to anyone, that it would hurt our investigation."

I took another small portion of lasagna and opened my second beer. "Think she'll keep quiet?"

"I think so," Mary said. "I told her that's how she could help with the investigation."

"So, basically, you've got nothing."

"Not a damn thing," Mary said.

13

At eight o'clock on most mornings, the diner was buzzing. This particular morning was no exception. I waited for the buzz to die down, as it always did when the big man entered. But it didn't. He arrived almost unnoticed through the back door. I say *almost* because Doris was there thirty seconds later with a mug of black coffee.

"Thanks, Doris," Big Bob said. "It's damn cold out there."

We ordered, and I waited while he enjoyed that first taste of coffee.

"Anything you can add to yesterday?" he asked calmly. I could tell he was over it.

"Only the obvious."

"Indulge me," he said.

"There were at least two of them. They were well acquainted with Howard Cox *and* Megan *and* Cindy. They took time planning it. At least one of them is a local. The cemetery was the perfect place to do the exchange. They never planned to hurt Cindy, and they're probably a thousand miles away from here by now. If you don't find a suspect among Cox Foods employees, you're not going to find one."

"Probably not," he said. "Mr. Cox is going to send us a list this morning. We'll check to see where everyone was. Maybe we'll get lucky. It's not out of the realm of possibility that a current employee is involved."

"About yesterday . . . ," I began.

He held up a hand to stop me. "As a parent, I'm telling you that you did the right thing. You got the little girl back. That's what counts. A lot of things could have gone wrong if you called it in. They could have spotted us, and things could have turned out badly. Or one of my guys could have gotten excited and blown it. As the chief of police, I can only say you should have trusted that I would not let that happen."

"I didn't want it to get complicated."

"I know," he said as Doris set our food in front of us. "Forget about it. Let's eat."

◆   ◆   ◆   ◆

I was in the office by nine o'clock. I locked the front door and went into my office, closing my door behind me. Gretchen would be in by ten. That gave me an hour to sort things out. I needed to process. The chances of tracking down Cindy Carter's kidnappers were evaporating by the minute. I had one good lead: the clown. A man didn't use a clown disguise on a whim. I would bet he had done it before.

I picked up my office phone and dialed Buckley Clarke's cell. Buckley was a junior G-man fast becoming a senior G-man in the Knoxville FBI office. He was also Gretchen's main squeeze. I had worked with Buckley on a couple of cases when I consulted with the bureau.

"Don," Buckley answered. "Everything okay?"

"Fine," I said. "Your lady love is not in yet. I need a favor."

"And you didn't want to bother the deputy director or Agent Glass."

"I've already bothered Agent Glass on another matter, and I'd rather bother you than David Steele. Him I save for the big stuff."

"Your wish is my command," Buckley said.

"See if, in your files, you have any unsolved kidnapping cases involving a clown."

"A clown?" Buckley said. "Like Bozo?"

"Probably not Bozo. A distant cousin, maybe."

I told him about Cindy Carter's kidnapping and about not calling the police and why.

"That was a good decision," Buckley said.

"Is this something you guys would get involved in after the fact?"

"Well, since state lines were not crossed, we would get involved only if local law enforcement asked us to," Buckley said. "Maybe not even then, since the child is back safe. Let me make some calls about the clown MO. I'll call you if I come up with anything."

◆ ◆ ◆ ◆

Gretchen arrived. As usual, we went over a to-do list, which was to say things she was going to do with my approval. Most of the time, I said, "Go ahead." On rare occasions, I said, "Let's hold up on that."

When I was alone again, I pulled out my notes on Lola Madrid. One scribbling struck me as curious. Lola had said something about growing up on P.E.I. I went online and Googled "P.E.I.," and it popped right up, big as life: Prince Edward Island. *Now I'm getting somewhere*, I thought.

I did some research. P.E.I. was about one-twentieth the size of Tennessee and had a population less that Tennessee's fourth-largest city, Chattanooga. If Lola Madrid had grown up on Prince Edward Island, then I should be able to find some trace of her. I searched for high schools. I found five. It was a start.

I buzzed Gretchen. She was in front of my desk in five seconds, note-pad and pen in hand.

"I need some more research on Lola Madrid," I said.

"You have another lead?"

"I do. I think she grew up on Prince Edward Island. There seem to be five high schools on the island. See if you can find if Lola Madrid graduated from one of them."

"I doubt that's her real name," Gretchen said.

"Maybe not, but it's a lead we have to follow. Maybe you can get into an annual file and look at pictures."

Gretchen nodded and returned to her desk.

I now had the wheels in motion on both cases. All I could do was wait.

14

I was up early Saturday sitting at my desk in my lake house office and looking at the Wall Street week in review on my desktop computer. I took a sip of freshly made coffee and opened my stock portfolio. Stocks had taken a roller-coaster ride during the week and had closed on Friday close to where they had opened Monday. I had no doubt that during the week fortunes had been won and lost; that was the nature of a wild up-and-down week. I had been oblivious, gaining nothing and, more importantly, losing nothing. In truth, my interest in investing was waning. Gretchen was becoming adept, and I was content turning that part of our business over to her. I would be macro to her micro. I needed the adrenaline rush of big cases. I didn't know if either of the two I had just started would turn into anything, but time would tell.

As usual on Friday nights, Mary and I had driven to the lake house and had a nice, relaxing dinner in front of the fireplace, followed by a close encounter of the coupling kind. Saturday morning, Mary was still sleeping, and the house was quiet. Quiet had taken up residence since Lacy had gone off to college two thousand miles away. The sounds of teenagers that had once dominated our weekends were no more. The house was lonely. We were suffering from off-to-college syndrome. Mary freely admitted it; I did not. *Toughness is all.*

I didn't expect the phone to ring, but it did. I certainly didn't expect it to be junior G-man Buckley Clarke, but it was. *Hope it's not a social call,* I thought. It wasn't.

"You're working on the weekend," I said when I answered. Caller ID allowed me to be clairvoyant.

"I am," Buckley said. "And I have some information I thought you'd be interested in."

"I'm all ears."

Buckley got right to it. "In 2006, 2009, and 2011, there were three kidnappings with the MO you described. All demanding one hundred thousand dollars the same day the child was abducted. All ransoms paid the same day. All the children returned safe by a clown. In every instance, it was a rich grandfather paying the ransom, and in every instance it was pocket change. They were all much wealthier than Howard Cox."

"So they were all reported after the fact," I said.

"Yes. One of the grandfathers was a heavy hitter and had friends at the bureau, so the FBI got involved. The trail was cold, no leads. That was the 2011 case. We uncovered the other two while canvassing local law enforcement for similar cases."

"I wonder how he picked his victims."

"Could be as simple as going online and researching the rich. Plenty of rich grandfathers in Texas," Buckley said.

"Did they all occur in Texas?"

"Every one."

"All girls?"

"As far as I can tell, all girls and all around the age of eight to ten."

"What do you want to bet this guy did some others that weren't reported?" I said. "Especially in 2007, 2008, and 2010. He could have been doing one a year. Not a bad little tax-free income. And I'd also bet he was from Texas or worked in Texas."

"I think you're right on all counts," Buckley said. "Because there's more."

"I'm listening."

"I expanded the file search to include anything with a clown reference." Buckley paused, waiting for my response.

"And?"

"Nothing. So the next logical step was to look at Texas law-enforcement files."

"I'm guessing you found something."

"You're right. I found a guy in the Texas Criminal Investigation Division computer files that did time for armed robbery. His name is Royce Rogers."

"Armed robbery," I said. "He robbed someone while dressed as a clown?"

"No, he robbed a casino in Texas and was caught only because the police got an anonymous tip."

"You're not going to tell me he took only a hundred grand from the casino."

"More than that," Buckley said. "But he left a lot behind. Maybe he thought they wouldn't notice. Or maybe he got scared. Or maybe he's just plain nuts. Who knows?"

"Or maybe he was on the clock."

"Could be. But I'd vote for just plain nuts."

"Or there's another reason we don't see," I said. "So how does the clown part fit in?"

"Because of the anonymous tip, the TCID got a warrant to search his house. They found some of the casino money hidden in the basement with a clown outfit complete with face paint and red nose. The report said the money was well hidden and that they were lucky to find it. They had some kind of money-sniffing dog."

"You can't fool those money-hungry dogs," I said.

"Apparently not."

"Did they make the connection to the clown kidnappings?"

"They did. Someone remembered the kidnapping cases. They looked but couldn't come up with any evidence to link Royce Rogers to them. No evidence that he had been anywhere near where they occurred. Rogers conveniently couldn't remember where he was at the time of the kidnappings, so no alibis either. They couldn't find any bank accounts or safe-deposit boxes, so no other money. Bottom line: he might have done the kidnappings, or he might not have done them."

"The kidnapping money could be anywhere."

"Here's the real interesting thing," Buckley said. "The last clown kidnapping was in 2011. No record of one in 2010, but he could have done one. I'm told Rogers was in prison from early 2012 until three months ago. No record of a clown kidnapping while he was in prison."

"That's a big coincidence. And I don't like coincidences. But why did he end up in Tennessee? There's much bigger game in Texas."

"I guess that's one thing you'll have to find out for yourself," Buckley said.

"I guess I will."

"One final thing. Rogers swore he was innocent on all counts."

"Don't they all?" I said.

◆　◆　◆　◆

I went to the kitchen, fixed a second cup of coffee, and returned to my office. The house remained quiet. I sat, drank coffee, and thought about everything Buckley had told me. Most law-enforcement personnel will tell you—off the record, of course—that luck is involved in breaking cases, like getting a search warrant for money and finding a clown costume. Could it be that Royce Rogers got out of prison, came to East Tennessee, and kidnapped Cindy Carter? That was a long shot, but if I could find a connection between Rogers and East Tennessee, then it might be a more reasonable assumption. Maybe his current partner knew Howard Cox.

I called Buckley.

"If you would, find out where Rogers was in prison," I said. "I'd like to talk to the warden, if you can set it up. Tell him I'm interested in information on Royce Rogers."

"You think he could be the guy that snatched Cindy Carter?"

"It's possible. But if I can't find an East Tennessee connection, then I don't think so."

"I'll get back to you," Buckley said.

15

"**I** found Lola Madrid," Gretchen said when she came in Monday morning.

"You did not," I said.

"Well, I found a Lola Madrid that went to high school on Prince Edward Island. I can't believe there would be two of them."

"So Lola Madrid is her real name."

"If it's the same Lola Madrid you're looking for. I couldn't find any pictures."

"Tell me all," I said.

"The Lola Madrid I found graduated from Souris Regional High School in Souris, Prince Edward Island, seventeen years ago."

"That would make her about thirty-five. She certainly doesn't look thirty-five."

"Probably all that makeup."

"Right," I said. "I'm sure it's the makeup. What else?"

"I didn't find any Madrids in the Souris town directory. Souris is a small town, so not surprising. But since the high school is regional, I searched the surrounding area and found a Selma Madrid in nearby Stratford. Stratford is not big either, but it's larger that Souris. Selma is the owner and manager of an upscale B&B. I took the virtual tour online. It's nice. You want her phone number?"

"No."

"I didn't think so," Gretchen said. "I'm guessing you'll want to see her in person."

"You guessed right."

"Mary might not like that. Especially if Selma looks anything like her daughter."

"Be sure to add a confidentiality clause to this partnership agreement we're signing," I said.

"Relax, my liege. What's said in this office does not get repeated by me, no way, no how."

"Right answer," I said. "See if you can get any more info on Selma Madrid."

"I'm on it," Gretchen said.

◆　◆　◆　◆

That afternoon, Buckley called.

"My main squeeze is on line one," Gretchen said over the intercom.

"Your main squeeze? Does that mean you have a minor squeeze?"

"Funny. Just answer the friggin' phone."

So I did. "Buckley," I said. "What have you got?"

"Warden Harold 'Call Me Hal' Dansk is all set to talk to you in the morning at ten," Buckley said. "I might have implied you're assisting the FBI, you being a top consultant and all. He said he would pull the file on Royce Rogers and review it before you call. He didn't seem too impressed you're an FBI consultant, so don't be expecting unbridled enthusiasm."

"You FBI guys do have a way with words."

"We try," Buckley said.

"Is that my ten o'clock or his?"

"Good question. I'm pretty sure it's his ten o'clock."

"Know anything about this guy?"

"Ex-marine, tough as nails, all business, been there for fifteen years," Buckley said. "I figured you'd ask."

"What prison?"

"Huntsville, the oldest prison in Texas, where they send all the death-penalty recipients off to the great beyond."

"A death house," I said.

"For lack of a better term," Buckley said. "Let's just say it's a serious place and Hal Dansk is a serious guy."

◆　◆　◆　◆

I sat at my desk after Gretchen left for the day and thought about my two cases. I was hoping a phone call would relieve me of traveling to Texas. If I had to go to Texas, I'd do so before going to Prince Edward Island. A kidnapping clown took precedence over a lovesick yuppie in the Big Apple.

16

The next morning, I called the number for Hal Dansk at exactly eleven o'clock my time, ten o'clock his. It must have been a private line. He answered on the second ring.

"Youngblood?"

"Yes, sir, Warden Dansk," I said. *Youngblood, the respectful private detective. Or is it FBI consultant?* I couldn't keep that straight.

"Prompt," he said. "I like that. I've got the file, ask your questions."

I wasn't sure where to start, so I tossed the ball back to him. "Did you have any dealings with the prisoner personally?"

"No, never met him."

He sounded like David Steele when he had been my drill instructor at Quantico: sharp, clipped, hurried words. No nonsense.

"Is there anything in the file you find interesting?"

"Well, he was never in trouble here," Warden Dansk said, seeming to relax a little. "No write-ups of any kind. Somebody always gets written up for something. And he had a high IQ—160, the file says. Must not have been that smart, he ended up here."

"Did he have visitors?"

"Yeah, thought you would ask that. I looked that up. No visitors," he said. "Most of our guys have visitors, so that's out of the ordinary."

"Was he housed alone, or did he have a cellmate?"

"He had two cellmates," Dansk said. "Harrison Cook and Richard Card. Cook was moved to a different block when he started working in the kitchen. The guy was actually a chef. Poisoned his wife and got life. He does more with less than any guy I know. Anyway, I digress. Cook was with Rogers for about a year, and then Card was with him until Card was released."

"When was that?"

"Richard Card was released a month before Rogers."

"What was Card in for?"

"Possession with intent to distribute," Dansk said.

"Was Card ever a problem?"

"Not that I can tell. I never met him either."

"Is Cook still there?"

"For the rest of his natural life," the warden said.

"I might want to come down and talk with him. Would that be possible?"

"Why not?" Dansk said. "I like you, Youngblood. You don't pussyfoot around. Call when you're ready, and I'll set it up."

"Thank you, sir. I appreciate it. I won't take up any more of your time."

"Over and out," Dansk said. He hung up.

◆　◆　◆　◆

Buckley called after lunch.

"Buckley on line one," Gretchen said.

"What happen to 'main squeeze'?"

"Don't push it," Gretchen said.

"Sorry."

I pushed line one. "Youngblood."

"How'd it go with Dansk?" Buckley asked.

"Pretty well. He invited me down for a tour of the place."

"You're kidding."

"Well, yes, but he did offer to set up a meeting with one of Royce Rogers's cellmates."

"You going?"

"Maybe. I'll have to think about it."

"Well, if you do, I'd like to tag along."

"Why?"

"I'd kind of like to see the place," Buckley said. "And if you're on to something, I'd like to position myself to get the case."

"You're a sly one," I said.

"I'm learning from the best."

"Flattery will get you everywhere," I said. "If I go, you go."

17

We went to Texas two days later. Roy arranged Fleet Industries jet number one with Jim Doak again at the helm. Buckley was in heaven flying the private jet on my dime. If I could prove that Royce Rogers was a serial kidnapper, then I might ask David Steele to reimburse me.

The flight took about two and a half hours, wheels up to wheels down. We left Tri-Cities Airport at eight and landed in Huntsville at nine-thirty Central Standard Time.

"Wait on us," I said to Jim Doak. "We certainly don't want to be stranded here. We shouldn't be long."

"I'll be here," Jim said.

The clerk at the rental car desk laughed when I asked for a Lincoln Navigator. "Our premium offers are a Chevy Impala or a Dodge Ram 1500. That's a truck, by the way."

Smartass.

I took the truck. We'd fit right in.

"Nice ride," Buckley said when we got in.

"When in Rome," I said.

The penitentiary was three miles from the airport, a straight shot onto Fourteenth Street and then a couple of turns to Twelfth. We parked in the visitors' lot. Five minutes later, we were sitting in front of Hal Dansk's desk. Try saying that fast three times. Unfortunately, Hal wasn't at his desk, but we were promised he would be there soon.

Five minutes later, he bolted through his door, a man in a hurry. "Sorry," he said.

We stood.

"Hal Dansk," he said, extending a hand.

Hal looked like a drill sergeant—chiseled face, short salt-and-pepper flattop, penetrating, dark eyes. He was about my height and appeared to be hard as nails.

"Don Youngblood," I said, shaking his hand. It was a firm shake, but he didn't overdo it. "This is FBI agent Buckley Clarke."

Hal shook Buckley's hand and went around his desk and sat. "I thought you would be alone," he said, clearly annoyed that I had an escort.

"Buckley's kind of an amateur historian," I said. "He wanted to see the place."

Dansk's mood changed immediately. "Well, I'd be happy to give you a tour while Youngblood interviews Cook."

"That would be great," Buckley said. I couldn't tell if he meant it or was just playing along.

Dansk pushed a button on his intercom. "Gail, is Harrison Cook in interview room three?"

"Yes, warden," the intercom responded.

Warden Dansk stood. "Let's go."

We followed him down a hall to a door on the right.

"In there," Dansk said to me.

"Is a guard in there?"

"Affirmative," he said.

"I'd like to be alone with Cook."

Dansk paused to think about that. "Since you're technically FBI, I guess I can allow that. Tell the guard I said it was okay. If you finish before Agent Clarke and I get back, let Gail know you're through, then go wait in my office."

"Will do," I said.

"Agent Clarke, you're with me," Dansk said, apparently forgetting he was no longer in the marines.

Buckley smiled at me and followed Dansk down the hall, around a corner, and out of sight.

◆　◆　◆　◆

I took a few moments collecting my thoughts before I opened the door to interview room three. Harrison Cook sat at a table handcuffed to an O-ring bolted to the table. The table was bolted to the floor. A guard stood in one corner at attention, a blank look on his face. There was no two-way glass for viewing. I wondered if the place was bugged. It looked like a room where a client might speak with his lawyer.

"I'd like to be alone with Mr. Cook," I said to the guard. "The warden said it would be okay."

The guard nodded and left, never changing expression.

I turned to Harrison Cook, who was decked out in bright orange. "I'm Don Youngblood. I'm a private investigator from East Tennessee."

"Harrison Cook," he said. "Pardon me if I don't get up." Cook appeared to be a tall man. He had brown wavy hair and a friendly face.

I nodded and sat.

"You must have some juice if you got in here for an interview," he said. "The warden runs a pretty tight ship." His voice was a rich baritone, the accent hard to place, although from the file I knew he had grown up in Norwalk, Connecticut.

"I sometimes do consulting with the FBI," I said.

He nodded. "Let's make this quick. I need to get back to the kitchen. A lot of mouths to feed. Why are you here?"

So much for small talk.

"I want to ask you about Royce Rogers," I said.

"Why? Royce in trouble?"

"Not that I know of."

"Why should I talk to you?"

"No reason. But if you do, it will not go unrewarded."

"How so?"

"You might want something for the kitchen—special spices or a piece of equipment, whatever. I could make that happen."

Well, maybe I can or maybe I can't.

He thought for a minute. "A Cuisinart stand mixer with a dough hook. That would be nice."

"Done," I said. Of course, I had no idea if the warden would go along, but I couldn't be sidetracked by a technicality.

"What do you want to know?"

"What kind of guy was Rogers?"

"Pleasant-enough guy," Cook said. "Quiet, smart, organized, meticulous. He was a neatnik. I am, too, so we got along."

"Sounds like the perfect cellmate."

Cook shrugged and said nothing.

"What?" I said.

"He was a little bit off, if you know what I mean. Sometimes, he wasn't all there. He'd start talking about being framed and who might do such a thing. He just could not believe he was in prison."

"Do you believe he was framed?"

He thought about it. "A lot of guys talk about being framed, you know. I think some of them talk about it so much they believe it's true."

"Was Royce one of those?"

"I don't know. But if there was one guy in here that might have been framed, Royce would be my pick."

"Did he ever talk about the outside?"

"Not specifically. We'd talk sports and politics sometimes, and places we had been, but never personal stuff."

"He never mentioned friends or family?"

"One time, he mentioned he had a sister," Cook said. "Then he quickly added that he hadn't seen her in years and didn't know where she was. It was like he was trying to take it back."

"Did he ever mention East Tennessee?"

"He never talked about anyplace but Texas and New Mexico," Cook said. "He was from Santa Fe."

"Did he ever mention dressing up as a clown?"

Cook laughed heartily. "A clown? Royce? No, never. Royce dressing up as a clown? Now, that's rich."

I was out of questions. I stood and placed a business card on the table. I said nothing. The gesture was self-evident. I headed for the door.

"Going to send that Cuisinart?" Cook asked from behind me.

"Sure am," I said. "Whether the warden gives it to you or not is your problem."

"I think he will," he said. "The warden's a foodie."

I closed the door behind me.

As I walked past Gail's desk, I said, "I'm done. The warden told me to wait in his office."

"They'll be a while," she drawled. "The warden loves to give tours of the place, and he hasn't given one in months."

"Not a problem," I said. "I have some calls to make."

◆ ◆ ◆ ◆

A half-hour later, I was still waiting. I had called Gretchen and learned there was nothing new. I had called Mary, who said she was in the middle of something and would see me tonight. Then I called Lacy, who said everything was great at Arizona State and she was headed to an English lit class.

After that, I got really bored. I paced the room and saw on the warden's desk two files: Harrison Cook and Richard Card. I picked up Cook's file and read it front to back, learning a few more details but nothing helpful. Cook was six-four and weighed 225. He was a few years older than I was and had been at Huntsville for over five years. He had been a chef in an upscale Houston restaurant. He had hired a private detective to follow his wife to see if she was having an affair. She was. Harrison rewarded her with a delicious home-cooked lobster stew laced with prussic acid, the liquid form of cyanide. She didn't last through dessert. He maintained throughout his trial that he had no idea how the poison had found its way to the stew. The jury was unconvinced.

I opened Richard Card's file and sat staring at the first page. I had made the East Tennessee connection: Richard Card's unmistakable mugshot. Unless he had an identical twin, I was looking at the face of the supposedly dead Ricky Carter, Megan Carter's father.

◆　◆　◆　◆

Buckley and the warden appeared as I sat reading the file of the man I was sure was Ricky Carter.

"How'd it go with Cook?" Warden Dansk asked.

"Fine," I said.

"Helpful?"

"Some."

"What did he get out of you?"

I laughed. "How did you know?"

"Information is the coin of the realm around here," Dansk said. "If you want it, it will cost you."

"A Cuisinart stand mixer," I said. "With a dough hook. I told him I would send it and it was up to you whether he got it or not."

"Hell, yes, I'll give it to him. I like homemade bread as well as the next guy."

"Can I borrow these two files for a few days? I'll send them back UPS overnight."

"I can allow that, since they're no longer guests at this fine establishment. Something in there interest you?"

"Maybe," I said.

Definitely, I thought.

"Anything else interesting come out of the interview?"

I sat and stared at Dansk and said nothing.

He waited. Then he didn't. "What?"

"Harrison Cook said Royce Rogers talked about how he didn't do it and how someone framed him. Why would he spin that story to Cook?"

"Lots of guys in here want us to think they're innocent," Dansk said. "None of them are. A few may be here on a bum rap for one reason or another, but none of them are innocent."

"Maybe you're right, but Rogers had no priors. Don't you find that strange?"

"I do," Dansk said. "But it happens."

◆   ◆   ◆   ◆

On the way back to Tri-Cities Airport, I told Buckley the story of my first encounter with Ricky Carter. He sat mesmerized.

"You found him in Bermuda?"

"I did."

"And up until an hour ago, you thought he was dead."

"Yes."

"So you have your East Tennessee connection."

"I do indeed," I said, feeling rather proud of myself.

In the long run, skill wins out over luck. When you have both, you're golden.

◆   ◆   ◆   ◆

That night, Mary and I went to the lake house. We usually went on Fridays, but Mary was working a case that took her outside Mountain Center, and she wouldn't have to make the drive back into town. The drive didn't bother me, as I enjoyed the lake house more than the condo.

The days were getting shorter. Daylight saving time had ended, and it was dark when I drove down the driveway and parked. The dogs perked up immediately. I turned them loose in the side yard, and we went inside. I turned off the alarm, turned on the water, and bumped up the heat. Fifteen minutes later, as Mary came down the driveway, I retrieved the dogs.

A half-hour after that, Mary and I sat in front of the fireplace eating Chinese takeout Mary had picked up on her way and drinking our beer of choice. About halfway through the sesame shrimp, I reached into my briefcase and pulled out the Richard Card file. We had not discussed my trip. Thanksgiving was approaching, and all Mary could talk about was the feast at the Fleet mansion next week. I dropped the file in front of her.

"What's this?" Mary said.

"A big clue in the Cindy Carter kidnapping."

She looked at the folder. "Richard Card?"

I smiled.

It took her only a few seconds. "Ricky fucking Carter?"

I nodded and ignored the profanity. It came with being married to a cop, and Mary kept it to a minimum.

She opened the folder and stared at Ricky's mugshot. "I thought he was supposed to be dead."

"So did a lot of other people."

18

Early the next morning, I was in the Mountain Center police station, in the office of the chief. I had come in with two large cups of Dunkin' Donuts coffee and a dozen assorted donuts. The donuts had a life expectancy of maybe fifteen minutes.

"Well, I know you want something," Big Bob said, taking his first drink of coffee while staring into the box of donuts. "I hope it's not more time off for Mary."

"Nothing like that," I said. "You're far too cynical."

"You come bearing gifts. You want something. What is it?"

I slid the Richard Card file across his desk.

He looked at the outside of the file, stamped, "Texas Department of Criminal Justice—Huntsville Unit," then back up at me. "What's this?"

"Open it."

He opened the folder and stared at the first page. "Are you fucking kidding me?"

"The chief of police shouldn't be using vulgar language," I said. "It sets a bad example for the troops."

Head never rising, he peered out at me underneath his thick eyebrows. His scowl was self-explanatory: *Fuck off*.

He eyes dropped back to the folder. "Ricky Carter?"

"Or his twin. You have his prints on file. I need your fingerprint expert to compare this file to yours and confirm this is who we think it is. I'd bet a million bucks it's Ricky."

"No bet," he said. "I assume you told Mary."

"I did."

"What was her reaction?"

"Pretty much the same as yours."

He rose from his desk and picked up the file and his coffee. "I'll be back in a few minutes."

Ten minutes later, he tossed the file on his desk and picked a Boston Kreme from the box of donuts. He sat and took a bite and then a drink of coffee.

"It's him," he said.

"Good to have confirmation."

"I thought Ricky was dead."

"I was misinformed," I said.

"Now what?"

"I don't know. I want to find Royce Rogers and shut him down. I don't want any more little kids subjected to this weird kidnapping scenario."

"Good luck with that," Big Bob said. "He's long gone."

"There's a trail somewhere. I just need to find it."

◆   ◆   ◆   ◆

The first thing I noticed when I walked into the office was a new door to the right of Gretchen's desk. It led from the outer office to the vacant office next to ours. Our expansion had begun.

I walked out in the hall and stared at the outer door leading to the vacant office. It read, "Cherokee Investigations—Use main door." A recently added line on the door that at one time was the only entrance now declared it as the "Main Door." Gretchen had been busy. I smiled to myself and went back inside, wondering how I had missed that in the first place.

I had a second cup of coffee and sat in my desk chair with my legs on the window sill, staring down at Main Street. Traffic was light, as it usually was that time of day. A light cloud cover was letting some sunlight through, giving the midmorning a soft, comfortable look. I thought about the clown and Ricky Carter, about what a lowlife Ricky was, setting up a kidnapping of his own daughter for profit. I wanted Ricky Carter more than I wanted the clown.

I dug into my card file and found the one I was looking for, a four-year-old business card from a Knoxville drug kingpin:

Rasheed Xavier Reed
President, Ace Security
Knoxville, TN 37996

Rasheed had been instrumental in Cindy Carter's return the first time she was kidnapped. I was still having a hard time wrapping my mind around the fact that one little girl had been kidnapped twice before her eighth birthday. She *should* have been in the *Guinness Book of World Records*.

I flipped the card over and looked at the number written on the back. I punched the number into my cell phone. Caller ID was blocked on my office phone, thanks to Gretchen, but it wasn't blocked on my cell, and I wanted Rasheed to see who was calling. I heard three rings and then got a recording, short and sweet: "Leave a message."

"It's Youngblood," I said. "Call me."

◆   ◆   ◆   ◆

Gretchen was in my office soon after ten for our morning meeting.

"I assume you saw the new doorway and new signage," she said.

"I am nothing if not observant."

"I'm so glad," Gretchen said. "With your approval, I'm going to post the job opening at The University of Tennessee and East Tennessee State. I'll request all résumés be in by a certain date—say, two weeks. I'll go through them and pick out three or four candidates to interview. If I find somebody I like, I'll ask you to interview them also. Does that sound like a plan?"

"It does," I said. "Proceed."

Gretchen smiled. "Good." She made some notes, then looked up at me, expectant.

I slid the Richard Card and Royce Rogers files across my desk. "Copy everything in these files. Duplicate the folders as close to the originals as you can. I want the whole files to look as authentic as possible."

"Why?"

"I don't know yet."

"Okay." She shrugged.

"When you're finished, put the copied files on my desk and send the originals back to Warden Dansk." I had paper-clipped the good warden's address to the Rogers file.

We discussed a few minor investment details and a few things she was working on for Rollie Ogle, and then Gretchen returned to her desk, leaving me thinking about the belly dancer and the clown.

◆　◆　◆　◆

Curiosity got the best of Rasheed after lunch. My cell phone rang. His number appeared on my screen.

"That you, Rasheed?"

"Long time, no talk, Youngblood. Is this a social call? You miss talking to the brother?"

"Exactly," I said. "How are you? How's business? How are things in the black community?"

He laughed. "Cut the bullshit, Youngblood. Why *did* you call?"

"I have an interesting file I'd like you to take a look at involving a former acquaintance."

"Who?"

"That would spoil the surprise. And believe me, you will be surprised."

He was silent a few seconds. "How early do you get in on Monday?"

"As early as you want."

"I'll be there around nine o'clock Monday morning," he said. "As long as you understand I am not coming especially to see you. I have to be in the area."

"Of course you do," I said.

He didn't wait for a confirmation. He hung up.

◆　◆　◆　◆

I called Roy Husky.

"Want to grab a beer at the Duck after work?"

"We haven't done that in awhile," Roy said. "What's up?"

"You're not going to believe it," I said. "I'll tell you when I get there."

"Now I'm curious. Six okay?"

"See you then," I said."

◆　　◆　　◆　　◆

The Bloody Duck was a combination blue-collar and biker bar-and-grill out on the highway that led from Mountain Center to Johnson City. I wore black boots, jeans, a black *X-Files* T-shirt proclaiming "The truth is out there" and a black leather jacket. As usual, I was overdressed. Inside the Duck were a bar, a few tables, a few booths, and six full-sized pool tables. The tables were vintage and immaculately maintained. The place was quiet.

Over the years, Roy and I had been in often enough so that no one paid attention to us anymore. Occasionally, Mary joined us. They paid a lot of attention to Mary. Roy and I sat at a vacant booth in the back.

Rocky, the owner, brought us mugs of beer. "Haven't seen you two in a while."

"From time to time, we have to mingle with the little folks," Roy said. He and Rocky went way back.

"How kind of you," Rocky said, sitting down. "I might as well take full advantage. How you doing, Youngblood?"

"No complaints," I said. I took a sip of my Michelob Amber Bock.

"You two want a burger and fries?"

In my opinion, the ten-ounce burgers and hand-cut fries at the Bloody Duck were the best around.

"Probably later," I said.

"You on a case?" Rocky said.

"Sort of. I was hoping to catch Butch Pulaski around."

"If Butch shows up, it'll be soon," Rocky said. "He's usually in three or four days a week."

"If he comes in, give him a beer and send him back here," I said.

"Will do," Rocky said, getting to his feet. "Gotta get back to the bar." He nodded at Roy. Roy nodded back.

"Rocky," I said as he started to leave. He stopped. "You haven't seen Ricky Carter around, have you?"

"Ricky Carter? Rumor has it he's dead," Rocky said. "Killed by some drug dealer."

"Maybe not," I said. "I take it you haven't seen him."

"If I do, you'll be the first to know." He turned and walked away.

"Ricky Carter?" Roy said.

"Drink your beer and listen."

I told him about the clown and Ricky Carter.

By the time I finished, Butch Pulaski was walking our way with a beer in hand. Butch was a working-class guy who had helped me the first time I crossed paths with Ricky Carter.

"Hey, guys," he said. "Thanks for the beer. Haven't seen you-all in here lately."

"We've been busy," Roy said. "Have a seat."

A waitress appeared.

"Want a burger and fries on us?" I said to Butch.

"Hell, yes," Butch said.

We ordered. The waitress sauntered away.

"What's going on?" Butch said. "If I'm getting free beer and a free meal, you guys want something."

"We always knew you were smart," Roy said.

"Have you seen Ricky Carter?" I said.

Butch's face showed total surprise. "Oh, my God. I didn't believe it."

"Believe what?" I said.

"A friend of mine told me that a guy he knew saw Ricky Carter, and I told him he was full of shit, that Ricky was dead. Are you telling me he's alive?"

"Might be," I said, not wanting to get into the details. "Think we could talk to this friend of yours?"

"Sure," Butch said. "If you hang around long enough, he'll probably show up sometime tonight."

So we hung around, drank beer, and ate burgers and fries.

◆   ◆   ◆   ◆

An hour later, Butch's friend Ken sat with us drinking a free beer and feeling important.

"Who was this guy who said he saw Ricky Carter?" I said, not wasting time with pleasantries.

"Mike," Ken said. "Friend of mine at work. Everyone knows Ricky is supposed to be dead, so we kind of blew him off, but he swears it was Ricky."

"You think I could talk with him?"

"Sure," Ken said. "I can call him right now."

So that's what he did.

"Mike," Ken said, "I'm at the Duck with Butch and that private investigator, Donald Youngblood." Pause. "Yeah, that's the one. He wants to ask you some questions about seeing Ricky Carter." Pause. "All right, hold on." Ken passed his cell phone to me. "He's excited," Ken said.

"Hello, Mike."

"You really Donald Youngblood?"

"Yeah, that's me."

"Man, you're famous. It's an honor talking to you."

Mike sounded a little buzzed. I wondered if I was wasting my time.

"Thank you, that's very kind, but I'm wondering if you could tell me about when and where you thought you saw Ricky Carter."

"In a parking lot at the mall. Could it have really been Ricky?"

"Yes, it could have been Ricky. Tell me about it."

"Not much to tell," he said. "I saw this dude going to his ride. He had on sunglasses and a baseball cap pulled low, but I thought to myself, *That dude looks just like Ricky Carter.* He was thinner and looked older, but the more I watched him the more I was sure it was him. Ricky had a special way of walking. I'd know that walk anywhere. I hollered at him, and he turned and looked at me and then took off toward his ride and got in, and it took off."

"What kind of ride?" I said.

"A black SUV. It looked new, but I don't remember the make or model."

"Was Ricky driving?"

"No, he got in the passenger side."

"Did you get a look at the driver?"

"No, it had tinted glass all around."

"Did you get a look at the license plate?"

"Not so I could read the number," Mike said. "But I'll tell you one thing: it wasn't a Tennessee plate."

"Anything else?"

"No, sir."

"Thanks, Mike. I have to go now. You've been a big help." I disconnected before he could say anything else.

"Did he help?" Butch asked.

"Maybe," I said, taking a drink of beer.

Butch took the hint. "Thanks for the beer and the food," he said. "I'm gonna shoot some pool."

After Butch left, Roy looked at me and said, "Well?"

"Did you know I'm famous?"

"Get over yourself, Gumshoe. What did he say?"

"He said he saw Ricky in the mall parking lot with a baseball cap pulled low on his head and sunglasses, but he recognized him anyway." I told Roy everything Mike had told me.

"Think it was Ricky?"

"Too much of a coincidence not to be," I said.

19

Saturday, I watched football as efficiently as possible. My DVR allowed me to watch three games. Mary liked to watch Tennessee football and got much more excited than I did. I tended to brood, question offensive play calling, yell at the refs, and feel uncomfortable until a minute was left in the fourth quarter and the Vols were up three touchdowns.

"Why do you yell at the TV?" Mary had once asked in the early days of our watching Tennessee games.

"Therapy," I said. "It reduces stress."

"Well, if it's that stressful, why watch at all?"

Was she kidding?

"That's part of the fun," I said.

Her only comment to that: "Men!"

This particular Saturday was relatively stress free because Tennessee was playing LSU and I knew there was no way they were going to win that game. I was right, of course, but it was closer than I anticipated.

◆ ◆ ◆ ◆

Sunday, we drove to Gatlinburg and had a late breakfast at the Mountain Lodge. Afterward, we took Highway 441 over the Great Smoky Mountains and down into Cherokee to visit Billy Two-Feathers, his wife, Maggie, and their young son, Donald Roy Youngblood Two-Feathers, otherwise known as "Little D." I, of course, was Little D's godfather and doted on him like a grandchild.

Billy took me to his studio to show me his latest painting. He worked in oil, sold the originals he didn't want to keep, and did not make limited-edition prints, thereby making the originals much more valuable. He had gained a reputation in the area, and his paintings sold almost immedi-ately. His only problem was finding the time to paint.

"Why don't you give up the deputy job and paint full-time?" I said.

"Painting wouldn't mean as much to me if I did it full-time," he said. "I'd get bored. Besides, I like being a deputy sheriff, and I think in some small way I've made a difference in our community."

"I don't doubt that," I said.

Billy's latest was a colorful, striking painting of a war-horse.

"How long have you been working on this?"

"Couple of months," he said. "It's almost finished."

"Going to sell it?"

"Yes," he said.

"How much?"

"Two grand. I already have a buyer."

"That's great, Chief."

I looked around the studio. It held a lot of paintings of Maggie, among them Maggie from the waist up wearing a colorful headdress, Maggie wading in a stream wearing an elaborate Cherokee Indian gown, and Maggie shooting a bow and arrow. All were magnificent. None, I was sure, was for sale.

"You are really talented, my friend."

"Thank you," Billy said. "It is a gift I do not take lightly."

We were quiet as I walked around and looked at everything. Some of the paintings I had seen before. Others were new to me. I knew I was looking at the work of a major talent who probably would never be dis-covered, because that was the way he wanted it. I said nothing. Billy was happy with his life, and I was happy for him.

"What are you working on, Blood?" Billy asked.

"Two very different things, Chief."

I told him about the clown and the belly dancer.

"So Ricky Carter is finally dead?" Billy said.

"I think the odds are pretty good."

Billy nodded.

"I can understand about the clown," Billy said. "That guy needs to be stopped. But why chase down a belly dancer who probably doesn't want to be found?"

"Because I'm a sucker," I said. "Bentley needs closure or he's going to mope around for years the way I did about Maureen Long. Although I must admit my romantic notion is starting to fade."

Maureen Long was a high-school crush I had elevated to goddess status over a period of twenty years until I met Mary. I later saw and had a brief conversation with Maureen and realized what a dope I had been. I certainly had not made the impression on her that she had made on me, and although my ego took a blow, seeing her in the flesh put an end to my fantasy.

Billy smiled. "Knowing you, you'll probably find something sinister. Be careful of what you're looking for."

I said nothing.

"Of course, if you need backup, you'd better call me."

"If I need backup, you'll be the first to know. And if you ever need backup . . ." I let the words trail off.

Billy turned, looked at me and smiled. "You'll be the first to know."

20

O n my way to the office early Monday, I stopped by the diner to pick up some fresh blueberry muffins. Doris fussed and complained about not seeing me often enough.

"I've been away on an important case," I said. "You may not see much of me for a while. I have two cases going."

"I understand," Doris said. "We just miss seeing you, that's all."

I took my muffins and beat a hasty retreat down the alley.

I had thought about bringing the dogs to the office, but I was afraid they might frighten Rasheed, or vice versa. When I was settled in, I popped a K-Cup of original Dunkin' Donuts into my Keurig, added the prerequisite amount of raw sugar and half-and-half, and brewed a nine-ounce mug. I took my coffee to my desk with one of the muffins, booted up my desktop, and spent my time waiting for Rasheed by visiting sports websites. The Tennessee Vols were having a disappointing season, having lost more games than originally predicted by the so-called experts.

At nine o'clock sharp, I heard my outer office door open and close.

"Come on back," I said, loud enough for him to hear.

A big black man filled my doorway, looking no different from the last time I had seen him, which must have been at least four years ago. He was impeccably dressed in a charcoal-gray suit with light gray pinstripes, a lavender shirt with French cuffs and silver cufflinks, and a lavender and silver tie in a full Windsor knot. His black shoes glowed.

"I see you dressed for the occasion."

"I dress for any occasion."

"You're looking well, Rasheed. Would you like a cup of coffee?"

"No, thank you."

"Take a load off," I said, motioning for him to sit.

Rasheed sat in the oversized chair nearest the door. "You're looking pretty good yourself, Youngblood," he said. "I've been following some of your escapades online. What's the big mystery?"

I slid the Richard Card file, which I had retrieved from Gretchen's desk, across my desk to Rasheed.

He looked at the outside of the folder. "Texas Department of Criminal Justice—Huntsville Unit," he said, more to himself than to me. "Richard Card. Who's Richard Card?"

"The mystery," I said. "Open it."

He opened it. His face showed no emotion. Same eyelids that drooped a bit, as if he were sleepy, same slack jaw. Same eyes that didn't miss anything as they stared at the first sheet in the folder.

He looked up at me, never changing expression. "Ricky Carter?"

"Back from the grave, it would appear."

"Is he still at Huntsville?"

"No. But he hasn't been out long."

Rasheed said nothing. Instead, he read the file front to back.

"It would appear that I was misinformed," he said.

"It would."

"Bad for business, me being lied to."

"I thought the same thing."

"I'll look into this," Rasheed said.

"I thought you might."

"Thanks for telling me. I owe you one."

"One thing and we'll call it even," I said.

"Name it," Rasheed said.

"If you find Ricky before I do, don't kill him before I get a chance to talk with him."

"Deal," he said. "And the same goes for me if you find him first."

"Agreed."

"By the way, what did he do to get you on his trail again?"

"Kidnapped his own daughter for ransom."

Rasheed shook his head and said nothing. He stood, walked to my door, and turned. "Some people just don't deserve a second chance."

"I couldn't agree more," I said. "I need you to keep the kidnapping thing quiet. I don't want that on the street."

"It's between you and me. No need for anyone else to know about that. Is the little girl okay?"

"Safe and sound."

"You got her back?"

"I did."

He nodded. "That's good."

Rasheed turned and disappeared into the outer office. Seconds later, I heard the door open and close. I picked up the file and placed it back on Gretchen's desk.

◆   ◆   ◆   ◆

The time had come to call David Steele. I called his direct line, the one reserved for us important folk.

"Office of the deputy director," an icy female voice answered.

"This is Donald Youngblood, ace FBI consultant," I said. "I need to speak to the deputy director at his earliest convenience." *Decorum is all.*

"The deputy director is in a meeting at the moment, Mr. Youngblood," the voice said, thawing a bit. *My reputation has preceded me,* I thought. "I'll be sure he gets the message. Would you prefer he call your office or your cell phone?"

She had obviously pulled me up on her computer. Were there no secrets anymore?

"Office until five o'clock," I said. "Cell phone after five."

"Very well, Mr. Youngblood. I'll pass that along also."

◆   ◆   ◆   ◆

Late that afternoon, close to five, David Steele returned my call.

"Must have been a long meeting," I said.

"I hate to put a dent in that ego of yours, but you weren't exactly first on my list of callbacks," he said. "How are you doing, Youngblood?"

"Fine. I'm working a couple of cases, one of which the FBI might be interested in."

"Tell me," he said.

I told him all of it.

"A serial kidnapper with a unique MO," David Steele said. "God, but you can really pick 'em, Youngblood."

"It's more like they pick me. What do you think?"

"Well, there was no movement across state lines, and the locals didn't ask for our help, so I don't think we can get involved. The FBI has enough to do as it is. Combine that with the fact that no one has gotten hurt and the girls have been returned on the same day, and the FBI will have to pass on this."

"I have a feeling this is not as benign as it seems."

"Explain," he said.

"Well, first, there is the emotional distress suffered by the victims. I've seen that firsthand. Then there are the clown's partners. I've been thinking about that. I know Ricky Carter didn't participate in any of the other kidnappings, which leads me to believe the clown had a different partner for each kidnapping. What happens to Ricky and the others after the job is done?"

"You're thinking he might be getting rid of them."

"Can't rule it out," I said. "Beats splitting the take."

"Any history of violence in Rogers's file?"

"No. But all that could mean is he hasn't been caught."

"At this point, it's a stretch, Youngblood. You need to turn up a dead body and link it to Rogers."

"Yeah, I know," I said. "Lucky me."

"Tell you what," David Steele said. "I'll talk to the SAC in Knoxville and tell him you're working on something special for me and to make Buckley available when you need him. You keep me posted on what you come up with."

"Thanks, Dave. I want to get this guy off the street."

"I hear you," David Steele said. "And I don't disagree. If Ricky Carter turns up dead, then we'll jump in."

"Good enough. By the way, thanks for those unique business cards."

"Don't let them go to your head, Youngblood."

◆ ◆ ◆ ◆

If Ricky Carter was dead, where was the body? The best place to get rid of a body around Mountain Center without going to the trouble of digging a grave was to dump it in the lake with enough weight to keep it under. The closest lake to Mountain Center fell under the jurisdiction of the county sheriff.

I picked up the phone and called Sheriff Jimmy Durham, a longtime friend and high-school basketball adversary. I used his private number.

"That you, Blood?" he answered.

"It is, Bull."

"Long time, no talk. What's up?"

"I have reason to believe, with no proof whatsoever, that someone recently dumped a body in your lake," I said. "If your guys find anything floating around out there—a shoe, a piece of clothing, anything—please let me know. If anyone reports seeing anything suspicious, let me know."

"I'll talk to the guys," Jimmy said. "If we find anything, you'll know."

◆ ◆ ◆ ◆

That night, Mary and I sat at the kitchen bar in our Mountain Center condo nibbling on cheese and crackers and sipping good red wine. Well, I was sipping. Sipping wasn't exactly in Mary's vocabulary.

"I talked with Megan and Cindy again today," Mary said.

"How are they?"

"Megan is mad as hell, and Cindy is having nightmares about the clown. Clown parties are not in her future."

I felt my anger flare. "Did you mention Ricky?"

"No. I think we should keep that under wraps for now."

"Sounds right," I said.

I took another drink of wine and had visions of my beating the clown to a bloody pulp.

Mary noticed. "You're having a bad thought."

"This guy thinks he's being cute, and he's not," I said. "I was just thinking I would love to get my hands on him."

"Maybe it's not about cute. Maybe it's about smart. If he's been doing this for as long as you think and getting away with it, then he's got to be pretty smart."

I said nothing. I knew she was right, and my silence confirmed it.

"He is pretty cool about it," I said.

"Sounds like sociopathic behavior to me," Mary said. "Why don't you run it by Sister Sarah Agnes?"

"And they say you're just another pretty face."

"Who is *they*?"

"The people who have seen you and don't know you," I said.

"Sweet talker."

We nibble, sipped, drank, and were quiet.

"I think Ricky Carter is dead or will soon be dead," I said.

Mary sat up straighter. "Explain," she said, refilling her glass. Mine still had half of what I had poured.

"Like you said, this guy is smart. If Ricky Carter is any indication of the kind of partners he's working with, then they're disposable. They would rat him out in a minute if it served their purpose. And if he's a sociopath, then he couldn't care less. So I'm betting that, soon after the payoff, he eliminates the partner and moves on."

"Sounds plausible," Mary said. "If you could find Ricky Carter's body, you could get the FBI involved."

"Needle in a haystack."

"Forget about it for a while. Something will pop up. For now, how about you take us out to dinner, and later on you can have me for dessert."

Well, there was an offer I couldn't refuse.

.

21

The next morning, the first things I noticed when I sat at my desk were the two files I had given Gretchen to copy. *My future partner must be coming in on Saturdays*, I thought.

I had been in the office about ten minutes when Buckley called. "I hear I'm helping you with the Clown case," he said.

"I heard that, too. Welcome aboard."

"What do you need?"

"Are you in town?" That was code for *Are you at Gretchen's?*

"Yes."

"Okay," I said. "Drop by later and we'll discuss the Clown case."

"Will do," Buckley said.

I hung up and called Sister Sarah Agnes Woods, a friend, nun, and advisor on things dealing with the human psyche. I wasn't sure she could help me with the Clown case, but I had promised Mary I'd call, and I knew I'd get grief if I didn't follow up.

She answered on the second ring.

"Do you still do consulting for wayward private detectives?"

She laughed. "Especially the wayward ones in Tennessee. This is a surprise. How are you?"

"I'm fine. And you?"

"All the usual stuff. Only the names change."

Sister Sarah ran Silverthorn, a treatment center for addictions of all kinds. Many of the rich and famous had been treated there, most successfully. They paid dearly.

"Got any of those failed presidential candidates?"

"Mercy, no," she said. "They are beyond help. So, how can I help you?"

"I need you opinion about a guy I'm chasing. Do you have a few minutes?"

"Oh, dear," she said. "Let's hear it."

I told her every detail from the time Howard Cox had sent me a text to my conversation with Mary last night.

"That's it so far," I said. "What do you think?"

"Hard to be specific without talking to the subject. From what you told me, I'd say he definitely displays some sociopathic behavior, but he is probably not a true sociopath. He appears to show some empathy for the victims, which leads me to a question: are they all pre-teen girls?"

"As far as I know, yes."

"I believe that's significant," she said. "No doubt, it's about something in his past."

"What else?"

"For what it's worth, sociopaths are smart, glib, charming, and pathological liars. They sometimes have a hard time distinguishing fantasy from reality. They want things the way they want them, and it becomes their truth. They cannot be trusted, and they usually don't have any regard for life other than their own. So this clown could very well be a killer, which makes him dangerous and unpredictable. Be careful."

"I hear you," I said.

"Why don't you just let it go?"

I said nothing.

"Sorry, stupid question," she said. "When you catch him, don't let your guard down. He might appear harmless, but he isn't."

"I'll keep that in mind. And thanks for the vote of confidence."

"Your track record speaks for itself," she said. "I just want you to be safe."

I second that emotion, I thought.

◆   ◆   ◆   ◆

Buckley was in my office at nine-thirty.

I slid the two files from Huntsville across my desk. He had initially looked at them on the trip back. "When you have some quiet time, take another look and see if anything pops."

He nodded, picked up the files, and put them in his briefcase.

"Find out everything you can on Royce Rogers and Richard Card—last known address, birth records, DMV records, family, credit cards, anything. And check out jails in Texas. Maybe they got in trouble and are locked up."

"One can hope," Buckley said.

"I think the alias, Richard Card, is dead, but we have to check him out."

"How urgent is this? I'm working something that might take up the rest of my week."

"We've got time," I said. "Looks like he's done his kidnapping for this year. But the sooner we catch this guy, the better."

Buckley nodded. "I've got to get going," he said. "See you Thanksgiving."

◆   ◆   ◆   ◆

Later that morning, I had another thought. What if Ricky Carter wasn't dead? I knew from experience that he wasn't real bright, so maybe we could track him.

I picked up the phone and called Roy Husky. After a brief wait, I heard his familiar greeting: "Hey, Gumshoe, what's up?"

"You never answer your own phone anymore," I said. "Forget how?"

"No, just spoiled. You need the jet?"

"No, I need to come for a visit and talk to one of your employees."

"Who?"

I told him.

"I'll let the gate guard know you're expected," Roy said.

◆   ◆   ◆   ◆

Stanley Johns was a unique little man Big Bob and I had befriended in high school. Short and round with dark, curly hair and a raspy, high-pitched voice, Stanley may have been the original geek. He was shy and sensitive and had an innocence usually found in small children. Stanley, however, was a computer genius. Had he wanted to, Stanley could have been a world-class hacker. Instead, he had turned his talents toward writing antivirus programs and becoming part-owner of a software company that had made him rich. I should know. I handled his finances. Stanley was one of the kings in the realm of antivirus protection.

Through an odd set of circumstances, Stanley was now working at Fleet Industries. Gone were the days of Stanley the hermit locked away in the basement office I had dubbed "Oz." Stanley was in charge of computer security—no small job, given that Fleet Industries often did classified work for the U.S. military.

"Don!" Stanley shouted when I walked into his office. "So good to see you." He got out of his chair, walked over, and gave me a hug. He was looking positively corporate, dressed in a white shirt and tie, sharply pressed slacks, and expensive black wingtips.

"You, too, Stanley," I said. "It's been a while."

"Well, what a nice surprise. Are you visiting Roy or Mr. Fleet?"

"No, I'm visiting you. I need a favor."

I told Stanley about Ricky Carter rising from the grave and participating in the kidnapping of his daughter.

"This is the same guy I found before?"

"The same one," I said.

"And you want me to try and find him again."

"If you have time. I'm interested in bus, train, and air travel. Also check rental cars and charter planes."

"I'll make time," Stanley said.

"Look for Richard Card or Ricky Carter taking flights in the last couple of weeks."

Stanley wrote the names on a personalized Fleet Industries notepad. "If he paid to go anywhere, I'll find him."

"I know you will."

"Is this an emergency?"

"No," I said. "I have reason to believe he probably didn't fly anywhere, but I need to be sure. Also, check for any credit-card use in East Tennessee under those names."

Stanley nodded and made another note.

"See you Thanksgiving?" I asked.

Stanley smiled. "Of course."

◆ ◆ ◆ ◆

That night, Mary and I picked up Lacy at Tri-Cities Airport. We waited for the plane while engaged in casual conversation with Biker's parents.

At baggage claim, Lacy kissed Biker goodbye. "See you tomorrow night," she said.

He nodded and left with his parents.

"Poor guy," Lacy said. "He has to eat two Thanksgiving dinners tomorrow."

"I'm sure he can handle it," I said.

We drove to the lake house. Mary had prepared crockpot lasagna. I contributed Parmesan garlic toast and Caesar salad. We ate around the kitchen island, enjoying the heat from our gas stove. The outside temperature had dropped into the thirties. Unfortunately, snow was not in the forecast. We ate and talked, happy to have Lacy back, even though it would be a short visit. I did the eating and the listening. Mary and Lacy talked and nibbled.

"Tell us about your classes," Mary said.

"The usual stuff," Lacy said. "You've seen my schedule."

"Grades?"

"Nothing worse than a B. Mostly A's."

It went like that for an hour. Every now and then, I got to utter a word or two.

"Hey," Lacy said to me, "I almost forgot. Guess who I met?"

"To make a reasonable guess, I'll need a few clues other than, 'Guess who I met?'"

Mary laughed. "You're the great detective. So detect."

"Okay," I said to Lacy. "Teacher or student?"

"Student."

"At ASU?"

"Yes."

I paused. It had to be connected to someone I knew or someone famous. I already had an idea.

"Someone famous?"

"I don't think so."

Then I had it. "Native American?"

Lacy frowned. "Yes."

"Male or female?"

"Male."

"Is his last name Wildfire?"

Lacy looked exasperated. "How did you know?"

"Some deductive reasoning, combined with a lucky guess. It pretty much describes what I do. His father told me he had a son at college. It made sense that he would be in-state. Tell me about him."

"William Wildfire. We call him Will. He's nice. He looked me up because his father told him to. He said his father knew you and Chief; that you had worked together. Of course, I knew that, but I played dumb. Biker and I went to a movie with Will and his girlfriend. He wants to take us rock climbing when the weather warms up."

"Rock climbing?" Mary said.

"Relax, Mom. Nothing dangerous."

Mary and Lacy were still talking at midnight when I gave up and went to bed.

22

Thanksgiving Day was cold and overcast, but inside it was warm and festive. Thanksgiving at the Fleet mansion had become an annual event. *Is this the sixth or seventh?* I wondered. No matter; it had grown from a small gathering to a major party, from a regular turkey-day dinner to a feast with a jazz ensemble playing softly in the background. Attire had evolved from casual to semi-formal/formal. I wore an Armani tuxedo I had purchased in New York years ago. Thankfully, it still fit, even after the big buffet. Mary wore a simple but elegant Oscar de la Renta black gown we had purchased when she dragged me to Saks Fifth Avenue during our New York trip. When she saw the price, she had said, "Forget it." When I saw her in it, I said, "Forget the price." When I told her how much the tux had cost, she said okay to the gown. It was floor length with a slit to her knee and a neckline that showed just enough cleavage without going too far. She wore the gown and a string of pearls and that was all.

"Mary looks especially gorgeous tonight," Wanda Jones said, strolling up beside me and looking rather gorgeous herself.

"She does indeed," I said.

"As a matter of fact, you look rather dashing yourself," Wanda said, taking a sip of her champagne. "How about a threesome?"

I laughed out loud. Wanda loved to shock and tease me, and I think she was a little buzzed.

"I thought you gave up women," I said.

"I have," she said. "But for Mary, I might come out of retirement."

"Go find Bruiser and stop harassing me," I said. Bruiser Bracken, a college friend and part of our inner circle, was her man. Their wedding plans had been on and off for a year.

"But it's so much more fun harassing you." She smiled as she seductively moved away.

Roy wandered over. "That's some tux," he said. "Must have cost a fortune. Glad you can mingle with us common folk."

"I wouldn't call that gorgeous redhead you're with common," I said. Roy rarely talked about his love life, and I didn't ask.

"No, you certainly wouldn't," Roy said. "I should probably go protect her from wolves like you."

"Good idea."

Roy smiled and moved away. He was working the room, something he never would have done before becoming president of Fleet Industries.

T. Elbert rolled by in his wheelchair. "I haven't seen much of you lately," he said. "What's going on?"

"Lots. I'll come by next week and fill you in. I'll send you an email and let you know when."

"Anytime," he said.

It went like that for the next hour. I basically stood in one place observing the small clusters of guests scattered around the ballroom while friends and acquaintances wandered by, exchanged a few tidbits of conversation, and moved on. Near ten o'clock, I caught Joseph Fleet staring at me. He motioned his head toward one of the ballroom exits, and I knew it was time for our annual Thanksgiving aperitif in his study. I nodded as I made my way toward the door.

"Baileys as usual?" he asked when we were alone in his study.

"Can't break that tradition," I said.

He filled a small wine goblet with ice and filled it to the top with Baileys Irish Cream. He poured himself a large cognac.

"Let's sit," he said.

We sat in two large leather chairs in front of the fireplace. The last time I was in this room, Joseph Fleet had asked me to be on the Fleet Industries Board of Directors. I had accepted. Soon afterward, Roy had been promoted to president of the company and Fleet had gone on a long sabbatical in Europe with a female companion. I hadn't seen him since.

"How was your trip?"

"It was so good that I wondered why I hadn't done it sooner," he said. "And I can't wait to do it again."

"Good for you." I didn't know exactly how old Joseph Fleet was, but I knew he was on the north side of eighty.

"Roy tells me you've been an excellent addition to the board," he said.

"I don't do a lot. I nod every now and then and try to look smart. I can tell you this: with Roy Husky at the helm, Fleet Industries is in good hands. He's a natural leader and much smarter than he realizes."

"I know," Fleet said. "But it's good to hear it, especially from you."

We sat in silence sipping our drinks and watching the flames dance in the fireplace, a Norman Rockwell moment.

Joseph Fleet broke the spell. "I need to tell you something." At that moment, he looked old and tired, a man bearing bad news. "Very confidential at this point."

"I don't like it already."

He smiled. "I told Roy once that what makes you such a great detective is that you're the most perceptive person I have ever met. You read people and situations like other people read books."

"How long do you have?"

He shook his head. "See what I mean?"

I took a deep breath. I didn't want to hear any more of this. Joseph Fleet was part of my world, and I liked my world just the way it was. No one had permission to leave.

"Cancer?"

He nodded. "Brain tumor, inoperable. Found out last week. They'll try to shrink it with radiation. How long I have depends on how it reacts."

"Does Roy know?"

"Yes," Fleet said. "I wanted to tell you because he's going to need emotional support."

"So am I," I said. "I'm kind of used to having you around."

"Well, let's not get too maudlin. I'm *not* dead yet, and I am very hard to kill."

"Amen to that," I said, raising my glass and taking a long drink of the Baileys.

23

Monday morning, I was on T. Elbert's front porch with Roy and T. Elbert. I had planned this parlay with Roy in hopes he might want to talk about Joseph Fleet. The morning was cold and damp, but the overhead heaters and ceiling fans kept us comfortable as we settled in to drink coffee and eat the assorted muffins I had picked up on the way over.

"So tell us what you're working on," T. Elbert said.

"And don't spare the details," Roy added before T. Elbert could.

I told them about the clown, who I was pretty sure was Royce Rogers. I told them about Ricky Carter, and that I thought he might now really be dead. Even though Roy already knew about Ricky, he didn't let on. I told it slowly and with great detail, as I always did with T. Elbert. I talked for half an hour.

"Incredible," Roy said when I finished.

"Sure as hell is," T. Elbert said. "This is one for the books. A serial kidnapper and possibly a serial killer all rolled up into one."

I said nothing. I sat wondering, once again, how I had managed to get pulled into this maelstrom of kidnapping and probable murder. We ate and drank in silence. I think T. Elbert sensed it was time to move to lighter conversation.

"What's going on with Lola Madrid?" he asked.

"Who's Lola Madrid?" Roy asked.

"A belly dancer," I said.

"Don's looking for her," T. Elbert said. "It's an affair of the heart."

"This I've got to hear," Roy said, looking at me.

I looked at T. Elbert. "You tell it."

He smiled, pleased. "So there's this guy, Bentley Williams, who works for Don's old boss in New York . . . ," T. Elbert began. He milked the story for all it was worth for a good fifteen minutes. "And she wasn't in any of the databases I had access to," he added as a finishing note.

Roy chuckled. "A belly dancer."

"She's quite a dish," I said.

T. Elbert looked at me. "So what's going on?"

"Well, Gretchen found out that a Lola Madrid grew up on Prince Edward Island. Since Lola mentioned P.E.I. to Bentley during some pillow talk, I have a feeling it's the right Lola Madrid. Guess I'll be making a trip there."

"Want Jim to fly you?" Roy asked.

"Maybe. Any problem for Jim to fly into Canada?"

"Don't know," Roy said, "but I'll find out." He stood as a black limo pulled up to the curb. The windows were dark, but I knew Oscar Morales was behind the wheel. "I've got a meeting."

So much for my best-laid plans.

"Thanks for stopping by," T. Elbert said.

"Anytime," Roy said. He was down the steps with a wave and out to his limo. Oscar was holding the rear passenger-side door open for him. Oscar closed the door and waved toward the porch. I waved back.

"Those two have certainly come up in the world since you met them," T. Elbert said.

"They certainly have."

"And you had a lot to do with it."

"It would be nice to think so," I said.

◆　◆　◆　◆

My office phone rang soon after I walked in. Caller ID let me know it was my old friend Rasheed, so I answered in my usual professional fashion: "Youngblood."

"If Ricky Carter is around here," Rasheed Reed said without preamble, "he is well hidden. He paid an *ex*-employee a tidy sum to look the other way four years ago. I will not be making that mistake again."

He emphasized *ex*. I didn't inquire about the ex-employee's health. I had the feeling he was terminal, if not already dead.

"It would appear," Rasheed continued, "that Ricky took the money, went to Texas, and got himself in trouble. No big surprise there. If I come up with anything else, Youngblood, I'll call you."

"I wouldn't waste too much time looking for Ricky, Rasheed," I said.

"You think he's dead?"

"Most likely. The guy that I think he partnered up with is too smart to let Ricky run around with too much cash and too much information."

"Yeah, I see what you mean," Rasheed said. "Well, good riddance."

"Can't argue with that," I said.

◆ ◆ ◆ ◆

Roy called before lunch.

"Jim says no problem going to Prince Edward Island. He's free Wednesday and Friday. You'll need your passport. You'll have to go through customs."

"Okay. Tell him to pencil me in for Wednesday, and call me tomorrow afternoon with the particulars."

"Will do, Gumshoe," Roy said. "Good hunting."

◆ ◆ ◆ ◆

That night, Mary picked up a pepperoni pizza on her way home, and I made Caesar salad and uncorked a bottle of very good French Bordeaux and let it breathe. I heated our pizza stone to four hundred degrees and placed half the pizza on the stone to keep it warm while I tossed the salad. I served us two pieces each and an ample amount of salad, poured the wine into goblets, and handed one to Mary.

She looked at the bottle and read the label out loud. "Château Leoville Barton St. Julien 2010."

"It came in my last shipment from Total Wine," I said. "Try it."

"You first."

I made a show of swirling the wine around the goblet and inhaling the bouquet. Then I took a drink, smiled, and nodded.

Mary followed my lead. Her eyes widened. "God, that's good," she said. "What did that cost?"

"More than I would normally spend on a bottle of wine. *Wine Enthusiast* gave it a one hundred rating. I wanted to see what a hundred rating tastes like."

"So tell me how much."

"That would spoil it. Eat your pizza."

She smiled and picked up her first slice. "I'll know before the clock strikes midnight."

"Think so, huh?"

"I do," Mary said.

"We don't have a clock that strikes midnight, or any other hour, for that matter."

"Figure of speech."

"What makes you think I'll tell?"

"I know your weaknesses," Mary said.

We ate and drank slowly. Good wine will do that, slow you down to savor every nuance.

"I'm going to Prince Edward Island on Wednesday," I said. "As you know, Gretchen found out where a Lola Madrid went to high school there. It's probably the Lola I'm looking for. Her mother lives there also. Lola may or may not have gone back home, but at least I can interview the mother."

Mary peered at me over her goblet. "I'll bet the mother is good looking."

"Probably."

"Don't get distracted."

"Never."

"I'll have to make sure."

"I would hope so," I said.

Much later, I told Mary what the bottle of wine cost. Well, I held out as long as I could.

24

On Wednesday morning, Fleet Industries jet number one lifted off the tarmac at Tri-Cities Airport just after eight o'clock. I was perfectly relaxed with a mug of coffee and a *USA Today*. I would afford myself the luxury of reading most of it, especially the Sports and Money sections. Jim Doak leveled off at thirty thousand feet and promised smooth sailing all the way to the Charlottetown Airport, also known as Upton Field, on Prince Edward Island.

When I finished with *USA Today*, I sat and pondered my strategy for my visit with Lola Madrid's mother. I was hoping to spend the night. Rather than announce myself as Donald Youngblood, private investigator, I decided it would be easier to get my foot in the door as Alexander Youngblood, freelance reporter for the National News Network, a fictitious news agency created by Amos Smith. Keeping the NNN website up to date had become a hobby for Amos, who wrote weekly articles under different names, including his own and Alexander Youngblood's. I wondered what the subject matter was for the latest article I had written. The jolt of wheels hitting tarmac brought me back to the here and now.

When I arrived at customs, no one was there except an agent and me.

"Welcome to Prince Edward Island," he said as I approached.

"Thank you," I said, handing him my passport.

"Are you here for business or pleasure, Mr. Youngblood?"

He kept his eyes on my passport as he questioned me.

"Business."

"What is the nature of your business?"

"I'm a private investigator," I said. "I'm working a case."

"Could I see your credentials?"

"Certainly," I said, showing him my PI license.

He looked at my creds and nodded. "What is your final destination?"

"Stratford."

"How long will you be there?"

"I might leave later today," I said. "But I'll probably spend one night."

"Very well," he said, stamping my passport. "Enjoy your stay."

"Thank you," I said, and headed for the rental car desk.

I picked up a Jeep Grand Cherokee from Hertz and headed toward Stratford on Route 1, otherwise known as the Trans-Canada Highway, a nearly five-thousand-mile stretch connecting Canada's Atlantic and Pacific shores. I crossed the harbor bridge and fifteen minutes later parked in front of the Waterfront B&B. I was surprised how fast night had come until I realized I was now in the Atlantic Time Zone and also farther north than I had ever been in my life, much less in wintertime. The sun had set, and the place was aglow in subdued outside lighting.

I was hoping I would not have a problem getting a room for the night. Winter in this area had to be a slow time for tourists, and I was counting on the place being empty. Whether or not Selma Madrid would rent me a room was another story. Jim Doak was spending the night on jet number one and had said he would be ready to leave anytime. *This should be interesting*, I thought as I carried my laptop and overnight bag up the illuminated walkway.

When I rang the doorbell, an attractive woman opened the door halfway and said, "May I help you?" She was indeed an older version of Lola Madrid. The extra years and a few pounds had done nothing to diminish her looks.

I handed her a business card: Alexander Youngblood, National News Network. "I wonder if you might have a room for the night," I said as she stared at the card. "I saw your B&B online, and it looked and sounded first class."

"Thank you," she said. "I usually do not rent rooms this time of year, but I suppose it would be okay for an overnight, if you don't mind being alone with me."

I laughed. "I'll survive," I said as she opened the door wider.

"Please come in." She held out her hand. "I'm Selma Madrid, Mr. Youngblood." She had a nice, firm handshake.

"Pleased to meet you."

"I have two rooms and a suite upstairs. The rooms are $150 a night, and the suite is $225. The price includes breakfast. If you want, you may join me for dinner at no extra charge. I hate to cook for one."

"I'll take the suite," I said. "And I would love to join you for dinner."

"Half past six," she said.

"I'm looking forward to it. Do you have Wi-Fi?"

"Of course." She smiled. "The password is *belly dancer*. Two words, all lowercase."

I smiled and said nothing, then turned and headed up the stairs.

The suite was first rate: a sitting room with a gas fireplace and a separate bedroom with a king-sized bed. I checked the mattress: firm. The bed with its high headboard and lower footboard seemed solid as a rock. I liked the place already. The sitting room had a comfortable couch and matching chair, two end tables with a lamp on each, a floor lamp, and a desk with a desk lamp. The furniture was well made and, no doubt, expensive. *Mary would love this place*, I thought.

I unpacked my meager belongings, set up my laptop, acquired the Wi-Fi network, and went online. Since I couldn't get a cell-phone signal, I sent Mary an email that I was safe and sound at the Waterfront B&B. I failed to mention that I was alone with a beautiful woman.

◆ ◆ ◆ ◆

Dinner was ready promptly at six-thirty. The food was simple but elegant: beef bourguignon served over white rice with a side Caesar salad.

"Fabulous," I said, taking the first bite. I wasn't lying.

She poured a good Cabernet Sauvignon, and we touched glasses. A warning light went off in the back of my mind. This was beginning to feel like a date.

"I'm alone in the winter, so it's nice to share a meal every now and again," she said.

"Tell me about your B&B." *Ask questions, talk less, eat more*, I thought.

Selma Madrid carried the conversation and still found time to eat almost as much as I did. Then she turned the table on me and started asking questions.

"What kind of stories do you write?"

I tried to be vague. "In-depth feature articles."

"About what?"

"Something current and controversial."

She stared straight at me, not breaking eye contact. "Such as?"

I looked at my plate. I was trapped until I remembered the last article Amos had written on my behalf. "My latest was about the effect of over-population on the future of our planet."

"I never thought about that," she said. "I'll have to read it."

I said nothing. Instead, I finished my Caesar salad. "The dressing on the salad is very tasty," I said.

"It's an old recipe handed down in my family for generations," she said. "More wine?"

"No thanks."

She poured the last of the bottle into her glass. I had sipped on one half-filled glass during dinner. Selma Madrid had consumed the rest. *Mary has a kindred spirit on Prince Edward Island*, I thought.

"I'll get dessert," Selma said.

Dessert was right on par with the rest of the meal, a dark chocolate mousse. I could have eaten three helpings. I sacrificed and had only one.

"Delicious," I said.

Selma smiled and stared at me over her wineglass. I glanced at the clock on the wall: 7:45.

"I really enjoyed the meal," I said. "I'm sorry to eat and run, but I have some work to do."

"Well, okay. I'll see you in the morning," she said. "Let me know if you need anything."

I wasn't sure what *anything* meant, so I simply said, "Thank you." *I sure hope my door has a lock*, I thought. I rose and headed for the stairs, seeking the sanctuary of my room.

"Breakfast is at eight," Selma Madrid said. "Is that okay?"

"That's fine," I said. "See you then."

My door did have a lock. When I turned it, I could have sworn I heard Mary say, *Good boy.*

25

The next morning a little before eight, I went downstairs with my overnight bag and my laptop backpack. I set them by the front door and went into the dining room. I noticed only a single place setting where we had enjoyed dinner the night before.

"Good morning," Selma Madrid said, coming from the kitchen. "Breakfast will be ready in a few minutes."

"You're not joining me?" I asked, trying to put some disappointment in my voice.

"I usually don't eat with guests. Last night was an exception."

"So make another exception," I said.

She paused. "Very well. Give me a few extra minutes."

She turned and went back toward the kitchen.

Breakfast consisted of a luscious ham and cheese quiche, fried potatoes, and scones that hinted of rosemary. The coffee was rich and full bodied, not bitter. Much to my surprise, there was raw sugar and real cream. For a moment, I forgot why I was there. We ate casually and engaged in small talk.

"I have a confession," I said.

"Let me guess. You are not who you said you were."

"What makes you say that?"

"You don't look or act like a reporter," Selma said. "More like a police inspector."

"Actually, private investigator," I said.

"So are you here to see me, or did you just need a place to stay?"

"Both," I said. "I'm trying to find Lola."

She looked startled and defensive. "Why?"

"Because an old friend asked me to and because a young man in New York City says he can't live without her."

"This I've got to hear," Selma Madrid said, seeming to relax. "Tell me all of it."

So I told her all of it. I couldn't think of any reason not to. When I finished, she was quiet, staring beyond me out the sliding glass door that led to the deck looking out on the harbor.

"What do you think of this young man?"

"I like him," I said.

"You think he really loves her?"

"I do."

She shook her head as if listening to a lost cause. "Unfortunately, I do not know where Lola is. I haven't seen her in years and haven't heard from her in a long time. She calls every year or two but never tells me where she is. I think she's running from something or someone, but I don't know what or who. She may be in some trouble. I just don't know. That's all I can tell you."

"Sorry to hear that." I switched gears. I wanted all the information I could get. *Better to know than not to know*, I could hear T. Elbert chiding. "Where did she learn belly dancing?" I asked.

"From me," Selma said. "And I learned from my mother. I come from a long line of belly dancers."

"What is the significance of the tattoo?"

"Lola thinks she's a white witch," Selma Madrid said. I could hear the sense of absurdity in her voice. "She became interested in witches in high school. I'm not sure why. Lola says that white magic is good and black magic is bad. She thinks white magic is more powerful than black magic. She has spent years studying it and developing her own book of spells."

"Do they work?"

"Apparently, one does." Selma smiled. "It sounds like Lola has cast a love spell on this young man, Bentley."

"Or maybe he just fell in love."

"Maybe."

I couldn't think of anything else to ask, so I handed Selma Madrid one of my *real* business cards. "If she gets in touch with you, tell her to call me. I'm well connected, and I might be able to help her with her problem if she'll let me."

Selma Madrid looked at the card and nodded.

I stood. "I enjoyed my stay, and the food was fantastic. And that's the truth."

"Thank you," she said.

I headed toward the front door and picked up my overnight bag and backpack.

Selma Madrid followed me to the door. "I have one question," she said. "Are you married?"

I flashed my wedding ring.

"Yes."

"I saw your ring but I wanted to be sure. Tell your wife I said you were the perfect gentleman."

"Thank you," I said. "I'll tell her."

"Safe travels, Mr. Youngblood."

◆ ◆ ◆ ◆

Leaving was much simpler than arriving. The sleek little jet was waiting with stairs down when I arrived. The day was overcast with temperatures in the mid-forties, accompanied by a stiff breeze. Jim was in the cockpit with engines idling. He gave me a wave as I approached. Moments later, I was in the cabin with the stairs up and we were taxiing to the end of the runway.

"We are number one for takeoff," Jim said over the intercom. "Buckle up."

As we lifted away from the small Canadian island, I sat back to replay my conversation with Selma Madrid. I thought most of what she told me was the truth, but I would bet a million bucks she had heard from Lola recently. Selma was much too interested in Bentley not to have heard about him already.

Forget about Lola Madrid, I told myself. *You gave it the ole college try, and now it's time to let it go.* I didn't have time to bring two lovers together. I had a clown to catch.

My thoughts turned to Mary. It seemed as if I had been gone for a week, and after the veiled innuendos of Selma Madrid I needed to be with my wife. The pre-Mary me would have bedded Selma Madrid in a heart-beat and come back for seconds. The married me hadn't even considered it, in fact had been frightened of it. That metamorphic miracle had me puzzled. There could be only one answer: Mary. That was the last thing I remember before the purr of the jet's engines caressed me to sleep.

◆ ◆ ◆ ◆

I called Mary once I was in the Pathfinder and on my way home.

"Back safe and sound," I said. "I'm going to the office to see what's going on. I'll be at the condo at my usual time."

"Don't hurry," Mary said. "I have some things to do."

No *Welcome home,* no *I'm going to jump your bones,* nothing. *Something's going on,* I thought. *Maybe the honeymoon's over.*

◆ ◆ ◆ ◆

"Welcome back," Gretchen said as I opened the hallway door and walked into the outer office. "You'll see a number of pink slips on your desk. I took care of most of them. Take a look and let me know if you have any questions."

Sitting at my desk, I went through the slips. A few interested me. Buckley and Stanley Johns had called and asked that I return their calls.

Another slip from Gretchen read, "We have an appointment tomorrow @ 10:30 with a potential new hire." Gretchen had interviewed a few candidates when I was out of the office. She was moving fast.

I buzzed her on the intercom. "Come on in when you have a minute or two."

Thirty second later, she was sitting in front of my desk.

"What's the guy's name we're interviewing tomorrow?"

"Chauvinist!" Gretchen said. "Not guy, gal."

Just what I need, another female in my life. I tried to play it cool. "Okay, what's this gal's name we're interviewing tomorrow?"

"The candidate's name is Ronda Sharkey."

"How many résumés did you look at?"

"Twelve," Gretchen said.

"How many did you interview?"

"Four," she said. "Two men and two women. All under twenty-five."

I nodded. "And you liked this one best. Why?"

"Wait for the interview and you can tell me," she said.

"Can I see her résumé?"

"Tomorrow," Gretchen said.

Well, I used to be in charge.

◆   ◆   ◆   ◆

After Gretchen returned to her desk, I called Stanley Johns.

"I completed my search for Ricky Carter and Richard Card," he said. "Neither turned up as having an airplane ticket, a rental car, or a bus ticket. He could have paid cash for a bus ticket, but it's almost impossible to rent a car or buy an airplane ticket these days without identification. If he had, I would have found him."

"Good work, Stanley."

"I'm going to do another search in about a week in case he's hiding out and then tries to leave."

I didn't think Stanley would turn up anything, but I had to let him try, just in case I was wrong about Ricky Carter being dead.

◆ ◆ ◆ ◆

"How was your trip?" Buckley asked when I got him on his cell phone.

"I see there are no secrets around here," I said.

"Not likely."

"The trip was fine," I said. "I'm returning your call."

"Okay," Buckley said, "down to business. There is no trail of Richard Card in Texas. However, he did have a legitimate Texas driver's license. Texas DMV said he must have had some acceptable form of identification to get it, but there was no record of what that might have been."

"Well, we know who he is, or was, so I guess it doesn't matter. I was hoping for one useful tidbit. How about Rogers?"

"Royce Rogers is an entirely different matter. I have a lot of information on him."

"Let's hear it."

Buckley enlightened me about the life of Royce Rogers. The short version was that Royce had been a loner in high school in Santa Fe but a good student, attended the University of Texas, and married in his sophomore year. The wife died three years later: pancreatic cancer. Royce graduated and started working on offshore oil rigs soon after the wife passed. No criminal record until the casino robbery, not even a traffic ticket.

"The strange thing is, the whole time he did the kidnappings and collected a hundred grand a year, he kept working oil rigs," Buckley said.

"Maybe the money went into his retirement fund."

"If so, he's going to retire in style," Buckley said.

"Family?"

"Parents are dead. One sister, still lives in their hometown of Santa Fe, Gloria Rogers Davis, divorced, lives alone. She is a vice president at a local bank. Get this: Loan Star Bank. As in L-o-a-n."

"Pretty clever," I said. "Nice play on words. Is Gloria older or younger than Royce?"

"Older by three years."

"How many people did you interview?"

"Five," Buckley said. "Two high-school teachers, two college teachers, and one oil rig foreman. They pretty much agreed that he was pleasant and smart but not memorable."

"That's good work, Buckley."

"Well, I had some help from John Banks," he said.

John Banks, FBI computer whiz, reported to Scott Glass. I had worked with John on more than one occasion.

"Do you have an address for the sister?"

"Of course," Buckley said.

"Cell-phone number?"

"Naturally."

"Great. Email those to me, please."

"Will do," Buckley said. "Anything else you need?"

"Do you do yard work?"

"Only for Gretchen," Buckley said.

◆   ◆   ◆   ◆

As I entered the condo, I heard soft music coming from the upper level, most likely the master bedroom. Mary appeared in the hallway overlooking our sunken living room wearing a short, black, see-through negligee.

"Hey, Cowboy," she said.

"Hey, yourself."

"Upstairs, now."

Sometimes, I love bossy women. "Yes, ma'am."

I bounded up the stairs as she backed down the hall. I caught her at the bedroom door and kissed her.

"I missed you," she said. "Were you a good boy?"

"I was very good."

"Then you get a reward," she said as she unbuttoned my shirt.

◆   ◆   ◆   ◆

An hour later, we were at the kitchen bar having dinner and sharing a bottle of a good red blend from Australia. Dinner was chicken parmigiana with angel hair pasta tossed in butter, olive oil, and fresh basil. Garlic bread and a fresh Caesar salad rounded out our meal. I ate and drank with gusto.

"Tell me about Selma Madrid," Mary said.

"What do you want to know?"

"Good looking?"

"Yes, but not in your league."

"Sweet talker. Did she try to seduce you?"

"Not exactly."

"What does 'not exactly' mean?"

I told her about dinner with Selma Madrid.

"So she was there for the taking," Mary said.

"Maybe."

"And you went to your room and locked the door."

"A guy can't be too careful."

Mary laughed. "Tempted?"

"No."

I knew Mary trusted me, but she did have a jealous streak. So, rather than get aggravated at her little inquisition, I just played along. Satisfied, she changed the subject.

"Learn anything?"

I told Mary what Selma had said about Lola.

"A witch?"

"A white witch."

"That's weird," Mary said.

"And then some," I said.

26

The next day, I went to the diner early to meet Big Bob. I had called him and offered to buy breakfast. Big Bob never missed a free meal. The diner was relatively empty and therefore quiet.

Before the big man showed up, Doris brought a mug of coffee and lingered at my table long enough to complain about not having seen me lately. She wasn't the only one.

"Haven't seen you in awhile," Big Bob said as he tossed his cowboy hat on an adjacent chair a minute later. "How's the Clown case going?"

"Slowly," I said. "Buckley found his sister. She lives in Santa Fe, New Mexico."

"You going out there?"

"Have to," I said.

"When?"

"Soon," I said.

Doris brought Big Bob coffee, took our orders, and hurried away.

"How's your ulcer?" I said.

"Under control."

"How was Thanksgiving?"

He shrugged. "Okay, I guess. Too much food and too much family. Honest to God, Blood, one of these days I'm going to leave town and spend Thanksgiving with the wife where no one can find us."

Our talk turned to family, his job, and sports.

"What's going on in Mountain Center I should know about?"

"The usual," he said, taking a drink of coffee. "Petty theft, domestic abuse, drug busts, and various motor vehicle violations. Pretty boring stuff. Thank God I'm not involved in the day-to-day."

"You are involved in the day-to-day," I reminded him. "You oversee all of it."

"The good thing is that I usually just get the highlights. I don't have to be bothered with every detail, and I have good people."

When our food arrived, Big Bob did get involved in the details, surveying his plate of ham, eggs, home fries, and biscuits and gravy. Our conversation slowed as the eating began. No denying it, the big man could eat.

"Why don't you let this clown thing go?" Big Bob said as we neared the finish line.

"Because I saw the look on Cindy Carter's face after he let her go," I said. "She tried to be brave about it, but she was scared. He could have killed her. I was mad as hell. Most kidnap victims end up dead. If I can stop that from happening to another child, I'm going to."

Big Bob drained his coffee mug. "Well, good luck. And if you find the son of a bitch, you have my permission to shoot to kill."

"I'd rather have him locked up. Child abductors endure a special kind of hell in prison."

◆　◆　◆　◆

Later that morning, Gretchen walked into my office, trailed by a big and tall young lady she introduced as Ronda Sharkey. Ronda was not a pretty woman but was attractive, well groomed and curvy. The curves seemed to originate from some well-defined muscles. Ronda was definitely in shape.

"I have work to do," Gretchen said. "Buzz if you need anything." She left me alone with the Amazon.

"Please sit down," I said.

Ronda sat.

"Tell me about yourself."

"You want the short version, I hope. When I get going, sometimes I can't shut up."

"Let's start with the short version. If I need more, I'll let you know."

"Well, I grew up in Knoxville, went to high school at Christian Academy of Knoxville, got a volleyball scholarship to UT, studied criminology and criminal justice, got a master's degree, and here I am."

She was pleasant enough, almost perky, which somehow downplayed her size.

"So why do you think you'd like to work here?"

She smiled. "Well, you're kind of famous. There's quite a bit about you online. I think I could learn a lot working for you. I would apply for my PI license if I get the job. I'm sure you could help me with that. Then I would go for a gun carry permit."

"I hope you would never have to use it."

"Me, too," Ronda said. "I don't know if I could shoot anyone."

Unfortunately, I didn't have to wonder about that.

"Does it bother you that there might be times when the job is dangerous?"

"No," she said. "I find that exciting. Besides, I can take care of myself. I'm a brown belt in karate and working toward my black belt."

Just what we need, I thought, *a female lethal weapon.*

"This might be politically incorrect," I said, "but how tall are you?"

"Why do you need to know that?"

"Because I have a rule never to hire anyone taller than I am."

She was speechless.

"Just kidding. I want to know because my wife is six feet tall. I think you're a bit taller, and if you come to work for us she's going to want to know everything about you, and 'I don't know' is not an acceptable answer."

"Oh, yes. Your wife, Mary, is a detective with the Mountain Center Police."

At that point, I was not liking the internet. "There are no secrets anymore."

"Some," Ronda said, "But definitely less that there were before. I'm six-one. How tall are you?"

"Six-two," I said. *Well, almost.*

"Well, that's a relief."

We talked for a while longer. Ronda's parents were both big people. Her mother had played basketball for Pat Summitt, and her father had played football for Phil Fulmer. Both had law degrees. Her father was now a judge, and her mother practiced corporate law. They still lived in the Knoxville area. Ronda was not married and was not in a relationship at present. The more questions I asked, the more information she volunteered. I could see why Gretchen liked her. Ronda was smart, had a pleasant personality, and with her size would not be easily intimidated. I had seen and heard enough.

"Wait in the outer office a few minutes," I said, "and ask Gretchen to come in here."

Ronda exited. Moments later, Gretchen entered and closed the door.

"What do you think?"

"I think she would make a good addition," I said. "I take it she's your choice."

"She is," Gretchen said.

"No need to make her wait for confirmation," I said.

"No need at all," Gretchen said. "I'll tell her she starts Monday."

27

Monday morning, I flew to Santa Fe. Unfortunately, I was not in Fleet Industries jet number one, or jet number two, for that matter. Jim Doak apologized; both jets were booked for the week. He promised to call if there was a cancellation. I was flying commercial, albeit first class, and hating it. I flew out of Tri-Cities Airport in the dark and arrived at Charlotte, North Carolina, in the dark. From Charlotte, I flew to Dallas–Fort Worth. From DFW, I flew to Santa Fe. It was an eight-hour-plus marathon. One I dreaded repeating.

I rented a Nissan Frontier pickup truck and drove to the Santa Fe Residence Inn. I checked into a one-bedroom suite and booted up my laptop to check the market, which I had ignored for weeks. The Dow was showing minor fluctuations, and I was in a holding pattern. I texted Mary to let her know I was safe and sound and then called Gretchen.

"Did our new hire actually show up for work?"

"She did," Gretchen said. "She's already in the field working a case for Rollie."

"Doing what?"

"Interviewing witnesses in a DUI case Rollie is handling."

"I didn't know Rollie handled DUI cases."

"Apparently, it's for the son of a friend of his."

"What else is going on?"

"Nothing I can't handle. Enjoy Texas."

"New Mexico."

"Right," Gretchen said. "New Mexico."

◆   ◆   ◆   ◆

After being dismissed by Gretchen, I called David Steele. He surprised me by answering.

"Must be a slow day in FBI land," I said. "Or you're trimming the budget."

"At some point, I have to allow for a bathroom break," he said. "Where are you?"

"New Mexico."

"Doing what?"

"Working the Clown case. I'm about to interview the sister."

"So I'm guessing you called to ask permission to flash your FBI creds," he said.

"I knew there was a reason you got that promotion. I think an FBI agent is a little more intimidating than an out-of-state private investigator."

"You're only a special consultant," he reminded me.

"True, but most people see only my mugshot and that big, bold *FBI*. Especially if you give them only a few seconds to look."

"Permission granted," David Steele said. "Find me a body, Young-blood, and I'll officially open a file on this case."

◆　◆　◆　◆

At five o'clock, I went downstairs to the Residence Inn's happy hour. I was looking to kill some time, hoping to catch Gloria Davis when she had just come home from work. Chips, dip, a selection of cheeses, carrots, celery, raw broccoli and cauliflower, and Italian meatballs adorned the buffet bar. Chardonnay, Merlot, and Evolution Amber Ale on tap were available to wash them down. I put a few things on my plate, drew myself a pint of Evolution, and found a small table in a far corner away from the food and drink.

As happy hour got busier, the buzz grew louder and seats became scarce. An attractive dark-haired woman approached my table with a plate and a glass of Chardonnay. She was well dressed, about five and a half feet tall, and appeared to be fit—a package I might have been interested in before Mary happened on the scene.

"May I share your table?" she asked. "There seems to be a shortage of seats."

"Certainly," I said, standing. "Be my guest."

"Emma," she said, extending her hand.

"Don."

"Pleased to meet you, Don. What brings you to Santa Fe?"

"Business," I said, nibbling a piece of cheese. "You?"

"Business," she said. "Our corporate offices are just up the block."

Emma munched on a carrot. Her plate was full of veggies—rabbit food, Mary would have called it. No wonder Emma was so fit.

"Where are you from?" she asked.

"East Tennessee," I said. "You?"

"Dallas."

We ate and drank and engaged in small talk. Both Emma's plate and glass were empty.

"Can I get you another glass of Chardonnay?"

"That would be nice," she said.

There were worse ways to kill time. The crowd was starting to thin, and I was back to our table soon with her wine.

"I don't mean to seem forward," Emma said, "but do you have plans for dinner?"

"I'm working," I said.

"Working after hours," she said. "What line of work are you in?"

"I'm a private investigator."

"No way."

"We do exist."

"Can I see your ID?"

I laughed. "You don't believe me?"

"I do. It's just that I've never seen one before."

I showed her my Tennessee private investigator's license.

"Wow," she said. "May I have your autograph?"

I laughed again. "I don't think so. That would be classified."

◆   ◆   ◆   ◆

Near six o'clock, I managed to disengage from Emma with a promise I would call if it wasn't too late. *Too late* was never defined. We both knew I wasn't going to call.

A few minutes after six, I drove past Gloria Davis's house—no car in the driveway and no lights inside. Daylight was receding fast, and the temperature was dropping. Fifteen minutes later, I made another pass—nothing. At six-thirty, I made my final pass, resolved that if I saw no signs of life I would try again tomorrow. As I neared the house, I saw lights inside and a car in the driveway. I parked on the street and called her cell phone. It rang four times and then went to voice mail. *Monitoring her calls*, I thought. I left a message.

"Ms. Davis, my name is Donald Youngblood. I am with the FBI. I am conducting a routine investigation and would like to ask you a few questions about your brother. It should not take long. Please call me as soon as possible."

I confirmed my cell-phone number, thanked her, and ended the call. I drove away and found a nearby McDonald's. I parked and waited.

Fifteen minutes later, she called back.

"Thanks for returning my call," I said.

"I really don't know anything about my brother," she said. "I have not seen him in years."

"I don't want to do this over the phone," I said. "Can I come by your house for a few minutes?"

"How close are you?"

"I'm at the McDonald's about a mile from your house."

"I'll be there in fifteen minutes," she said. "Go inside and get a booth."

She didn't wait for an answer. *Cautious lady*, I thought. *And very cool.*

I staked out a corner booth in the back and waited.

◆   ◆   ◆   ◆

Gloria Davis was an attractive, slender, athletic-looking blonde with a pleasant face that wore a curious look. She was tall, maybe taller than Mary. She wore jeans, a long-sleeved T-shirt, and calf-high leather boots. The jeans fit well, showing off a curvy backside. She looked around and spotted me. I gave her a perfunctory wave, and she headed my way, moving like an athlete. I stood as she approached. *Courtesy is all. Taller than Mary*, I thought.

"Mr. Youngblood?"

"Ms. Davis," I said. "Please sit down."

She sat. "May I see some ID?"

I showed her my FBI creds.

"Special consultant," she said. "So what's your specialty?"

The lady takes her time and pays attention, I thought.

"Finding trouble," I said.

She smiled.

"Want anything?" I asked. "The FBI will pay."

"Coffee," she said. "Black."

"Be right back," I said.

I bought two coffees and took them back to the booth and sat. I slid her cup across to her. The place wasn't busy, and no one was sitting near us.

"Careful with that," I said. "It's hot."

She took a cautious sip and nodded. "So what does your case have to do with Royce?"

"Maybe nothing. I would just like to talk with him."

"Like I said, I haven't seen him in years."

"Did you know he was in prison?"

She laughed. "Santa Fe is not that big a town. A lot of people knew Royce went to prison. It was a real shocker."

"Were you shocked?"

"Yes and no," she said. "Royce never showed who he really was. I'm surprised he had the guts to rob a casino but not surprised he'd take the money."

"Did you visit him in prison?"

"No. But I saw him once in jail before he went to prison. I wanted to ask him why he did it."

"What did he say?"

"All he said was that he wanted the money."

"Has he called you?"

"Once," she said. "Right before he got out. He wanted to know if he could come see me. I told him no. I haven't heard from him since."

"Why did you tell him no?"

"None of your business," she said. "It's personal."

"Do you have any idea where he might be?"

"None. We were never that close, and once he left Santa Fe we didn't stay in touch."

I drank some coffee and stared at her. She stared back. If she was lying, she was doing a good job of it. Then again, I am easily lied to by women.

"Okay," I said. "If he calls, tell him I want to talk to him." I handed her a Cherokee Investigations business card.

She looked at it. "So this is your full-time job, and you consult on the side?"

"Or vice versa," I said. "It's really hard to say."

"If he calls, I'll give him your number. But I wouldn't hold my breath."

She stood without a hint of goodbye, turned, and walked away, leaving her coffee on the table. More than one set of male eyes watched her go.

That's a cold one, I thought.

28

The trip home from Santa Fe wasn't any more fun that the trip out. The phone call from Jim Doak I was hoping for never came, so I spent most of the day getting back to Mountain Center.

"Changing planes twice is for the birds," I said to Mary as we sat at the bar in the condo and enjoyed a bottle of good French red.

"Poor baby. Besides, birds don't change planes. They fly direct."

"Cute. I'll have to remember that one."

"I'm going to pick up the pizza," Mary said. "You just sit there and relax. You've had a hard day in first class." She kissed me on the cheek.

"I was in first class only from Dallas to Atlanta," I called as she headed out the door. I was getting no sympathy.

I heard the front door shut and felt a gust of cold air. Junior had followed Mary to the door. He came into the kitchen, looked at me, and went to lie down. Jake, already comfortable, didn't waste the energy. We had three sets of dog beds at the condo—one in our bedroom, one in the kitchen, and one in the den. Each set was personalized with *Jake* and *Junior*. I didn't think the dogs could read, but they always managed to get on the right beds.

In between running around airports, I had found time to think about the Clown case. Something didn't add up, but I wasn't sure what. Gloria Davis had not wanted me in her home. Was she hiding Royce? I didn't think so. That would be too obvious. But there was something she was not telling me. I'd bet she knew where Royce was. I wondered if she knew about the kidnappings. I didn't think so. *So where is Royce, and how do I find him?* I wondered.

Lola Madrid was another matter. I'd given it the ole college try and come up empty. I wondered if she might still be in New York. It would be easy to hide in the Big Apple. Somebody needed to nose around and see if she was still there, or at least locate her last known address. Somebody, but not me. I knew just the right guy. I sat there relaxed, hatching a plan.

I heard the front door open and shut. Mary was back, and soon the kitchen filled with the fragrance of pizza. Jake and Junior were on their feet, looking longingly at the box in hopes that a crumb or two might escape. I looked longingly at the box and was told I had to toss a Caesar salad. I did so post-haste.

Twenty minutes later, the box was empty, the salad bowls were empty, and our wineglasses were empty. The dogs had been rewarded for their patience with the crusts Mary would not eat.

"That was great," Mary said. "Pour me some more wine."

I emptied most of the bottle into her glass, saving a splash for myself. The dogs, convinced no other crust was forthcoming, went to their beds and lay down.

Mary smiled at me over the top of her glass. I knew that look.

◆   ◆   ◆   ◆

Much later, we were in bed reading.

Mary put down her book. "Tell me about Gloria Davis."

"Tall, attractive, cautious blonde."

"How attractive?"

"Not in your league, sweetheart," I said in my best Bogie.

"You always say that."

"It's always true."

"Good answer," Mary said. "Cautious how?"

"Didn't want to meet me at her house. We met at a McDonald's."

"Maybe there was something or someone she didn't want you to see."

"Maybe. Or maybe she just didn't want a strange man in her house."

"Guess you'll never know."

"Guess not," I said.

"Did you learn anything else?"

"Not much. I think she knew more than she told me. I'll bet she knows where her brother is."

"Probably," Mary said. "So now what?"

"Await developments. Maybe Royce will call me."

"How long will you wait?"

"A few days."

"And if he doesn't call?"

"I'll use my influence with the FBI to help me find him."

"What about Lola Madrid?"

"Same thing. I'll wait and see if she calls. In the meantime, I'm going to see if I can locate her last known address."

"How are you going to do that?"

"I'm going to call Phil Vance," I said.

"That good-looking private eye from New York?"

"Not that good looking," I said.

"A real hunk," Mary said.

I feigned annoyance.

"And I should know," Mary said, "because I married a real hunk."

"That's more like it," I said, rolling toward her.

29

The next morning, I called Phil Vance on his private line as soon as I got to the office. I was counting on his being an early riser. I was right.

"Vance," he answered.

"Youngblood, from Tennessee. Remember me?"

"How could I forget? How did that thing turn out that we were caught up in?"

Phil Vance had been hired to find out if Lacy was the granddaughter of Elizabeth Durbinfield. He was good looking, knew it, and was a bit of a smartass. I had not exactly cooperated with his investigation. Things had worked out in the end, and I was hoping he had no hard feelings.

"It turned out fine," I said. "Elizabeth Durbinfield and my daughter, Lacy, have decided they are grandmother and granddaughter without any scientific proof."

"That's pretty nice for your daughter. Rich grandmothers like Elizabeth Durbinfield are hard to find."

"It's not about the money, Vance," I said, letting my displeasure show.

"Relax, Youngblood, I was kidding. You called for a reason. How can I help?"

"I need to hire you or one of you associates to find the last known address of someone I'm looking for."

"Tell me about it."

So I did.

"A belly dancer," Phil Vance said. "Good looking, of course."

"And then some."

"All right, send me your file."

"I'll get it out today. Thanks, Vance."

"No problem, Youngblood. Glad to help a fellow PI."

◆   ◆   ◆   ◆

I knew Scott would be in early, so I called, even though his day was two hours behind mine.

"SAC Glass," he answered curtly.

"Friendly as ever, Professor."

"Well, if you wouldn't block caller ID, I could be a lot friendlier."

"Or ignore the call."

"There's that," he replied. "My first assumption when you call is that it's not social. Right or wrong?"

"Right," I said. "I want to give John Banks a chance to do some moon-lighting at a hundred bucks an hour. It will be computer work. He'll be helping me with a case."

"I'll ask him when he comes in," Scott said. "How's that Lola Madrid thing going?"

"At this moment, it's at a standstill. I need another lead or to just get lucky and have her walk into my office."

"Knowing you, that's exactly what will happen."

I heard a phone ring in the background.

"Got to go, Blood. I'll have John call you."

◆   ◆   ◆   ◆

John called two hours later.

"I hear you're offering a hundred bucks an hour," he said. "Who do I have to kill?"

"For killing, I pay two hundred. This is strictly research. Or, more specifically, search."

"Who am I looking for?"

"A guy named Royce Rogers. He was in prison until about three to four months ago. I've scanned the file I have on him. I'll attach it to an email and send it later today. See if he has any credit cards. Look for charges for gas, restaurants, hotel stays, bus tickets, rental cars, airline tickets, anything. I want to know where and when."

"It's going to take a while."

"I'm not going anywhere," I said.

Turns out, I was wrong about that.

◆   ◆   ◆   ◆

Every case, it seems, has a surprise or two—a shocker, even. The two cases I was working would prove to be no exception.

The first surprise came late that afternoon after Gretchen left. The phone rang. All caller ID told me was that it was an incoming call. Well, that was helpful.

"Cherokee Investigations," I said, trying to sound bright eyed and bushy tailed.

"Mr. Youngblood?"

Female, trace of an accent I could not identify.

"Yes."

"I hear that you are looking for me."

It took me a few seconds to sort it out. "Lola?"

"Yes."

I took a deep breath. I never really thought she would call. I hadn't found her, she had found me. Well, sort of.

"You're a hard lady to find," I said.

"I've been running and hiding for over a year now."

"Why?"

"There is someone looking for me who is very evil," she said. "If he finds me, he will kill me. Can you protect me?"

"Where are you now?"

"At my mother's house on Prince Edward Island. Mother thinks I can trust you to deal with my problem. She is usually right about these things."

"Let me think about this and call you back," I said. "Give me your number."

She gave me her cell number and then added, "Don't take too long deciding. He is on his way here."

"When do you expect him?"

"Late tomorrow at the earliest."

"How do you know that?"

"I got a call from a friend," she said. "She risked her life for me. If he finds out that she called me, he will kill her."

"I'll call you tonight."

"Thank you so much, Mr. Youngblood."

◆   ◆   ◆   ◆

As darkness fell on Mountain Center, I sat and thought about Lola's predicament. Was is perceived or real? Hard to tell, but if Selma Madrid thought it was real, then it probably was. It took some time, but I formulated a plan. Meanwhile, a light snow appeared in the streetlights on Main Street. There was no prediction of accumulation, but I could always hope.

I picked up the phone and called Roy.

"Hey, Gumshoe. Shouldn't you be home with the wife having drinks and dinner?"

"I need the jet, and I need it tonight," I said.

"I'm assuming this is urgent."

"You assume correctly."

"Life-and-death urgent?"

"Possibly, but not likely."

"Need backup?"

"Not this time," I said. "I'll have backup."

"Jim is due to land in an hour," Roy said. "He had a day trip. I'll tell him to stay put and get ready to go out again."

"Make sure he's ready for an all-nighter."

"To where?"

"Prince Edward Island."

"Weren't you there just last week?"

"I was."

"So this case of yours is heating up," Roy said.

"Seems to be heating up fast."

◆　　◆　　◆　　◆

Ten minutes later, I made another call.

"I don't exactly need backup, Chief," I said. "But I need your help. Put Maggie on the other line."

I waited maybe ten seconds.

"Hey, Don," Maggie said as soon as she picked up. "How can we help you?"

"I need someone to stay with you for a while. Let me tell you her story."

Billy knew some of the Lola Madrid story, but I had no way to know how much he had shared with Maggie, so I told all of it. When I finished, I said, "I don't think it will be long, but it could be dangerous."

Without hesitation, Maggie said, "We'd be glad to have Miss Madrid stay with us, wouldn't we, Billy?"

"We would," Billy said.

◆　　◆　　◆　　◆

I called Lola Madrid.

"I'll be there tonight to pick you up," I said.

"How?"

"Private jet, Charlottetown Airport, sometime after midnight. I'll call when we're close. Can you meet me where the private jets deplane?"

She paused. I heard muted voices.

"Mother says no problem," Lola said.

"Okay, wait for my call. I'll call when we're half an hour from landing."

"Thank you so much for doing this, Mr. Youngblood."

"Glad to."

All in the name of love, I thought. *And, of course, the adrenalin rush.*

◆　◆　◆　◆

Mary had just returned from walking the dogs when I came through the front door of the condo. She was in the kitchen, and I heard the unmistakable sound of a cork popping. A bottle of wine had just been violated.

"Whatever it is, pour me a glass," I said as I hung up my topcoat. "I have a story to tell."

I walked into the kitchen, draped my blazer over the back of one of the barstools, loosened my tie, and sat. Mary placed a glass of red in front of me and sat facing me across the bar. She managed to look tired and gorgeous at the same time. Her hair was in a ponytail. She wore faded jeans and a sweatshirt I had purchased in Utah.

"Tough day?" I asked.

"Not especially. A couple of break-ins and lots of paperwork. I hate the paperwork. It wears me out." Mary took a long drink of the red.

I said nothing. I didn't do paperwork, so what was to hate?

"Let's hear this story," Mary said.

I smiled and took a drink. "Lola Madrid called."

"You're kidding."

"Nope. Wants me to protect her from the bogeyman."

Mary took a drink and gave me the cop stare. "I don't think so. Let her find someone else."

"Hear me out first."

"Okay, talk."

So I told her about the phone call and my idea. She listened without interrupting.

"I guess that'll work," Mary said. "I especially like the part about me going with you."

"I thought you would."

"What about the dogs?"

"Gretchen will come by later and take them out and also first thing in the morning."

"Have you talked to Billy?"

"I have. He and Maggie agreed."

"Big Bob?"

"Yep," I said.

"What did he say?"

"Not to get you killed. That he couldn't afford to lose you. Me getting killed, on the other hand, he never mentioned."

"He meant both of us," Mary said. "He's just too macho to say it."

"Probably."

"Have you scheduled the jet?"

"Yes, ma'am. Jim Doak is on his way to the airport."

"You've been a busy boy," Mary said.

"I have."

"When do we leave?"

"Wheels up in two hours."

"Good God," Mary said.

30

We sat on stools at a bar-height table at the Tailwind Grill inside Tri-Cities Airport. I was eating a burger with bleu cheese and bacon and a side order of fries and washing it down with a beer. I told myself the beer would counter the fat and cholesterol. Mary was having a cheeseburger with Swiss cheese and a glass of house red.

"The burger is pretty good," Mary said.

"You're hungry."

"Starved."

Jim Doak had promised to call when the jet was fueled and ready. He had to go through his checklist and was not about to be rushed. Mary was right: the burger was good. I was looking forward to this little adventure. I felt the excitement.

"Do you think there will be trouble?" Mary asked.

"I hope not, but it pays to be ready."

"And we are."

"We are indeed," I said.

We were both armed. I was carrying a Glock Nine and Mary a Glock Ten. We were not going through customs, so bringing the hardware should not be a problem. I was not planning on leaving the tarmac at Charlottetown.

◆   ◆   ◆   ◆

An hour later, we were cruising at thirty thousand feet. We were sitting side by side. Mary was reading, and I was on my laptop reviewing portfolios.

I leaned over and whispered, "Want to join the mile-high club?"

Mary laughed. "How do you know I'm not already a member?"

"Well, if you are, I'm sure your membership has expired."

"I'm not that kind of girl. Unless, of course, we can lock Jim in the cockpit."

"It's a thought, but I don't think the FAA would approve."

"Harness that libido and go back to your laptop," Mary said. "My book is getting good."

So I went back to the Street, reviewing earnings per share, quarterly dividends, and fifty-two-week highs and lows in search of some jewel I might have missed. I found none.

Sometime later, Mary said, "Are you?"

Oh, boy, Youngblood. You and your big mouth.

"Am I what?"

"A member of the mile-high club?"

Rather than explaining the details, I lied. "No," I said. It was what my father would have called a little white lie. It was definitely the right answer.

"You better not be," Mary said, and went back to reading.

The fact that it had happened years before we met would have no bearing. Knowing it would bother her, it was my little secret, and worth keeping close. I had never shared it with anyone and was not about to start now. I stared out the window at the lights below as the little Learjet streaked through the night. At some point, I fell asleep.

"Buckle up," I heard Jim say somewhere from a distance. "We're on final approach."

I slowly came out of it, my mind swimming to the surface. When my eyes opened, I saw Mary awake and alert. I fumbled for my cell phone. "I need to call Lola," I said to no one in particular.

"Already taken care of," Mary said. "I sent her a text fifteen minutes ago."

"Of course you did. How silly of me."

Mary smiled. "We're a team, remember?"

"Always," I said, the sleep falling away.

The jet banked to the right, and I saw the lights of Charlottetown Airport in the distance. Then the airport disappeared as the jet came around, leveled, and began its descent. A few minutes later, the wheels touched, the engines reversed thrust, and the jet braked. We taxied toward the private hangars and were soon parked and waiting. Jim lowered the stairs, and Mary and I walked down to the tarmac. The light breeze made it feel near or below freezing. We could see our breath in the air. I was glad I had worn a turtleneck. We waited by the stairs.

We didn't wait long. Far down the tarmac, we heard the mechanical sound of a gate opening and saw a police cruiser slowly pull through.

"Well, that's not good," I said. I turned and gave Mary my Glock. "Take the hardware back on board."

She turned and went up the stairs.

The cruiser crept toward the tail of the aircraft, did a slow turn to the left, and came to a stop near the stairs. The rear passenger-side door opened, and out stepped Lola Madrid. Then the front passenger-side door opened, and Selma Madrid joined us. The driver stayed behind the wheel, motor running. I heard Mary descending the stairs behind me.

"Mr. Youngblood," Selma said, "this is my daughter, Lola."

"Nice to meet you." Lola was even better looking in person than in the video. Mary had come all the way down and was at my side. "My wife, police detective Mary Youngblood," I said. The women nodded at each other as I said to Mary, "Lola and Selma Madrid."

"Thank you both so much for taking care of my daughter," Selma said. "I know you will resolve her problem."

"Take Lola on board," I said to Mary. "I'll be right there."

Lola went up the stairs, followed by Mary. They disappeared into the jet.

Selma Madrid stepped close to me and said, "Now I understand why I could not seduce you. I thought I was losing my touch. Mary is gorgeous and a handful, I'll bet."

I smiled and said nothing.

Selma smiled back. "I must go now."

"Will you be all right? Is this man Lola is running from a threat to you?"

"He is no threat to me. I am well protected. He wants Lola, not me. And he is a bad man, so be careful. Sooner or later, he will come for her."

She turned toward the cruiser, and I opened the door for her. The driver was not in uniform. He had both hands on the steering wheel. From my angle, I could not see his face, and I didn't feel the need to. I closed the door gently, and the cruiser eased away and headed back to the gate. I turned and hustled up the stairs and into the jet. Jim stood at the cockpit door. Mary and Lola we in quiet conversation, sitting mid-cabin.

I looked at Jim. "Let's get out of here," I said, pushing the button to raise the stairs.

"Roger that," he said, turning and closing the cockpit door behind him. A moment later, I heard the engines rev. Then Jim came over the intercom: "Buckle up."

I sat across from Mary and Lola and fastened my seatbelt. We were quiet as the Learjet taxied to the end of the runway, turned, and waited.

Seconds later, Jim said, "Here we go."

We streaked down the runway, and I felt the nose lift. We were airborne. Jim banked left and gave us one last look at Charlottetown Airport. We climbed, leveled off, and got the okay to move around the cabin.

"I'll make coffee," Mary said. "You two have a lot to talk about. Would you like coffee, Lola?"

"Yes, please. Black."

Mary smiled at me and headed to the galley in the rear of the aircraft. I knew what the smile meant: *You big sissy, why can't you drink your coffee black?*

"How did you manage a police escort?"

"A friend of my mother's," Lola said. "My mother knows many people in important positions."

"So your mother told you that I was looking for you?"

"Yes, and she told me you could solve my problem."

"How does she know that?"

"She knows things," Lola said. "She has psychic powers. She has actually helped the local police solve some cases."

A white witch and a psychic. Oh, boy! I said nothing.

"Where are you taking me?"

"To stay with a friend who lives with his wife on the Indian reservation in Cherokee, North Carolina. You'll be safe there. He's a deputy sheriff, and he also knows things."

"Is he psychic?"

"Sometimes, I think he is."

Mary returned with the coffee, black for them, cream and sugar for me.

"Tell me about the man chasing you," I said.

Lola took a sip of coffee. "Can we talk later? All of a sudden, I'm really, really tired."

Mary took Lola's coffee and placed it on a nearby table. "I'll get you a pillow and blanket. You can take a nap on the couch."

We got Lola situated and moved to the rear of the cabin.

"What do you think?" I said.

"I think she's scared," Mary said. "What are you going to do?"

"I don't know yet. I'll know more once I talk to her."

31

We sat in the Tailwind eating breakfast. The café had just opened, and we were the only customers. Lola had slept the entire trip to Tri-Cities. Mary and I had managed naps, and although the coffee and food were reviving me I knew I would hit the wall later. Everyone in our little group had an appetite, and we grew more animated as we consumed the food.

"Tell me about this man," I said to Lola.

"His name is Levi Pickingill," Lola said. She spelled if for me.

I removed a small spiral notebook from my backpack and wrote it down. "Are you sure that's his real name?"

"That's the name on his driver's license. He claims to be a male witch and a direct descendant of George Pickingill, a notorious male witch of the eighteen hundreds."

I wrote down *George Pickingill*. "Does Levi practice black magic?"

"I'm sure of it," she said. "I haven't seen him cast spells, but I've seen the results."

"What results?" Mary said.

"Power over women, mostly," Lola said, avoiding eye contact. "He makes them submit."

"Submit to what?" Mary said.

"Everything," Lola said. She was looking straight at Mary, as if I had disappeared. Her eyes were tearing. I did not do well with female tears. I was content to fade into the woodwork.

Mary nodded and said nothing. She took Lola's hand and held it. "How did you get away from him?" she asked.

"I cast a spell to break his spell," Lola said. "It worked. He came home one day, and he could tell. He was furious. He said my spell was weak and wouldn't last and I would be back under his power in twenty-four hours. That evening, when he wasn't looking, I drugged his drink and managed to slip away. I took half his money. He'll kill me just for doing that."

"What happened after you left?" Mary said. "Tell us all of it."

Lola told her story. She had taken a series of buses and ended up in New York City. She had been there once before and loved it. She found an apartment in Greenwich Village and realized she had to get a job. She got a hostess job at an upscale restaurant in Midtown but soon discovered she could make some nice side money moonlighting as a belly dancer. Levi had not known about her belly-dancing skills, and she thought it would be safe. Somehow, he found her. The day she had left Bentley's apartment, she got a call from one of the waitresses at the restaurant that a handsome, dark-haired man was looking for her. She knew it was Levi, and she knew he would find her soon if she didn't run. So she ran. She went back to Canada and stayed with some friends, eventually going home.

"Why didn't you call Bentley?" Mary asked.

"Because I was afraid for him," Lola said. "I have no doubt that Levi is capable of killing. He would have killed Bentley if he knew about us. He'll kill me if he finds me."

"If he finds you," I said, "he'll find more than he bargained for, spells or no spells."

Lola looked at me. "I believe that. So does my mother. That's the reason I came with you."

◆ ◆ ◆ ◆

We roared down I-81. Mary was driving. If Levi Pickingill was following us, he'd have a hard time keeping up. I looked at the speedometer—steady on eighty-five. Lola was asleep in the back, oblivious to Mary's reputation behind the wheel. I called Gretchen to let her know I may or may not be in.

I ended my call and looked at Mary. "If you don't back it down, you're going to get pulled over."

"Not only will I not get pulled over," Mary said, "we're going to get a THP escort."

Seconds later, a Tennessee Highway Patrol cruiser passed us and took position a hundred feet in front of us, matching our speed. Its rack lights were on.

Mary's cell phone rang. "Yeah, eighty-five is good," she said. "We're going to I-40 East. If you can get us to the border, that would be great. I'll try not to get pulled over in North Carolina. Really, that's very good of you. Thanks, Harry."

She hung up and kept driving. I said nothing, knowing she was dying for me to say something. Obviously, she had made a call when I wasn't looking.

Keeping quiet was not Mary's strong suit. It didn't take long. "That was Harry in the cruiser up ahead."

"I gathered."

"He's taking us to the North Carolina border."

"I heard. Nice to have friends in the THP."

"Well, one thing you didn't hear, smarty pants, is that we're also getting an escort in North Carolina."

"Really?" I said. "Are we in a hurry?"

"I'm in a hurry," Mary said. "I need to get back to work. Besides, I don't get to do this much. I kind of like it."

We made it to the North Carolina border in record time and had a brief but exciting twenty-mile trip on the curvy highway doing seventy until we left I-40 East at the Maggie Valley exit. Billy was waiting for us at a nearby gas station. We followed him into Maggie Valley, past the Cataloochee Ski Area exit, and up the mountain. We crossed the Blue Ridge Parkway and coasted down into Cherokee. Lola Madrid remained asleep in the back. We drove past the casino, took a left at the next light, and headed toward Bryson City. A few miles later, we were on a backcountry road and officially in the boondocks of North Carolina.

The Two-Feathers' house and property, inherited by Maggie from her parents, sat a half-mile off the secondary road. There were enough trees that the house could not be seen from the road in summer, but as Mary turned into the driveway I saw that it had been rendered partially visible by the effects of a cold winter. We followed Billy and parked in front of the modest but well-kept ranch house. The roof of Billy's studio peeked over the top of the ranch.

"Lola," I said.

Lola stirred and opened her eyes.

"We're here," I said.

"I slept the whole way?"

"You did."

"Thank you. That's the best sleep I've had in a long time."

"Let's get you situated," Mary said, opening the driver's-side door. "I'll introduce you to your hosts."

◆   ◆   ◆   ◆

Billy and I were on the second floor of his studio. The ladies were in the house, Mary and Maggie getting to know Lola. Mary seemed in no hurry to leave, so I waited patiently. I shared with Billy what Lola had told us about Levi Pickingill.

"Are you expecting trouble?" Billy said.

"Eventually."

"Here?"

"Probably not. I don't think Pickingill is psychic. Just a charmingly bad dude that knows how to manipulate women, a con artist hiding behind a myth. If people believe he's a warlock or male witch, then he is one. The perception is in the eye of the beholder. He'll never find Lola here. If he does, then I'll change my mind about him."

"If he comes here uninvited," Billy said, "he will regret it."

It was not an idle threat. I said nothing.

"Hey, Cowboy!" I heard Mary call from below. "Let's ride."

"On my way!" I called back. I looked at Billy and shrugged. "Now she's in a hurry."

All he could do was smile and shake his head.

◆   ◆   ◆   ◆

Mary let me drive back to Mountain Center—nice of her, considering it was my ride. I dropped her at the station.

"Remember, it's girls' night out tonight," she said. "You're on your own for dinner. And don't forget that Lola wants you to call Bentley."

She shut the door to the SUV before I could respond. I waved and watched her walk away and didn't stop watching until she went through the station door. I drove away smiling.

I made it to the office five minutes before Gretchen was due to leave. Our new hire was nowhere to be seen. I had not had the chance to welcome Ronda officially to Cherokee Investigations. Maybe she didn't really work here.

"Where is Ronda?"

"I sent her to the post office," Gretchen said.

"How is she working out?"

"Great," Gretchen said. "Rollie loves her."

"He would. Be sure he pays dearly for her services."

"My pleasure," Gretchen said. "What have you been up to?"

"Plenty."

"So enlighten your junior partner."

"Want to take a few minutes and hear it now?"

"Certainly. As a junior partner, I am no longer on the clock."

I hit the high spots. She listened and said nothing, but her expression said, *You've got to be kidding me.*

"Do you ever have a dull moment?" Gretchen said.

"Not since Lacy walked through my office door," I said.

◆   ◆   ◆   ◆

Sometimes, I get to make calls that aren't bad news. This was one of those. After Gretchen left the office, I dialed his direct number.

"Bentley Williams," he answered.

"It's Don Youngblood. I have Lola Madrid." *No sense beating around the bush, just drop it on him.*

Dead silence. Processing.

"What?" Bentley said, not believing he had just heard what he thought he would never hear. "My God, really?"

"Really. If you call her cell, she will answer. If you want to come down here, let me know and I'll pick you up at the airport."

"As soon as I can get a flight," Bentley said. "What airport should I fly into?"

"Asheville, North Carolina."

"I'll be in touch," Bentley said.

32

The Christmas lights on Main Street came on at exactly five o'clock, reminding me that the holidays were a few weeks away and I was totally unprepared. It was hard to think about Christmas when I had two cases going, two puzzles that I needed to solve. They were not likely to be solved before Santa made his appearance. I thought about what to do next. The clown had disappeared, and Levi Pickingill was hunting Lola Madrid. How much of a threat he was, I could only guess, but Selma Madrid did not seem like a woman who exaggerated. I needed information on Pickingill, and I didn't mind using the big gun to get it. I called his private line. Since it was after hours, I knew if he was there he would answer his own phone.

"Steele," he said.

"Working late again? Why don't you go home and have a drink and dinner with your wife?"

"Because I wouldn't be here to answer your calls, Youngblood. What is it this time?"

My timing is not good, I thought.

"Having a bad day, Dave?"

"Sorry, Youngblood. Just a really long day. What can I do for you?"

"It can wait, Dave. Go home. That's an order from friend to friend. Call me in the morning."

"Thanks, Don," he said. "Leaving now."

I made another call.

He answered on the second ring. "Roy Husky."

"If you're free for dinner, I'm buying."

"Raincheck, Gumshoe," Roy said. "I've got a date, and she's a hell of a lot better looking than you."

"Must be a stunner."

"You're correct. Call T. Elbert. He doesn't get out much."

"Good idea. I haven't seen him since we were on his front porch about ten days ago."

I hung up and called T. Elbert. I had asked him out on a number of occasions, and he rarely said yes, so I needed a hook, something so unique he couldn't pass it up. When he answered, I said, "What are you up to?"

"SSDD," he said.

"Well, I'm about to change that." I told him my proposal.

"Hell yes, I'm interested," T. Elbert said. "Come on over and we'll take the Black Beauty."

The Black Beauty was T. Elbert's specially equipped Hummer H2. It had hand controls for gas and brakes and a power lift for putting him behind the wheel. The front bucket seat had been removed. Once inside, his wheelchair locked in place in the driver's position.

"On my way," I said.

◆   ◆   ◆   ◆

"That's damn good shootin', Donald," T. Elbert said, looking at my target. "Especially with that cannon you're using. You haven't lost the touch."

I was using my .357 Ruger, a five-shot revolver with the kick of a mule. I was cheating a little by firing .38 caliber rounds. They kicked a little less and were also less noisy, but not by much on both counts.

"You're not doing so bad yourself," I said. "Comes back in a hurry, doesn't it?"

"Damn right," he said, smiling. He was like a kid in an amusement park.

We were in the basement of the Mountain Center Police Station. Being best friends with a small-town chief of police has its privileges. I came to the range as I pleased, and no one paid any attention to me. My contribution was seeing that the lockers were well stocked with an assortment of ammo.

T. Elbert was firing an old Police Special, a long-barreled .38 manufactured by Smith & Wesson. The model had been manufactured in 1911.

The pistol was in pristine shape. The cylinder held six rounds. We were shooting from thirty feet.

He fired his last round and laid down the pistol. I flipped a switch and reeled in his target. We took a look.

"Not as good as yours," he said. "But not bad."

"Every one of those would have been fatal," I said.

I took his old target, laid it on a table behind us, clipped on a new one, flipped the switch, and sent the target down the range. I did the same for myself.

After we had fired a hundred rounds, T. Elbert said, "That's enough. Let's go eat."

◆   ◆   ◆   ◆

A half-hour later, we were at my favorite table at the Mountain Center Country Club ordering steaks with fries, Caesar salads, and draft beer.

"I've got to tell you," T. Elbert said, "I haven't had that much fun in years."

"We'll do it again after the holidays."

"Something to look forward to," T. Elbert said.

The beer arrived in frosted mugs. We raised them, touched them, and took the first long, cold drink. Perfect.

"Tell me the latest on your cases," T. Elbert said.

Every now and then, I liked dropping bombs on T. Elbert, just to see his reaction. I waited until he swallowed his beer. I didn't want it spewed all over the dining room. "Lola Madrid is staying with Maggie and Billy."

"What?" he said as if he couldn't have heard me right. "Say that again. This I really have to hear."

So I told him all of it: the phone call, the flight to Canada, Lola's police escort, Levi Pickingill, even Mary's wild ride with her police escort.

"That Mary's a pistol," he said.

"More like a loose cannon."

"What are you going to do about this Pickingill? You don't believe in this witchcraft stuff, do you?"

"Not yet."

"He'll never find her at Billy's," T. Elbert said. "But you'd hate to have this guy out there looking for her. She can't stay with Billy forever."

"I know. Eventually, I'll have to find him or draw him in. I'll worry about it after the first of the year. Wish I knew someone in the Royal Canadian Mounted Police. I'd like to see if Pickingill is in their records. I'm hoping David Steele might be able to help."

"I might," T. Elbert said. "I'm still friends with the director of the TBI. He has a relative that's an inspector for the RCMP. Let me check it out."

I knew T. Elbert relished every small thing he could do to assist me in an investigation. It made him feel like he was still in the game. The firing range had regenerated his desire for police work.

"That would be great," I said. "I'd rather not bother David Steele."

T. Elbert smiled and took a long drink of beer as our food arrived. We dove in, eating and saying little.

After a while, T. Elbert said, "What about the clown?"

"Buckley's doing some follow-up research. We'll see where that leads."

"Sounds like you're in a holding pattern on both cases."

"Not the first time," I said.

"Yeah," T. Elbert said. "But sooner or later, things will start to roll."

I had no doubt about that.

33

I was in the office early. Soon after I had made that first steaming mug of coffee, David Steele called.

"Did you get some rest?" I said when I answered.

"I did. What can I do for you, Youngblood?"

"Absolutely nothing. I don't think I'll need your involvement right now."

"Is this about the clown?"

"No," I said.

"Well, as long as we're talking, what's going on with that?"

I told him the latest.

"So you're at a dead end," he said.

"For now."

"Is Buckley helping?"

"Some."

"Okay, then," David Steele said. "I have to get going. If anything significant happens, like turning up a body or two, let me know."

"Will do," I said.

◆　◆　◆　◆

Later that morning, Bentley called back, a man in a hurry.

"I'm at LaGuardia," he said. "I'm flying American to Charlotte and then American Eagle to Asheville. I'm due in Asheville at 3:32. I'll rent a car. Maggie is going to set us up in a nearby cabin that belongs to a friend of hers. I'm supposed to drive into Cherokee and call Lola. I cannot thank you enough, Mr. Youngblood."

"Calm down, Bentley. Everything is going to work out just fine. How long are you staying?"

"As long as I have to."

"How much do you know?"

"Not much," Bentley said. "Lola said she'll explain when I get there."

"Safe travels," I said. "I'll be in touch."

◆   ◆   ◆   ◆

That afternoon, the office phone rang. Seconds later, Gretchen's voice came over the intercom: "Ben Shoney on line one."

"Youngblood," I said.

"I hear you're a miracle worker," Ben said.

"Just lucky. I take it you talked to Bentley."

"As he blew out of here like a tornado late yesterday. I've never seen such an attitude change. I take it you'll bill me plenty."

"Or I can bill Bentley," I said.

"No, bill me."

"Glad to," I said.

"Good work, Don. We'll talk later."

After hanging up, I buzzed Gretchen two quick blasts. Seconds later, she was sitting in front of my desk, pad and pen in hand. I got the get-on-with-it look.

"The Lola Madrid case is officially over," I said. "You may bill Ben Shoney for time spent plus expenses. Be fair but thorough."

"Always," Gretchen said. "What does 'officially over' mean?"

"I have some loose ends to tie up, but my time won't be billable," I said.

"Loose ends?"

"A bad guy needs to be taken care of."

She stared at me. I said nothing.

"You be careful," she said.

I smiled. "Always."

◆   ◆   ◆   ◆

My last call of the day was from John Banks.

"I can't find a trace of Royce Rogers anywhere," he said. "It's like he walked out of Huntsville and disappeared."

"Wait a week and try again," I said. "Maybe he's hiding out somewhere."

"Will do, Youngblood. In case you're interested, I spent five hours on this."

"Check's in the mail," I said. "Have a good weekend."

34

The holidays played out without any surprises. The weather turned warm and dry, and those of us looking for snow before Christmas were disappointed. The temperature stayed well above freezing, doing nothing to enhance the Christmas spirit. Gretchen continued to find work for Ronda Sharkey, most of it coming from Rollie Ogle.

Mary, Lacy, Biker, and I went to a Christmas Eve service at the local Methodist church and then for a late dinner. Mary and Lacy did most of the talking and Biker and I most of the eating. Surprising how much you can learn by keeping your mouth shut.

Christmas Day, after we opened presents, T. Elbert picked Mary and me up in his H2 and we went over the Great Smoky Mountains and down into Cherokee to have dinner with Maggie and Billy. Bentley and Lola joined us. Lacy and Biker had other plans.

Bentley was unclear on how long he intended to stay, but it was apparent he was in no hurry to leave. "I have my laptop and my cell phone," he said. "I can work from here, and no one will know I'm not in New York. If I have to see a client, I'll make a day trip."

"Sounds like a plan," I said.

Lola had received word from New York that a tall, dark, handsome man was still looking for her. Levi Pickingill, it seemed, was not going to give up easily. I mulled that over as Maggie and I were in the kitchen rinsing dishes and loading the dishwasher.

"Lola and Bentley make a nice couple, don't they, Don?" Maggie said. Her voice had a soothing, unhurried quality that made me feel at ease, like water flowing over river rock. The more I got to know her, the more I realized what a special person she was.

"They certainly do."

"I'm worried about this Levi," Maggie said. "He does not sound like a nice person."

"No, he doesn't. I think he'll have to be dealt with."

"How will you do that?"

"I don't know yet, but I'll think of something."

"You always do, Blood," Billy said, standing in the doorway. "You always do."

35

New Year's tiptoed past us like a thief in the night. Mary and I spent New Year's Eve quietly at the lake house alone. Lacy and Biker had places to go and things to do. The weather turned cold and it snowed. The snow caused me to look longingly at my skis. They would have to wait. I had two cases to resolve.

The following Monday, I was back in the office with two New Year's resolutions: find Royce Rogers and dispose of Levi Pickingill. I was pondering both when the phone rang. Caller ID said it was the county sheriff's office.

"Youngblood," I answered.

"Hey, Blood," Jimmy Durham said, his slow country drawl unmistakable.

"What's up, Bull?"

"Something you might be interested in. A couple of fishermen were out late yesterday afternoon and snagged something."

"People fish in this weather?"

"The crazy ones do," Jimmy said. "Anyway, one of them thought at first he had a big one on the line. Maybe a big cat or a carp. So he started bringing it up, and he began to think it wasn't a fish, since he wasn't getting any fight. Then the line went slack, and he knew he'd lost it. So he reeled in the line, and on the hook was part of a shirt sleeve and what might be a little flesh, so he called it in. I've got three pro divers coming in from Knoxville. I'm meeting the guy who hooked the sleeve in an hour, and he's going to show us the exact location. Looks like there may be a body down there. You want to join us?"

"Damn right I do," I said. "Where?"

He gave me the name of the marina and the directions.

"One hour," I said.

◆　◆　◆　◆

I met Jimmy at the marina. I parked and walked down the long dock to where he was standing near his patrol boat. Written on the side was "Sheriff's Patrol."

"Where are your guys?" I said.

"Already out there with the divers," he said. "I got three divers deep, in about ninety feet of water. They said if anything is out there, they'll find it."

"Let's go," I said.

We got in the patrol boat, and Jimmy took the wheel. He pulled away from the marina slowly until he passed the no-wake zone. "Hang on," he said. Then he gunned it, and we flew across the water so fast that the wind chill felt like ten below zero. My ski jacket, zipped up tight around my face, fought to keep me warm but lost. I squeezed near Jimmy behind the windshield.

Ten minutes later, we were at the site. I made a mental note to check for frostbite when I got to someplace warm. Two other boats were bobbing in the water. One was another sheriff's boat. The other held two men I assumed were the fishermen who had called the sheriff's department.

"How many patrol boats do you have?" I said.

"You're lookin' at 'em," Jimmy said.

He shouted to the deputies on the other patrol boat. "How long have they been down?"

"About fifteen minutes!" one deputy shouted back.

Ten minutes later, a diver surfaced, looked at Jimmy, and stuck a thumb in the air. One of the deputies threw a harness attached to a rope into the water. The diver took it and went under. Again we waited. Ten minutes later, another diver surfaced and made a circle gesture in the air. Two deputies began pulling on the rope. A short time later, a body popped to the surface, followed by the two remaining divers. The body was loaded on the other patrol boat and zipped up in a black body bag. Then the three divers were helped on board, and our little band of boats cruised back to the dock.

◆　◆　◆　◆

The body bag lay on the dock, a big, black blob nobody wanted to go near. A few bystanders stood on the fringes, knowing what was in the bag but looking for confirmation.

"Want a look?" Jimmy said.

"Not really," I said. "But I guess I'd better."

We walked over, and Jimmy unzipped the bag. The corpse was face down, cold and pale, drained of color from death and the dark abyss from which we had pulled it. The body looked in remarkably good shape, given that it had probably been in the water for over six weeks. I leaned in and looked at the bullet hole in the back of his head, a small entry wound. *Twenty-two caliber*, I thought.

"I don't think he drowned," I said.

"Good guess," Jimmy said. "Know him?"

I was sure I did but I rolled him over just the same.

I stood and nodded. "Ricky Carter. Once believed to be dead. Now officially dead."

◆   ◆   ◆   ◆

On my way back to Mountain Center, I called Wanda Jones.

"Medical Examiner's Office," the female voice said.

"That you, Amber?"

"Who's this?"

"Don Youngblood," I said. "Is Wanda in?"

"Hold on, Mr. Youngblood."

"Hello, handsome," Wanda said.

"Hello, second-best-looking woman in Mountain Center."

Wanda laughed. "The best-looking woman in Mountain Center being your red-hot wife."

"Correct."

"You didn't call just to give me a back-handed compliment. What do you really want?"

"A body is coming your way," I said.

"Did you shoot another one?" She sounded way too excited.

"No, someone else shot this one and dumped him in the lake. As soon as you can, please tell me how long you think he was in the water."

"Will do," she said. "Give number one a big kiss from me."

"And more," I said.

"Pervert," Wanda said, and hung up.

◆   ◆   ◆   ◆

I called David Steele. By some miracle, he was in, not on the phone, and willing to take my call.

"Happy New Year, Dave."

"Uh-huh," David Steele said without much enthusiasm. "Don't tell me you found a body."

"Well, somebody else found it. But it's the one I've been looking for."

"Ricky Carter?"

"Fished out of the local lake. Dead as a mackerel."

David Steele did not laugh. In fact, he said nothing.

"You said—"

"I know what I said," David Steele snapped. "It's still not enough. It's all circumstantial. He could have drowned."

"He had a .22 caliber bullet hole in his head."

Dead silence for a few seconds.

"It's a local murder. Could have been that drug guy you told me about."

I said nothing because David Steele was right. It could have been Rasheed. I had tipped him to the fact that Ricky Carter was still alive and maybe in the neighborhood. I was still betting on Royce Rogers, but it could have been Rasheed Reed.

"How long the body has been in the water will tell us if it could have been Rasheed Reed," I said. "He's known about Ricky for a month. I'm betting on six to seven weeks."

"Assuming you're right about that, you can flash your FBI special consultant ID around, and you can ask John Banks to do some moonlighting for you. Whatever deal you two agree to is fine by me. That's the best I can do right now. Don't bother Buckley. He's working something more important. Call me when you have something else. Give my best to Mary."

I said nothing. There was nothing left to say. The deputy director obviously wasn't impressed with the body, and now he was backpedaling. To him, it was circumstantial. To me, it was too much of a coincidence not to be connected.

36

"Ricky fucking Carter?" Big Bob said.

It was early the next morning, and we were in the Mountain Center Diner at my table in the back. Luckily, no one was close enough to hear Big Bob's expletive.

"Pretty much the same reaction Mary had," I said. "But I don't think that was Ricky's middle name."

"Well, it should have been," Big Bob snorted. "Good riddance."

"Easy for you to say. I really wanted to talk to him."

"So you think Royce Rogers killed him and dumped him in the lake?"

"Well, he didn't drown by accident. The bullet hole in the back of his head proves that."

"But at this point, it's just a theory. You don't have any concrete evidence that it's Royce Rogers."

"Not yet, but I'm working on it."

Doris brought breakfast, and we dug in.

"This means Jimmy Durham has an open murder investigation," Big Bob said. "I'll bet he's thrilled."

"Not very."

"I was being sarcastic," Big Bob said.

"I know."

"He probably thinks you'll solve it for him."

Jimmy wasn't lazy, but he did like to keep things simple. I said nothing. Rather, I took a big bite of feta cheese omelet.

"Who knows about this besides the county sheriff's department and Wanda Jones?" Big Bob asked.

"Mary and you," I said.

"You should probably tell the Cox family."

"You're right," I said. "I should."

◆   ◆   ◆   ◆

I sat outside Howard Cox's office waiting for him to get off the phone. As soon as that happened, his assistant was quick to let him know I was waiting.

Howard appeared in the doorway. "Donald, come on in."

I sat in front of his desk. Howard sat across from me in a big black leather chair that showed quite a bit of wear. It looked comfortable.

"The county sheriff's department pulled a body out of the lake yesterday," I said.

Howard Cox looked puzzled. "Who?"

"Ricky Carter."

"What? I thought Ricky was already dead."

"So did a lot of other people," I said. "Turns out, Ricky was probably one of the kidnappers, and his partner killed him after they got your money."

"What?" Howard was having a hard time keeping up. The news was too incredible.

I told him how my investigation had led me to Texas chasing Royce Rogers and how I had accidentally stumbled across Ricky. He listened like a man watching a train wreck. I finished. We sat quietly for a while.

"I hope the little bastard burns in hell," Howard Cox said.

I didn't particularly like the imagery, so I said nothing.

"You going to continue looking for Royce Rogers?"

"Probably," I said.

"Hell, you know you will. And I want it on my dime. I want this guy brought to justice for what he did to my granddaughter and those other granddaughters."

"Okay," I said. "Your dime. But I'd do it for free."

"I know you would," he said.

◆   ◆   ◆   ◆

I went back to my office, sat at my desk, and waited for an epiphany. I didn't expect one, but a guy can hope. *Think*, I told myself. *Okay*. Fact: there had been a number of kidnappings for ransom of grandchildren of rich men in Texas by two men, one dressed as a clown. Fact: Cindy Carter was kidnapped by two men, one dressed as a clown. Fact: when Royce Rogers had been arrested for the casino heist, officers had found a clown costume in his basement. Conclusion: the clown was Royce Rogers. Fact: Ricky Carter shared a cell with Royce Rogers in prison. Fact: Ricky Carter knew that Howard Cox would pay the ransom for Cindy. Conclusion: Royce Rogers's accomplice for the Cindy Carter kidnapping was Ricky Carter. Fact: Ricky Carter was dead. Conclusion: Royce Rogers had killed Ricky Carter. Final conclusion: Royce Rogers had probably killed his partners after each kidnapping and disposed of the bodies.

Then an idea popped into my head. I called John Banks on his FBI direct-dial number. "It's your favorite consultant," I said. "Want to earn some extra dough?"

"Always," he said.

I told him what I wanted.

"How many do you need?"

"Two would be a good start."

"I'll start tonight. Might take a while. I might get lucky, or I might not ever find anything. How many hours am I authorized to spend on this?"

"As many as it takes. I trust you, John. Who could be more trustworthy than an FBI agent?"

"Yeah, right," John said. "I'll be in touch, Youngblood."

◆　◆　◆　◆

It was late when I made my final phone call of the day.

Rasheed Reed answered on the second ring. "Yeah?"

"It's Youngblood."

"You found Ricky Carter?"

"I did."

"Never let it be said you're not good at what you do, Youngblood."

"This time, it was pure luck."

"When can I talk to him?"

"In the next life," I said.

"He's dead?"

"Most sincerely dead."

Rasheed was quick on the uptake. "Somebody drop a house on him?"

"Very good, Rasheed. No, somebody put a bullet in his head, weighed him down, and dropped him in the lake. We were lucky to find him."

"You see the body?"

"I did."

"No doubt it was Ricky?"

"None," I said. "DNA will confirm it, but it was Ricky."

"I didn't do it," Rasheed said, "if that's why you're calling."

"I didn't think you did. Just thought you should know."

"Appreciate it," Rasheed said. "Know who killed him?"

"I think it was probably his partner in the kidnapping."

"It figures. No honor among thieves."

"Do tell," I said.

◆   ◆   ◆   ◆

I was walking out the door when my office phone rang. I normally would have ignored it, but I had too much going on, so I did an about-face and grabbed the desk phone.

"Youngblood," I said. *The annoyed private investigator.*

"Jeez, Mary cut you off?"

"Sorry, Wanda," I said. "Long day."

"In my humble opinion," Wanda said, "Ricky Carter had been dead six to seven weeks. I, of course, being the consummate professional that I am, took water temperature into consideration."

"I am in awe," I said. "Good work. That's exactly the answer I was looking for."

◆   ◆   ◆   ◆

That night, Mary and I sat at the kitchen bar in our Mountain Center condo eating a sausage calzone and drinking beer, Blue Moon for her,

Amber Bock for me. Occasionally, Mary shared some of her crust with the dogs. Being the food hog that I am, I shared nothing. We were recounting the day. Most of the time, Mary's day was more interesting than mine, but not today.

"Rasheed Reed sounds like quite a character," Mary said. "Think you could count on him if you needed to?"

"Maybe. Especially if it was dangerous."

"Sounds like you. A danger junkie."

"Look who's talking," I said.

Mary smiled and took a drink of her Blue Moon. Seconds later, my cell phone rang. I checked caller ID and answered.

"Hey, Chief."

"This Levi Pickingill is starting to annoy me," Billy said.

"Too bad for him. What did he do now?"

"Lola got a call this afternoon from her friend that he is offering five thousand dollars to anyone who knows Lola's whereabouts."

"Where did he get the five Gs?"

"Lola says he doesn't have it. She says it's only a ploy for someone to rat her out. My words, not hers."

I paused for a minute, then concluded it was time to deal with Levi. He was not going away. The opportunity was being presented to us, and we'd be fools not to take it.

"I think maybe we ought to find out if Levi has five big ones," I said.

"My thinking also," Billy said.

"Got a number where we can reach him?"

"I do," Billy said.

"Can you and Lola meet me in the office tomorrow morning?"

"We can. You got a plan?"

"I'm hatching one as we speak."

"What time?"

"Nine o'clock," I said.

"See you then," Billy said.

37

The next morning, I went to Walmart and bought the cheapest pre-paid cell phone I could find. I was in the office waiting with my second cup of coffee when Lola and Billy showed up at exactly nine. I pointed out the coffee, and they both took a cup and sat in front of my desk. Both were quiet. Both drank coffee and stared at me.

"You have a plan?" Billy said, breaking the silence.

"I do. It will require some acting from Lola and me."

"Tell us," Billy said.

I did.

"Might work," Billy said.

"Nothing to lose," I said.

"It scares the hell out of me," Lola said.

"No harm will come to you," Billy said.

Lola smiled. "I believe you," she said, then turned to me. "Let's rehearse."

◆　◆　◆　◆

An hour later, we were ready. I had a Sharper Image sound machine with a variety of sounds, one of which was big-city traffic. I started the sound machine, turned up the volume, and called the number Lola had been given. The speaker phone option was on. We heard four rings, and then a pleasant baritone voice said, "This is Levi. Leave a message."

"I have what you want," I said as mysteriously as I could muster. "You have the number. Call back if you're interested." I disconnected and turned off the sound machine. "Now, we wait," I said.

We sat sipping coffee.

"What route did you take today?" I asked Billy.

"The long way," Billy said. "Four forty-one over the mountain was closed due to ice and snow."

"No ice and snow down here," I said. "It's warm for this time of year."

"Global warming," Billy said.

"Tell that to the Northeast," I said.

A winter storm was currently wreaking havoc in New England. But East Tennessee was having an unusually warm and dry winter. Wildfires were at an all-time high, many of them set on purpose. A few cool days and a few showers had reduced the threat, but the forests around Mountain Center and the lake were still dry and susceptible to fire. The area needed more rain—or, better yet, snow. Global warming or a weird weather pattern? Who knew?

The pre-paid cell phone ripped me away from the weather debate. I let it ring twice while turning on the sound machine.

"Speak," I answered.

"Exactly what do you have that I would be interested in?"

"A lovely package named Lola Madrid."

"And how do I know this?"

"She's with me now," I said. "Say hello, Lola."

As rehearsed, Lola said nothing.

"I said to say hello." I hoped I sounded angry and annoyed.

"Stop it, you're hurting me," Lola said, just the right amount of pain in her voice.

"Don't hurt her," Levi said. He sounded sincere.

"As you wish," I said.

"Where are you?"

"Close," I said. "Do you have the money?"

"Of course," Levi said, probably lying through his teeth. "I'll meet you in Central Park. Go to the Sixtieth Street and Fifth Avenue entrance in one hour and call me."

"I have a better idea," I said. "Main concourse at Grand Central Station at five o'clock this afternoon."

"Too crowded," he said. "I'll never find you."

"Sure you will. Call me when you get there, and I'll tell you exactly where we are."

Silence. He was calculating the risk. Just how badly did he want Lola? I waited. More silence. I was sure he was listening to the traffic sounds. I didn't want to give him time to figure out that it was a machine with a repeating loop.

"Yes or no?" I said.

Silence.

"Answer or I hang up."

"Yes," Levi said.

"Five o'clock," I said. I disconnected.

"Grand Central?" Billy said.

"Let's go," I said. "We have a plane to catch."

◆　◆　◆　◆

Two hours later, we were in the air. Jim Doak had Fleet Industries jet number one pointed toward New Jersey's Teterboro Airport. Once again, Frankie Pastore, in Carlo Vincente's limo, would be there to meet the jet. I was using up favors right and left with Carlo. Evidently, they were unlimited.

I had instructed Lola not to tell Bentley she was coming to New York. I did not want him in the way. He had gone back the day before to meet with a client and had promised to return as soon as possible. Lola understood about not getting Bentley involved. "A very good idea," she had said.

As soon as we were in the air, I called David Steele on his private cell phone.

"This better be good, Youngblood," he said.

"How would you like to score points with the Royal Canadian Mounted Police?" I said.

"You've got to be kidding me."

"Interested?"

"I'm listening."

When I finished, he said, "I'll make some calls."

• ◆ ◆ ◆

The flight was uneventful, the landing perfect, and the limo waiting, glistening in the cold New Jersey sunshine. Frankie was leaning on the front fender, arms folded, rear door open. He sprang to attention as we exited the jet and held the door handle as Lola walked toward him. She nodded and climbed in. I nodded at Frankie and followed Lola into the limo.

Billy stopped in front of Frankie. It was a long time since they had seen each other. We had crossed paths with Frankie on our first big case.

"How have you been?" Billy said.

"Good," Frankie said. "You?"

"No complaints," Billy said.

"Me either," Frankie said.

Billy climbed in beside me and shut the door.

As the limo headed to the big city, my cell phone rang.

"Four of my guys will be there," David Steele said. "Tell me how you're going to play it."

I told him.

"By the way," I said, "according to the county medical examiner, Ricky Carter has been dead at least six weeks. That fits the time frame of the kidnapping."

"One thing at a time, Youngblood. We'll talk about this later."

◆ ◆ ◆ ◆

Grand Central Station was every bit as busy as I remembered. We stood in the shadows near a wall on the upper level, looking down into the chaos, people hurrying in all directions, somehow managing not to knock each other down, ants thick on an ant hill. We were not invisible, but we would be difficult to spot. Two big electronic boards displayed departure and arrival times and corresponding gates. A large clock over the information desk showed the time to be four-thirty. Arrivals and departures were announced. We scanned every nook and cranny for Levi Pickingill. Five o'clock came and went.

At five-fifteen, Billy said, "Is he going to show?"

"He'll show," I said. "He's probably already here, trying to spot us and convince himself it's not a trap."

"Which it is."

I started to comment that we certainly had lovely bait, but Lola interrupted: "There he is."

"Where?" I said.

"Coming down the escalator," she said.

At that moment, his fate was sealed.

I saw a tall man in a black leather jacket that was open to reveal a black T-shirt. He wore matching black pants and black boots. He reached the bottom of the escalator and headed for the Forty-second Street exit.

"He's leaving," Lola said.

"I doubt it," I said. "Let's wait and see."

Five minutes later, Levi slowly made his way back to the main concourse, hugging the wall and pretending to read a newspaper. He looked up more than he looked down, scanning the crowd. I called his cell and watched as he reached into his pocket to answer.

"Levi," he said.

"Show me the money," I said.

He reached inside his jacket, produced an envelope large enough to hold five grand, and put it away.

"Look up," I said, "at about ten o'clock."

It took him maybe twenty seconds. "I see you."

"Come to me, and let's get this over with," I said.

He started across the concourse toward the stairs that led to us. He never made it.

◆   ◆   ◆   ◆

We were cruising at thirty thousand feet on our way to Tri-Cities Airport, less one passenger. Since Levi Pickingill was now in the custody of the FBI,

Lola had called Bentley, and they had decided to stay in the city—young love. I could still see the anger on Levi's face as the FBI closed in on him from four sides. By the time he realized what was happening, it was too late to run. I could still hear him yelling at me from the floor of Grand Central: "I'll rain hellfire down on you for this!" He had said it more than once, and it echoed off the walls of the historic train station. His arrest and tantrum were barely noticed by the commuters, intent on catching their trains home. I guessed they had seen and heard everything. It was, after all, New York.

"Levi was most unhappy," Billy said, sitting across from me.

"Stalkers usually are when they get caught," I said.

Billy looked out the window, distracted. "Something about him bothers me. I'll have to think about it."

Something about Levi bothered me also, but I said nothing.

38

I've always hated goodbyes, even temporary ones. Mary couldn't stand watching Lacy fly off into the morning, so I had the task of taking Lacy and Biker to Tri-Cities Airport for their return trip to Arizona State. I regretted that Lacy and I had not spent more time together, but she had places to go and people to see and a small window of time. I understood that. She was the only child I would probably ever have, and my time with her over the few years she'd been with us had been like the blink of an eye, gone before I realized it.

I parked in the short-term lot, locked my Ruger in the glovebox, and escorted them to their gate, still smelling smoke in the air from distant wildfires. I was able to get through security thanks to my FBI creds and the fact that I knew most of the people working the checkpoint.

"You carrying, Don?" a security guard asked.

"Not today, Al. Just seeing the kids off. I won't be long."

We walked unhurriedly to their departure gate. No one said anything. When the flight was announced, Biker shook my hand, said goodbye, and went to board.

Lacy hung back. "It was great being home," she said. Tears were in her eyes.

I smiled. *Hold it together, tough guy.* "But it will be good to get back."

"It will," she said. "We love it there."

"If you need us to come out, or if you want to make a trip back before the end of the school year, just say the word."

"I will," Lacy said.

The last call was announced, and she hugged me fiercely. "I love you."

"I love you, too," I said. It was not a reflex, it was the truth.

She turned and without looking back went through the door, down the ramp, and onto the plane. I stood there frozen, feeling that sense of loss I always experience when someone I care about says goodbye and leaves me standing alone feeling sorry for myself.

I found my way to the observation deck and watched as Lacy's plane lifted off the tarmac, banked to the left, and flew westward. I stayed until the aircraft was a speck on the clear western sky and then disappeared. I took a deep breath and headed toward the Pathfinder.

◆　◆　◆　◆

I arrived at the office before Gretchen. Ronda Sharkey was already at her desk. I poked my head in. "Hey, Ronda, how's it going?"

"Great," she said. "I just got my PI license in the mail. I'm really excited."

"Congratulations."

"I want to get a gun-carry permit. Can you tell me how to go about that?"

"Sure," I said. "Look up Mountain Center Indoor Range online. They give classes for carry permits. The classes are on Saturdays and are about eight hours long. When you complete the class, they'll run a background check. In the meantime, you have to fill out some paperwork at the DMV and then have a photo taken. After that, you wait. Should take three or four weeks but could be longer."

"I'll call today and get signed up," Ronda said.

"You may want to take a shooting lesson before you do the class," I said. "I know a couple of Mountain Center cops that give lessons."

"Thanks. By the way, Buckley Clarke called this morning. He said he had some information for you."

◆ ◆ ◆ ◆

I got comfortable at my desk and called Buckley. "You called," I said.

"I did. I have two names for you. I'll email them with some contact info."

"How do they connect?"

"One was at the University of Texas at the same time as Royce Rogers," Buckley said. "The other worked for Texas Oil at the same time as Rogers. I have no idea if Rogers knew either one of them, but he could have. You'll have to find out that for yourself."

"And they were both reported missing?" I asked, just to confirm.

"Yes, they were."

"Thanks, Buckley. That's good work."

"You're welcome, but John did the hard part. I just pointed him in the right direction. I made a few calls, but they didn't lead anywhere."

"Guess I'm going back to Texas," I said. "Want to come?"

"Not this time. I'm working a fraud case. It's taking up a lot of my time."

"Good luck with that," I said. "We'll talk soon."

◆ ◆ ◆ ◆

When Gretchen arrived, I buzzed her to come into my office. She sat across from me looking every bit the junior partner in a tailored pantsuit, ready to take notes.

"You're looking swell, doll," I said.

She held a serious look for about two seconds, then burst out laughing. "Have you been watching those old private-eye movies again?"

"They don't make them like that anymore."

"Well, I must admit, you do a pretty good Bogie. Now, big boy, what can I do for you?"

I stared at her. "Mae West?"

She smiled. "You're not the only one who watches old movies. Now, enough goofing around. What do you need?"

I gave her what Buckley had given me.

"Find out what Glenn Evans majored in at the University of Texas and if any of the professors he took classes from are still there. If anyone asks, you're assisting a special consultant from the FBI in a missing person investigation. The office of the dean of students should be a good place to start."

Gretchen nodded and made notes.

"See if you can find out Jerry Altman's foreman on the oil rig, and if the foreman is still there."

"Anything else?"

"No."

"Then I'll get started," Gretchen said.

◆　◆　◆　◆

That night, I prepared dinner. Mary sat at the counter, drank white wine, and watched. We engaged in idle conversation as I put the meal together: fried catfish, coleslaw, hushpuppies, and French fries. The only part of the meal that required effort on my part was the catfish, which had been soaking in buttermilk since I arrived at the condo. The fries and hushpuppies were baking in the oven. The coleslaw was chilling in the fridge. A stick of butter was softening on the bar. The dogs were lying on their beds in the adjoining dining area, waiting patiently in anticipation that some morsel might come their way.

"I smelled smoke when I came in," I said.

"Me, too," Mary said. "We're concerned about that."

"Who's we?"

"The town. We've got a plan if the fires get too close."

I heated peanut oil in a large cast-iron skillet as we talked. "It's good to have a plan."

"It's also scary. There's a high-wind warning for the next few days. High winds and fire are a bad combination. The good news is there's a big storm on the way that should produce a lot of rain, but it won't get here until Monday night."

I took the buttermilk-soaked catfish fillets, rolled them in a white cornmeal mix of my own creation, and waited for the oil to get hot. "The rain sounds good," I said.

Mary's response was finishing her glass of Chardonnay. She poured herself a second. I opened a bottle of Amber Bock and took a drink. A drop of water in the oil let me know it was ready. I gently slid each fillet into the skillet and set the timer. Newspaper surrounded the skillet to protect against splatter.

"I love it when you fix dinner," Mary said. I could tell she was starting to mellow.

"Why is that?"

"Because I can sit and watch and drink wine and relax."

I removed dinner plates from the cabinet and set them near the frying fish. I took two forks from the drawer and set them on the bar with napkins. I took another drink of beer. When the timer went off, I carefully turned the fillets and reset it.

"I have to go to Texas on Monday or Tuesday."

"Why?"

I told her.

The timer for the hushpuppies and fries went off. I turned off the oven and cracked the door. I took the coleslaw from the fridge and set it on the counter with two small Pyrex bowls I had retrieved from another cabinet.

"How long will you be gone?"

"Couple of days. I have to go to Austin and then Galveston."

"How long have those men been missing?"

"Years," I said.

"Years is a really cold trail."

"Yes, it is. But if I can find someone that can tell me Royce Rogers knew one or both of those guys, then I might be able to get Steely Dave to open an official case."

"I wouldn't bet on it," Mary said. She drank more wine.

The timer for the fillets went off. I drained them on paper towels, gently patting the top sides to remove any excess oil. I removed the fries and hushpuppies from the oven, then filled our plates with food and set them on the bar. I sat opposite Mary.

"God bless this food and the hands that prepared it," Mary said.

"Amen."

We ate in silence for a while.

"This is so good," Mary said. "You deserve a reward."

"What do you have in mind?"

"A nice little send-off."

"I don't leave until Monday."

"Why put off until Sunday night what could be done tonight?"

"It's only Thursday."

Mary took another drink of wine. "Minor technicality," she said.

39

The next day, I was in the office early reviewing the two files Buckley had emailed me. Glenn Evans had been a student at the University of Texas at the same time Royce Rogers was there. He went missing between his junior and senior years.

Three years later, Jerry Altman went missing. Altman had worked on the same Texas Oil offshore rig as Royce Rogers. Altman went missing two years after Rogers started working there. Buckley had managed to get the name of the foreman working the rig during that time: Bud Jeneau.

I picked up the phone and called my local travel agent.

Surprising me, he answered his own phone: "Roy Husky."

"Did you lose your assistant?"

"Too early for her," Roy said.

"How's business?"

"Almost too good, Gumshoe. But I'm not complaining. Better swamped than dead on your ass. What's up?"

"I need to go back to Texas. What's Jim's schedule look like?"

"Don't know," Roy said. "I don't pay attention to that much anymore. I'll have Jim call you. Still working the Clown case?"

"Still working it."

"Well, watch your ass down there," Roy said. "It's the Wild West."

◆　◆　◆　◆

That afternoon, Jim Doak called. "I heard you're looking to hitch a ride to Texas."

"You heard right," I said. "What are my chances?"

"Where in Texas?"

"Austin, then Galveston."

179

"I could do Austin on Tuesday," Jim said. "You'd be on your own for the rest of it."

"I'll take what I can get. What time?"

"Eight o'clock in the morning. Usual spot."

"See you Tuesday," I said.

40

Saturday morning, I was sitting on the lower deck drinking coffee from a Yeti mug that Lacy had given me for Christmas. Evidently, Yeti was all the rage with the younger generation. It was a clear, dry day, but everything appeared as if I were looking through a filtered lens, and the smell of smoke was stronger than in the last few weeks. Sensing the air quality could not be healthy, I was about to go in when my cell phone rang. I recognized the private number. I rarely saw it, and never on a Saturday.

"This can't be good," I said.

"It's not," David Steele said. "Levi Pickingill escaped sometime during the night, and a guard is missing."

"Female guard?"

"How'd you know?"

"Supposedly, Levi has a special power over women."

"Lucky him."

"At least he doesn't know who I am," I said. "But he might go after Lola Madrid."

There was an awkward silence on the other end.

"Dave?"

"Pickingill might have overheard some of the guys commenting on how high-profile cases seem to find their way to the door of the infamous PI Donald Youngblood. Said personnel got a major ass chewing from me personally."

I had visions of David Steele, my FBI instructor at Quantico, reaming a few asses of new recruits, mine included. I smiled to myself and said, "Ass chewing was always one of your strong suits."

"Still is. Listen, I'm sorry about the loose lips."

"Not your fault." I could feel my anger coming to the surface. "But if Pickingill comes after me, I'll kill him."

"I would expect no less," David Steele said. "Watch your back, Youngblood."

◆　◆　◆　◆

I went inside and refreshed my coffee. Mary was still sleeping, so I returned to my spot on the lower deck and made a call. The air quality seemed better. Or was I getting used to it?

Bentley Williams answered on the second ring.

"It's Don Youngblood," I said. "Where are you?"

"In my apartment. What's going on?"

"Levi Pickingill escaped last night. I doubt he knows who you are, but you might want to get Lola out of the city."

"I'll take her to my parents' house on Long Island," he said. "They live in a gated community. Security is really good—guards on duty twenty-four/seven and cameras everywhere."

"Sounds good," I said. "I'll keep you posted."

◆　◆　◆　◆

Fifteen minutes later, Mary came down carrying her first cup of coffee. She sat and took a drink. "I don't like smelling smoke every time I walk outside," she said.

"It was worse earlier."

"How long have you been up?"

"Couple of hours."

She drank more coffee and looked out at the lake. "Hazy," Mary said.

I said nothing.

Mary looked at me. "What?"

"David Steele called."

"Is he going to open the Clown case?"

"No."

Mary gave me the cop stare.

"Levi Pickingill escaped last night," I said.

"How?"

"It would appear with help from a female guard."

"Well, shit," Mary said. "Did you call Lola?"

"I called Bentley." I told Mary about Bentley's plan. "There's more," I said.

She stared at me again as I told her the rest of my conversation with David Steele. Her face got red. "If that son of a bitch comes around here, I'll kill him."

"Not if I kill him first," I said.

Little did I know that Levi Pickingill was the least of my worries.

41

Monday morning, I went to Moto's Gym and worked out. My visits had been sporadic of late, and Moto, his usual surly self, let me know about it. After a hard hour, I rewarded myself with breakfast at the Mountain Center Diner.

Doris seemed preoccupied as she took my order. "The usual?" she asked.

"Sure," I said. "You okay?"

"Just worried about all these fires around here. I hear a lot of them were started on purpose. Can you imagine such a thing?"

"No, I cannot."

She shook her head and went to place my order. I picked up the *Mountain Center Press* and read the main headline: "Fires a Serious Threat in East Tennessee." I read the article as I waited for breakfast. A staggering number of fires had been reported. Many of them—the estimate was about half—had been set on purpose; others were controlled burns that got out of hand. A number of arrests had been made, and investigations were ongoing. Conditions for wildfires were at the most critical level. There was presently more ground fuel than there had been in my lifetime. The public was asked to report any fire, no matter how small. Rewards were being given for information that led to the arrest and conviction of anyone purposely starting a fire.

My breakfast arrived, and I turned to the sports page.

Afterward, I left a twenty on the table and slipped out the back door. I went down the alley toward the office. Downtown Mountain Center was engulfed in a smoky, wind-driven haze. Air quality was undoubtedly at a critical level.

I climbed the back stairs with my Ruger in my hand. I didn't think Levi Pickingill would show up at my office, but I had learned by experience that it paid to be careful. Not paying attention could land me in the hospital or worse.

No one was lurking in the shadows, so I went inside and locked the door. I had just turned on the lights and sat at my desk when the phone rang. Caller ID was blocked.

"Cherokee Investigations," I answered.

"I'm not coming in," Gretchen said. "Buckley is worried about all these fires, and there is a high-wind warning for later. He wants me to come to Knoxville."

"Good idea. Call Ronda and tell her to stay home or go somewhere safe. Heavy rain is expected later tonight, and that should settle things down."

"Will do," Gretchen said. "Be careful, boss. This could get ugly."

◆　◆　◆　◆

I tried to stay busy by thinking about my two cases and reviewing the portfolios of various clients, but I was distracted. I had to read some things twice. I couldn't shake an unsettling feeling that something was wrong or about to go wrong. I had left the dogs at the lake house because I intended to spend the night there, the lake house being closer to the airport.

At four o'clock, Mary called. She got right to it. "Fires are getting close to Mountain Center. Big Bob has called everyone in. The wind is picking up, and a front bringing rain is moving slower than anticipated. We're going to evacuate problem areas as a precaution. You need to get home and get the dogs. I think our condo is going to be safer than the lake house."

"I'm on my way. You be careful, and keep in touch."

"I love you," Mary said. I heard fear in her voice.

"We'll be fine," I said.

"You promise."

"I promise," I said.

◆　◆　◆　◆

Fifteen minutes later, I was on the road. As I drove out of Mountain Center, I heard an emergency siren go off. Sirens were scattered about town in enough locations so that every resident should be able to hear one. If you heard a siren, you were supposed to tune to the local radio station. I turned on the radio. Big Bob was giving instructions for certain areas of the city to evacuate as a precaution. Evacuation there was mandatory. I knew that couldn't be enforced, but better safe than sorry. I put the pedal to the metal and sped out of Mountain Center toward the lake house.

It took me forty-five minutes to get to the foot of our driveway. The smoky haze was thicker than it had been, and the wind was stronger, carrying ash that looked like snow falling at a furious pace. Trees danced around me as I made my way up the driveway. I parked in the center of our parking area; if a tree came down, it was the safest place to be. I trotted to the front door, called the dogs, and put them in the side yard. It was a routine they were familiar with, and they went about their business.

I climbed the stairs to my office. I spent a minute surveying it and deciding what to take. I put my Glock Nine and all the cash I had into my backpack, along with some zip drives that contained most of my computer files. I went to my ski closet, removed a pair of old goggles hanging on my ski rack, and put on a black baseball cap from Brighton Ski Resort. I grabbed the suitcase-sized safe from my clothes closet and headed back down the stairs to the utility closet, where I had surgical masks on hand from spray-paint work. I put on a mask. I stopped at the front door and put the safe down. I turned the baseball cap around and put on the goggles. I picked up the safe and headed outside, looking like an alien or someone who might be ready to rob a bank. I took the safe and backpack to the Pathfinder.

It was getting dark, but there was a faint glow on the other side of the ridge that led down to the lake house. Fire was getting closer, and the smoke was heavier. I had a brief thought about trying to save the house and then realized it would be futile. The wind was howling, and sparks were all around.

I went back for the dogs. Not taking any chances, I put Junior on a leash. As we approached the SUV, I heard a loud crack, and then a large tree landed with a thud over the mouth of the driveway. Junior spooked, turned toward me, and backed right out of his collar, leaving me holding a leash and no dog. He bolted toward the downed tree, hurdled it, and ran up the driveway. I raised my surgical mask and shouted after him, but my words were swallowed by the wind. I stood frozen with Jake, my mind numb. Another muted crack, farther away, and a distant thud snapped me back to reality. Another tree down. *Junior will be okay*, I thought. *Animals have great survival instincts.*

"The houseboat!" I shouted at Jake. He knew the word.

Leaving the safe in the Pathfinder, we went back through the house, out the back door, and down to the dock. I was glad I had the backpack. It afforded me more weight against the wind. Down near the water, visibility was better than in the driveway.

"Come on!" I shouted at Jake through the mask.

He followed me out on the dock to the side door of the boathouse. I pushed it open and latched it. When I turned to get Jake, he was gone. I looked in the water, but he wasn't there. I looked back toward the house and saw him at the edge of the dock barking furiously. I went inside the boathouse, opened the big double doors that would allow the houseboat out, and latched them to the side walls. I started the twin engines; thankfully, they turned right over. I put my cell phone in my backpack for safekeeping and put the backpack in the storage bin. At the same time, I pulled out a life jacket and put it on. I maneuvered the houseboat out of the boathouse, drove to the end of the dock, and tied off. I went back down the dock toward the house to get Jake. I couldn't believe what I saw next: Jake and Junior were coming down the dock toward me.

I raised the surgical mask. "Come on, let's go!"

Seconds later, a powerful gust blew both dogs into the water. I ran to the spot where they had been, ripped off the mask, and jumped in. The water temperature hit me like a stun gun. The dogs were not far away, and I called to them. They began paddling furiously toward me. I prayed that Jake had the strength in that old body to make it. Junior reached me first. I got his front paws on the dock, then boosted him from the rear, and he was on, shaking water all over me. I turned for Jake and did not see him. Then his head came out of the water, and he gasped for air as I grabbed one of his front legs. I maneuvered Jake the same way I had Junior, got him on the dock, and finally got myself up. A flaming piece of wood the size of a golf club landed near us, then blew off the dock into the water. I got the goggles back on and started to stand, but another gust knocked me down. I held on to the dogs and waited for a break in the wind.

Maybe a minute later, the wind calmed a bit, and we made a dash for the houseboat. I got the dogs on just in time. Another gust bowled me over, but I was able to grab the houseboat's railing or I would have again been in the lake. I pulled myself aboard, closed the gate, and sat there a moment or two catching my breath. The dogs were huddled in a corner of the covered section on beds we kept there for them. I looked toward shore and observed the woods on fire to the right of the lake house. The fire was a hundred yards away. I could only hope the side yard would act as a buffer.

I fought the wind to the helm, hung on to the steering wheel, and gunned the engines. We moved swiftly toward the center of the lake. I did not look back.

When I finally did, I could not see the shoreline, only an orange glow that probably spelled doom for the house I grew up in.

◆　◆　◆　◆

A few minutes later, the visibility in front of me improved. I could see the distant lights of Pete's Marina. I turned toward them and slowed to a crawl. I went to the storage bin for towels to dry the dogs. I gave them a good rubdown and left the towels on them.

Then I heard my cell phone ring in my backpack. I dug it out just in time. "Call from Mary Youngblood," a female voice informed me.

I removed the mask. The air was more breathable. I kept the goggles on. They protected me not only against the smoke but against the wind as well.

"We're okay," I answered.

"Thank God," Mary said. "I've been trying to call when I had a second, but the circuits have been busy."

"How's downtown?"

"Fine so far. There's a fire on the outskirts, and we're going to lose some homes on High Mountain. Our firefighters are doing their best to contain it. The wind has calmed some. Now, we're praying for the rain to get here. How is the house?"

"Probably gone," I said. "That whole shoreline is one orange glow."

"Oh, no. That's awful. Where are you?"

"On the lake with the dogs in the houseboat. A tree came down and blocked the driveway, and then all hell broke loose. I'll tell you about it later. Get in touch with T. Elbert and tell him to pick me up at Pete's Marina."

"I will," Mary said. "He'll love the opportunity to help. If I can't get him on the phone, I'll send someone over."

I put the mask back in place, revved the engines, and headed for Pete's. It was a hell of a lot farther than it looked. I seemed to be making little progress. That happens on the water. Depth perception is challenging.

Half an hour later, I pulled alongside the dock. Pete himself came out and tied me up. I took off the mask and goggles. I didn't want to scare Pete.

"What are you doing out here this time of night?" Pete said.

"Running for my life," I said as I climbed from the houseboat. The dogs leaped on the dock and stayed by my side.

"Is your house okay?"

"I doubt it, Pete. It looks like that whole side of the lake is on fire."

"Sorry to hear that. Can't tell much from here with all the smoke. I'm closin' up, Don. Do you and the dogs need a ride somewhere?"

"No thanks, Pete. I've got a ride coming."

"Well, I'll leave the lights on. Flip that switch there when you leave."
I put the mask and goggles back on and sat on a bench to wait.

◆　◆　◆　◆

An hour later, I saw headlights in the distance. It looked like the Black Beauty, so I cut the lights, and the dogs and I headed down the fifty-yard-long dock toward the parking lot. I could feel the dock rise and fall beneath my feet. Jake and Junior walked tentatively behind me.

The black H2 arrived about the same time we did. T. Elbert made a wide sweep and came around to us on the driver's side. The window slid down.

"That's quite a getup," T. Elbert said. "Need a ride, Donald?"

I opened the rear hatch and patted the bottom three times, and the dogs jumped in. I joined T. Elbert in the front of the Black Beauty. I removed the mask and goggles; only a faint hint of smoke was inside the Hummer.

"That's pretty smart," T. Elbert said. "The mask and goggles."

"I have my moments."

"Sorry I didn't get here sooner. A lot of people were leaving town."

"Not a problem," I said. "We're just glad you made it."

"Where to?"

"The condo, please."

"You got it," T. Elbert said. "Just sit back and enjoy the ride."

I did just that. I even took a short nap.

◆　◆　◆　◆

A few minutes past nine o'clock, we were at the condo. Traffic into town was light. Traffic out had also slackened. Mountain Center was starting to look deserted. Visibility was poor due to the smoke, and in certain directions I could see a faint orange glow.

T. Elbert pulled into underground parking and let me off by the elevator. He waited while I took the dogs up, got them in the condo, and came back down.

"Where to?" T. Elbert said.

"Police headquarters," I said.

42

I didn't recognize the woman running dispatch, but she was all business. She was in the middle of a 911 call. I waited. She wrote something down, thanked the caller, and looked up at me. The phone rang. She answered and said, "Please hold."

"I'm Don Youngblood," I said hurriedly. "My wife is Detective Mary Youngblood. I need to let her know I'm safe, but cell-phone service is out."

She didn't hesitate. "Dispatch to Mary Youngblood, over," she said into the mic in front of her.

"This is Mary, over."

"Your famous husband is here, over."

"That's good to hear. Put him to work. I'll catch up with him later. Over and out."

The dispatcher went back to the phone. She was doing double duty. "Thank you for holding," she said. "What is the nature of your emergency?" Pause. "What is your name and location?" Pause. She wrote down a name and address on a notepad. "Are you alone?" Short pause. "Stay where you are. We'll have someone there as soon as we can." She ripped the top sheet off the notepad and handed it to me. "She needs to be evacuated. She's up on High Mountain. Can you handle it?"

"On my way," I said.

"Take her to the community center."

"Will do."

I was about to ask her name, but she was already taking another call. I went to Mary's desk, retrieved the keys to her truck, and headed for the parking lot. Once inside the vehicle, I activated her route guidance system. I knew High Mountain well, but finding a specific house if the smoke was heavy would be a problem.

I turned on the emergency flashers and drove out of the parking lot. Five minutes later, I was on High Mountain Road, one of only two roads leading up and down High Mountain. High Mountain was not that high—maybe thirty-five hundred feet above sea level—but it was the highest point in Mountain Center, hence the name. A lot of nice homes were on High Mountain.

Visibility was not good, but I could still see the road. Off to my left and higher up, I saw an orange glow. The wind had picked up again, and sparks flew everywhere. I drove through some heavy smoke and then out of it. The route guidance system—in a female voice, of course—ordered a right. I turned right and drove on. Another left, then another, then a right, and soon I heard, "You have arrived at your destination."

A mailbox confirmed that I had indeed arrived. I pulled left into the circular driveway and stopped a few feet from the front door. I started to get out when the door opened and a tall, thin, white-haired woman emerged carrying a large purse. She moved quickly to the truck, opened the door, and got in. She was wearing a mask and what appeared to be swimming goggles. At that moment, I remembered I had left my mask in T. Elbert's Hummer and silently cursed myself for my stupidity. My ski goggles were hanging around my neck.

"Are you Edna Gates?"

"Yes, I'm Edna," she said in a muffled voice. "Thank you so much for coming to my rescue."

"I'm Don Youngblood, and you're welcome."

"The private detective?"

"Yes, ma'am."

"Oh, my," Edna said.

I pulled away toward the other driveway exit, intending to make a left and head back the way I had come, when I heard a sharp crack and then an earth-shaking thud. Twenty feet away, a large tree had succumbed to the wind, falling to block our path. Turning left was no longer an option. I turned right and prayed I could find a clear route off the mountain.

Miss Edna's street looped around and connected to another road farther down. From there, I connected back to High Mountain Road. Visibility was deteriorating. Down to our left, we could see a house on fire. We said nothing. I made a left on High Mountain Road and headed off the mountain. To our right, the woods were on fire—mostly ground fire, but still unnerving. The smoke was getting thick. All of a sudden, I could no longer see the road. I stopped and put on my goggles.

"I'm going to have to open the door and try to follow the centerline."

"Hang on," Miss Edna said. She opened her purse and handed me a mask. "What is it you-all say? 'It never hurts to have backup'?"

"God bless you," I said, putting on the mask. I opened the driver's door and looked down. The centerline was a few feet to my left. "Watch the road, Miss Edna. If you see anything in front of us, yell, 'Stop!'"

Smoke was seeping into the cab, but it couldn't be helped. I crept down the mountain, following the centerline. It looked newly painted. *God bless Mountain Center maintenance*, I thought.

We had gone maybe a quarter-mile when Miss Edna yelled, "Stop!"

I stopped and looked up. No more than three feet from my front bumper were the taillights of a car, glowing red. I backed up and started around, then pulled up alongside.

"Is anyone in there?"

"I don't think so," Miss Edna said.

I started to roll when she again yelled for me to stop. "I saw someone," she said.

Through the smoke, I saw a woman's face pressed against her driver's-side window. She appeared to mouth the words, *Help me*. Miss Edna

rolled down her window, raised her mask, and yelled, "Follow us!" in a
voice so loud I was astounded. The woman's head bobbed up and down.
Miss Edna's window went back up.

I proceeded around the car, relocated the centerline, and continued
slowly down High Mountain. The smoke gradually subsided enough that
I could close my door and follow the line from inside the cab. I gained
some speed. At the bottom of High Mountain, the smoke was considerably
less. Driving through the deserted Mountain Center was not a problem.

"You okay?" I asked.

"Just dandy," Miss Edna said.

◆   ◆   ◆   ◆

We drove to the Mountain Center Community Center, the car we had
passed on High Mountain Road following us. The farther we drove from
High Mountain, the better the visibility.

The community center was hopping. Cots were set up in the double
gymnasium. The air inside was breathable, with only a hint of smoke. Coffee, sandwiches, and various snacks and drinks were being handed out.

I left Miss Edna with a volunteer and went to talk to Big Bob, who had
just arrived. "How you doing?"

He shook his head, a tired man doing an impossible job. "Not one of
my best days, but I think we controlled it without losing anyone. Heavy
rain should arrive anytime, if you can trust radar. That will certainly help
things. I heard you volunteered to go on the mountain. How was that?"

"Touch and go," I said. "But the lady I went for is smart and tough and
was a big part of our getting out alive."

The woman who had driven the car behind me came over. "Chief, this
man saved my life." Turning to me, she said, "Thank you so much."

"You're welcome." I couldn't think of anything else to say. She hugged
me and kissed me on the cheek, then turned and walked away.

Big Bob stared at me. "I think there's a lot you're not telling me."

"Another time," I said. "You have work to do."

"You're right," he said, turning and heading toward the exit.

I went to the coffee station and poured myself a cup. All they had was powdered cream, so I took it black with sugar. It smelled okay but tasted terrible. I added some powdered cream. The improvement was minimal. I didn't care. I took another drink and carried it to an empty chair and sat. I felt like I had been awake for a week. I drank the hideous brew and leaned back to rest.

Soon, I saw a vision walking across the gym toward me—Mary Young-blood in jeans and a black T-shirt, her blond ponytail pulled through the back of a black baseball cap with *MCPD* on the front. She smiled as she came toward me. I stood. We hugged.

"There's a rumor you're a hero."

"Let's not spread that around," I said. "I don't need any more press."

"Still, I'm proud of you."

"There are a lot of heroes out there tonight."

"You're right about that," she said, and kissed me. "I'm so thankful you're okay."

"Likewise."

Out of nowhere, Miss Edna appeared. "You're his wife, I assume," she said to Mary.

"Yes, ma'am."

"He saved my life."

"Couldn't have done it without you," I said.

She ignored me and focused on Mary. "When this all blows over, I want you two to come up for dinner. I make a mean pot roast."

"We'll be honored," Mary said. "Don's never met a pot roast he didn't like."

"My husband was the same way," she said. "I'm going to get some coffee. You two stay safe. I'll be in touch."

"I've got to get back at it," Mary said. "Want to ride with me? We can get my truck later."

I followed Mary out to her unmarked squad car. The wind was still blowing hard. A bolt of lightning lit up the night sky, and I felt a heavy random raindrop, then another and another. We just made it to her car when the heavens opened and the rain came in buckets.

43

At nine the following morning, Mary and I sat at the kitchen counter having coffee and listening to the local radio station. We had finally gone to bed at three, right after I texted Jim Doak that our trip was on hold. I had also texted the inner circle to let them know we were okay. By the time I was up, I had heard back from everyone. Billy texted that there were also fires in his jurisdiction.

The heavy rain had pretty much brought the fires under control, and behind the front came calmer winds. But many trees and power lines were down and the roads to High Mountain were closed, so we brought Miss Edna to our condo and put her in our guest room. She was still asleep.

The city and county were under Big Bob's version of martial law. Everyone was told to stay where they were until damage and accessibility could be determined for various neighborhoods. A five o'clock curfew was in place. The radio station was broadcasting only public-service and law-enforcement announcements.

There was an elephant in the room: the lake house. Neither of us mentioned it until the announcer read, "It is estimated that at least fifty homes were lost in Mountain Center and the county. Residents will be allowed back to their property as soon as possible. Visitors will not be allowed into areas where fire has occurred until further notice from local law enforcement."

Mary and I made eye contact. I could read her mind. I picked up my cell phone.

"Sheriff's office," a female voice answered.

"Jimmy Durham," I said.

"Sorry, he's busy right now. Who's calling?"

"Don Youngblood."

"Hang on, please."

I was on hold for maybe thirty seconds.

"Make it fast, Blood. I'm swamped," he said.

"I can imagine. Listen, Bull, I just barely made it out alive last night. I had to take the dogs in the houseboat across the lake. The lake house is probably gone, but I'd like to know for sure. Can you have someone in the area take a look when they have a chance?"

"I'll do it myself," he said. "I have to be over that way."

"How bad is it in the county?"

"Bad enough. To make matters worse, we had a call that someone saw a guy with a gas can setting fires over your way."

"Did you get a description?"

"Tall man dressed in black. That's all we got. Not much to go on."

"Tall man dressed in black," I repeated for Mary's benefit. "If you happen to catch him, I want to be the first to see him."

"I understand," Jimmy said. "You'll be my first call. Got to go, Blood. Call you later."

I disconnected and looked at Mary. I'm sure I looked like I wanted to kill somebody.

"Pickingill?"

"Maybe," I said. "But how did he get here so fast?"

◆　◆　◆　◆

Miss Edna joined us an hour later, and Mary fixed breakfast: bacon and eggs, biscuits and gravy. *Oh, my!* One by one, the news came of different residential sections of town being opened to residents. Finally, word arrived that High Mountain residents could return to their homes.

"I'll call someone from my church to come and get me," Miss Edna said.

"You will not," Mary said. "I'm taking you. I want to hear all about your escape, and I want to make sure you have power."

"Well, let's go, then," a smiling Miss Edna said.

◆   ◆   ◆   ◆

Having nothing better to do, I took Mary's truck and went to the office. Late that afternoon, I got the call I didn't want.

"I wish I had better news," Jimmy Durham said.

"Not a real good way to start a conversation, Bull." He had said all I needed to hear. I had a sick feeling in the pit of my stomach.

"I know," he said. "I'm sorry, Blood. I'm afraid it's a total loss."

Even though I was expecting it, the news of the loss of my boyhood home hit me like a death in the family. A connection to the past had been lost forever. A black cloud passed over me. I knew that if I found the man who started the fires that took my home, I would kill him. That thought scared me.

"Thanks for checking," I said. "Any news on the man in black?"

"None," Jimmy said. "I know what you're thinking, Blood. Forget it. If I find him, I'll deal with it."

I said nothing.

"Don?"

"I hear you Jimmy," I said. "Keep in touch."

◆   ◆   ◆   ◆

I didn't want to ruin the rest of Mary's day, so I decided to wait until I got back to the condo to tell her about the lake house.

I drove to the condo in a steady rain, parked in the underground garage, and took the elevator to the fifth floor. I entered to the fabulous smell of meat cooking. I went into the kitchen to find Mary and Miss Edna sitting at the kitchen bar, half-filled wineglasses in hand.

"Well, hello ladies."

"Miss Edna doesn't have power, so I invited her to stay with us until she does," Mary said.

"You are most welcome," I said to Miss Edna.

"As a reward," Mary continued, "we get pot roast."

"If it tastes half as good as it smells, it's going to be terrific," I said.

I went upstairs to our bedroom to change into jeans, a T-shirt, and a pair of worn-out Nike Monarchs.

A minute later, Mary came in. She looked at me.

"It's gone," I said, trying not to lose it.

"Oh, Don, I am so sorry. I know that must be devastating. It was my home, too, and I'll miss it terribly, but I cannot imagine how you must feel."

She came to me, and we held each other. I felt like crying, but we private investigators are tough and don't cry, so I didn't. I had been so focused on myself that I had forgotten Mary and Lacy also lost things that were important to them.

"We'll get through this," I said.

"Damn right we will," Mary said, releasing me, her face getting red. "And if Levi Pickingill did this, I will kill the son of a bitch."

"You'll have to wait your turn," I said, kissing her lightly. "Let's go eat some of that pot roast."

44

The next day, Mary called Big Bob and asked to come in late. "The lake house is gone," I heard her say. She listened, then handed the phone to me.

"You have no idea how upset that news makes me," he said. "If there's anything I can do, just ask." Big Bob had spent considerable time at the lake house as we were growing up. I knew how he felt about the place.

"Give Mary the morning off," I said.

"You don't even need to ask. Go do what you have to do. Mary can come in when she's ready—today, tomorrow, or next week."

◆   ◆   ◆   ◆

As Mary drove down the lake house driveway, I had the feeling I was going to a funeral. Through the trees, I saw the chimney standing defiantly alone amid a pile of ashes. Some brick and stone work on the front of the house was still standing. Everything else was gone. To make matters worse, the Pathfinder was a burned-out piece of rubble buried beneath a giant oak. Evidently, the tree had collapsed on my SUV, rupturing the gas tank, which then caught fire and exploded. The safe I had left inside the Pathfinder was lodged in a large boxwood twenty feet away looking intact, blasted clear of the carnage. We stopped in front of the downed tree that blocked the driveway from the parking area. Trees near the house were black, some resembling burned matchsticks stuck randomly in the ground.

"My God," Mary said.

I said nothing. I got out of the car and stood looking in disbelief, arms folded. I slowly walked around and observed the damage. There were large, deep holes maybe three feet wide in the surrounding woods that were still smoking, hemlocks that had burned to the ground and all the way down to their root systems. Shrubs near the house were gone. Those farther away looked like they had been roasted by the heat. Around back, both decks were gone, along with the hot tub. The gas grill was a puddle of twisted metal. The dock and the boathouse were intact. I walked back around to the front yard to find Mary sitting on the trunk of the fallen tree and slipping on a pair of knee-high rubber boots that she kept in her truck.

"I'm going to poke around," Mary said.

She turned and walked toward the rubble, carrying a big stick. I went to the fallen tree in front of Mary's truck and waited.

◆   ◆   ◆   ◆

Fifteen minutes later, she was back, carrying something. She held out her hand and opened it. A small, white porcelain figurine of a baby in a crib rested in her palm. I gave her a questioning look.

"It's the baby Jesus from our nativity scene. It's a sign that everything is going to be okay." She had tears in her eyes.

I swallowed hard and set my jaw. There would be no tears from me. I stared at the tiny figurine and said nothing.

Mary turned and went back to poke around some more. A half-hour later, she had found most of the figurines from the nativity. She put the pieces in a plastic bag, sat beside me on the fallen tree, removed her boots, and put on her shoes. We sat in silence staring at the house and remembering what we had lost.

"You ready?" I said.

"Yes."

As Mary backed up the driveway, my cell phone rang. I recognized the number.

"That you, Bull?"

"I'm about a mile from you," Jimmy Durham said. "There's something you need to see."

"The last time you told me that, I ended up with a case I wish I'd never had."

"Not this time. You'll like this."

"Where are you?"

He told me.

"On my way," I said.

◆　◆　◆　◆

Jimmy was waiting for us, leaning on his cruiser on the side of the road. He was parked behind one of his deputies. Their light bars were on. Mary parked behind him and turned on her emergency lights. We got out.

"Follow me," Jimmy said.

We followed him onto scorched earth, the remains of burned-out trees and bushes all around. Many trees were down. The smell of charred wood was prevalent. In the distance, a deputy I recognized stood beside a large fallen tree. As we got closer, I saw a pair of burned legs protruding from under the trunk. A blackened five-gallon gas can lay not far away. I reached the trunk and peered over the other side to see the burned face of Levi Pickingill. His eyes were gone. *Poetic justice.* I resisted the urge to sing "Ding-Dong! The Witch Is Dead."

Mary was on my wavelength. "Looks like the good witch dropped a tree on the bad witch."

"You know this guy?" Jimmy said.

"No," I said. "But I know who he is."

"Enlighten me," Jimmy said.

I let Mary handle the enlightenment.

"Crazy son of a bitch to be out in this firestorm," Jimmy said.

"I guess he thought he was invincible," I said.

"He was wrong," Jimmy said.

45

The next day, I was back at the house sitting on the same downed tree and waiting on the insurance adjuster. His van came slowly down the driveway and stopped a few feet from Mary's truck. He got out and introduced himself as Ken Book. We walked to where the front of the house used to be and stopped a few feet from the ashes.

"Yep, that's a total loss," he said. "Is your automobile insurance with us also?"

"It is," I said.

He removed a camera from a carrying case and started taking pictures. I went back and sat on my fallen tree.

Ten minutes later, he joined me.

"I have to email these pictures so I can get approval to cut you a check for the full insured dwelling amount," he said. "It won't take long."

"You're going to write me a check today?"

"Two checks, actually. One for the dwelling and one as partial payment for your possessions. The car insurance will take a few days. I'll be back soon."

I watched as he went to his van and slid the side door open. The inside was set up as a small office, complete with desk, chair, and computer. I spun back around on my tree and stared at the rubble, refusing to acknowledge what had happened.

Thirty minutes later, I was handed two checks.

"Give me twenty-four hours before you deposit those," he said.

"Not a problem."

"You'll have to do a detailed inventory if you want to collect more on the possessions policy," he said.

"Forget it," I said. "We're too busy to mess with that. This will do just fine."

He looked disappointed. "You sure? I know you could get more money."

"This will do."

"Well, you've got two years if you change your mind. Do you think you'll rebuild?"

"Absolutely."

"Well, then, I've got more work to do. Would you happen to have a set of building plans for the house?"

"In my office," I said.

"Fantastic. That will certainly make my job easier. Do you have a place to stay while you rebuild?"

"I have a condo in town."

"Fantastic," he said again.

◆   ◆   ◆   ◆

That night, Mary and I were alone in the condo sharing a bottle of Cabernet Sauvignon. Mary stared at the two checks. "I've never seen this much money. Not even close."

"We'll spend it all to rebuild and refurnish," I said. "And probably more."

Mary took a drink of wine. "At least we have a place to live. Some people don't."

"What's the town going to do about that?"

"They're starting a fund to rent available housing—apartments and hotel rooms. Some people are stepping up and offering places to stay for free until the displaced can be housed. You'll hear about it in the next few days."

"We'll make a sizable donation," I said.

She took another drink of wine. I took a sip.

"Lacy called," Mary said.

"What was her reaction?"

"She was pragmatic. She said, 'I'm thankful you two are okay. It's only a house. Rebuild it.' "

I smiled. "That's just what we're going to do."

◆　◆　◆　◆

Later that night, I called one of the best builders in East Tennessee. He had been a few years ahead of me in high school and was a fine basketball player. He was in my pickup basketball group.

"I thought I might be hearing from you," he said when he answered. *Caller ID tells all.* "Sorry about your house."

"Thanks, Tim," I said. "Can I persuade you to rebuild it?"

"I'd be hurt if you didn't ask. You're on the top of my list. Do you have the plans?"

"I do. I'll probably tweak them a bit, but that won't take long. Can you handle cleaning up the property?"

"Sure," he said. "Whenever you're ready."

"I'm ready now."

"Next week, then," Tim said. "Was your house on a slab?"

"It was."

"I'll need to check the slab and make sure it's buildable. If not, I'll have to tear it out and start over."

"Call me if you need anything," I said.

46

The next day, Friday, was clear and cold. Early that morning, I was in the back of the Mountain Center Diner at my usual table. From my vantage point, it still looked dark outside. I was nursing a mug of coffee and reading the local paper when a shadow blocked my light. The big man tossed his cowboy hat and a leather chief of police jacket on a nearby chair and sat down. I folded the paper and set it aside. Doris arrived with a mug of coffee for Big Bob and hurried away with our orders.

"Have you been out to the lake house?"

I nodded.

"Anything left?"

"The chimney."

He shook his head unhappily and took a drink from the mug.

"I need to tell you a story," I said.

"This can't be good," Big Bob said.

"Actually, it's got a pretty good ending. I just haven't had time to tell you about the case of the missing belly dancer."

He chuckled. "Belly dancer. Go ahead, I'm listening."

I recounted the Lola Madrid case and the involvement of Levi Pickingill right up to the time that a tall man in black had been seen starting fires in the vicinity of the lake house. At that point, our food arrived. We began to eat.

"So you think this Pickingill started the fires?"

"I don't think, I know," I said.

"How?"

"I stood over his cold, dead body."

"You killed him?" He spoke so nonchalantly he could have been asking me to pass the pepper shaker. I had developed a bit of a reputation for shooting first and asking questions later.

"No, I didn't kill him. But I must admit, the thought did cross my mind, and Mary's."

"So who killed him?"

"God, maybe."

He looked at me curiously and waited.

"A tree fell on him while he was setting the fires. I guess the high winds took it over at exactly the right time. Divine timing, if you ask me."

I told Big Bob about the gruesome aftermath and the charred body of Levi Pickingill.

"A fitting end," he said.

"A perfect end," I said. "Just perfect."

I hated to gloat about anyone's death, but in Levi Pickingill's case I would make an exception.

◆　◆　◆　◆

"Bobbie Summers in the Dean of Students Office seemed to be thrilled to assist in an FBI investigation," Gretchen said. "Evidently, Glenn Evans finished his junior year, left for summer break, and never returned. She remembers investigators asking questions around campus, but no one questioned her. She's going to see who might still be there that taught classes taken by Mr. Evans. I'm to let her know when you'll be there, and she'll try to get you appointments, but you have to see her first."

"Good work," I said.

"Thanks. There's more."

"I thought there might be."

"As you know, Jerry Altman was with Texas Oil at the same time as Royce Rogers, and worked on the same rig. Their foreman, Bud Jeneau, died while Royce was in prison. The general manager of the rig is a guy by the name of Cort Nelson. He'll talk with you when you come down. He'll fly in from the oil rig and meet you in their Galveston offices."

"Impressive work," I said. "I'll go to Galveston first. Set something up for Tuesday afternoon with Nelson. Let Bobbie Summers know I'll be on campus Wednesday morning."

47

The following Tuesday morning, I was thirty-three thousand feet above firm ground reacquainting myself with the Clown case file. I had not thought much about Royce Rogers, due to the events of the past week. Mary and I had spent considerable time on the weekend with an architect friend of mine tweaking the old lake house plans with ideas for improving the new lake house. Although I mourned the loss of things that represented my family history, I must admit I was excited to build a new and better lake house, a second-generation Youngblood dwelling on the same spot as the original, the beginning of a new history. Mary was equally excited, and we couldn't wait to get started. On Monday, the architect had confirmed that our ideas were indeed doable.

Having done all I could about the lake house, I was, again, ready to pursue Royce Rogers. I read the file front to back and had the feeling I was missing something, a feeling that was not unusual for me on big cases. Sooner or later, it would surface. Then I looked at the file Buckley had sent on the missing Texas men who could be connected to Royce Rogers. There were pictures of both men, and their stories were remarkably the same. They had disappeared without a trace. I put the files back in my briefcase and thought about what I had read. Then I called David Steele's private number.

"I'm headed for Texas as an FBI consultant," I said. "That is, if it's okay with you."

"Doing what?"

"Buckley connected Royce Rogers to a couple of missing persons. It's possible Royce knew one or both of them. I'm going to find out."

"Okay," David Steele said. "Don't embarrass us."

◆　◆　◆　◆

We landed in Galveston before noon, and I rented an SUV from Hertz. After my meeting with Cort Nelson, I intended to drive to Austin and spent the night.

Traffic was light, and I found the Texas Oil building with ease. The modern structure in the heart of the city had underground parking, and I followed the signs to the visitors' slots. Reception was on the first floor. A pretty blonde with a Texas drawl asked how she could help me.

"I'm here to see Cort Nelson," I said.

"Are you Mr. Youngblood?"

"I am."

"Mr. Cort Nelson is not in at the present time, but our president, Will Nelson, will see you on his behalf."

"Father?"

"Uncle," she said. "Have a seat, and I'll let him know you're here."

Fifteen minutes later, I was riding the elevator to the top floor. When the doors opened, a tall, lean man—in his sixties, I guessed—was waiting on me. He wore a tan Western-style suit with a blue dress shirt open at the neck and, of course, cowboy boots. Everything he had on looked expensive.

"Mr. Youngblood?"

"Don," I said.

He extended a hand, and we shook; his handshake was maybe a little too firm, but thanks to Moto's Gym my hand survived.

"Will Nelson," he said. "Call me Will. Let's go to my office and talk."

I followed him down the hall to a corner office that took up at least a quarter of the floor. Not surprisingly, the décor was typically Western. We sat in leather chairs separated by a coffee table made from a cross-section cut from a large tree. An attractive young woman appeared.

"Would you like coffee?" Will said.

"Sure," I said. "Cream and sugar."

"I'll have some, too, Trish," Will said.

Trish nodded and disappeared through a side door.

"So you're with the FBI," Will Nelson said.

"Sometimes," I said. "I consult." I was guessing Will Nelson already knew as much about me as the internet could tell him.

"So you're working an FBI case."

"I'm working a private case that has gained FBI attention. They are as interested in my solving it as I am."

"Is Cort in any trouble?"

"Not as far as I know," I said. "You have my word on that. I just need to ask him a few questions about a couple of guys who worked for Texas Oil and reported to Bud Jeneau. At the present time, they're both missing. Since it's been a while since they worked for Texas Oil, and since they didn't report to him directly, Cort might not remember anything that can help me, but I have to pursue every lead."

"I understand," Will said. "Cort is on a deep-water rig right now. If you're not afraid of helicopters, we can fly out there."

I smiled, remembering the last time I had been on a helicopter with Billy and a team of FBI agents taking down a homegrown terrorist group. It had been a hair-raising experience. "I think I can handle it."

Will Nelson smiled back at me. "I thought you could. The executive helicopter is on the roof. Let's get to it."

I grabbed my briefcase and followed Will out of his office.

We were over Galveston for a couple of minutes, and then the Texas city was in our rearview as we headed out over the vast expanse of the Gulf of Mexico. We passed a few rigs below us as we headed away from shore.

"As you would expect, the deep-water rigs are farther out," Will Nelson said over the headphones we were wearing.

I nodded and said nothing.

"An impressive body of water," Will said.

"It is," I said.

Out my window and below us, I saw a few scattered boats. They looked like toys in a bathtub. An oil rig passed underneath. It looked like a Tinkertoy.

Half an hour later, Will said, "Straight ahead. That tiny dot is the Deepwater Blue Dolphin."

I nodded and said nothing. What was there to say? I watched the dot grow larger, turning from a Tinkertoy into something that looked like it belonged on another planet. We closed in and hovered over a helicopter pad with the Texas Oil logo, then descended and touched down with only the slightest bump. The engine wound down and then was quiet. The door opened, and stairs unfolded.

"Cort will be in the operations center," Will said as he stood. "Follow me."

◆ ◆ ◆ ◆

Cort Nelson looked like a younger version of his uncle, tall and lean. He was dressed in jeans and a T-shirt. His work boots looked expensive. Everyone in the operations tower looked busy, a phenomenon that can happen when the president of the company shows up. Will did the introductions.

"Is there someplace we can talk?" I asked.

"We have a small conference room," Cort said. "This way."

I followed Cort, and Will followed me. Down a hall and away from the operations center, Cort opened a door to a small room with a table and six chairs. He went in. I stopped in the doorway and turned to face Will.

"Is there something you need to check on, Will?" I said.

He looked surprised, then recovered and said, "As a matter of fact, there is. Have Cort page me when you're done." He smiled and walked away.

I turned and went into the room and shut the door behind me. I sat and removed the files from my briefcase.

"What's this about?" Cort asked.

"It's complicated," I said. "I started out investigating a kidnapping, and the case has turned into something bigger. I'm looking for at least three missing people, two of whom are probably dead." I opened the Royce Roger file and slid a picture across to Cort Nelson. "Do you recognize this man?"

Cort studied the picture, then nodded. "Looks like Royce Rogers. He worked for us a few years and then was arrested for robbery. It's been awhile, maybe four or five years."

"Seven," I said.

"That long?"

I nodded. "What can you tell me about him?"

"Well, he was the last guy I would have believed would rob a casino. He didn't seem to have that kind of moxie. He was quiet, did his job, and never caused trouble."

"How about this guy?" I slid a picture of Jerry Altman across the table.

Cort nodded and smiled. "Jerry Altman. Now, him I could believe it if you told me he robbed a casino."

"Did they know each other?"

"Probably."

"So you wouldn't know if they were friends."

"No, I was too busy with the job," he said. "During shift hours, we were all business. I was here day shift, same as these guys. That's why I know who they are. They reported to a foreman that reported to me. There are workers on this rig I am not even aware of, those that don't work the day shift."

"Anyone who might know if they were friends? Anyone been around that long?"

Cort paused a moment. "Hammer might. He's been with us forever and knows everyone *and* their business."

"Any chance I can talk to Hammer?"

"You'll have to wait for the shift change," Cort said. "I need to get back to the job."

"How long?"

"Couple of hours."

"Can I wait here?"

"Sure," he said. "We're connected to the internet by satellite, if you have a smartphone or iPad."

"I brought an iPad."

He gave me the access code.

I spent the next hour checking out various portfolios and looking for the next great stock purchase. As usual, no luck. Then I checked national news and sports. The second hour went faster.

◆   ◆   ◆   ◆

Hammer evidently did not have a last name.

"I'm Don Youngblood," I said when he walked into the room and looked at me.

"Hammer," he said. "Boss said you was FBI and wanted to talk to me about a couple of guys I might remember."

Hammer was about five and a half feet tall. One might describe him as swarthy—a Cajun, maybe. He would have made a good extra in a pirate movie. He was a dark-haired, dark-skinned man who was wiry and fit, somewhere on the high side of fifty.

"Know his man?" I said, showing him a picture of Royce Rogers.

"Sure," Hammer said. "That's Roy Rogers. His first name was really Royce, but we nicknamed him Roy. You know, like the cowboy. He didn't seem to care." His accent was Southern, with inflections of the bayou. I wasn't an expert, but I would have bet he was Louisiana born and bred.

"Did you know he went to prison?"

"Yeah, I did, but that was a bullshit charge. No way that guy robbed a casino."

"How about this guy?"

Hammer looked at the next picture. "Jerry Altman. A real piece of work. Not a bad guy, but he always had some scheme goin' to make money."

"Think he could rob a casino?"

"I doubt it. Not his style. I could see him stealin', but it would be sideways, not straight ahead, if you know what I mean."

"Like selling a little old lady the Golden Gate Bridge?"

Hammer pointed a finger at me. "There you go."

"Were Royce and Jerry friends?"

"Seemed to be. They hung out together. Always seemed to be in the same poker game. That Roy was a hell of a poker player. Got so no one would play with him."

"Anything else you can tell me?"

Hammer thought for a minute. "Jerry quit workin' here about the same time Roy went to prison."

"Did you know Jerry went missing?"

"No, I didn't."

"Any thoughts about that?"

"Well, I can see him gettin' mixed up with the wrong people," Hammer said. "Then shit happens."

Cort Nelson appeared in the doorway. "Are you about done? Uncle Will is ready to leave."

"I'm done," I said. "Thanks, Hammer."

"You bet," Hammer said, and left the room.

"One more question for you before I go," I said to Cort. "Was Jerry Altman fired, or did he quit?"

Cort smiled. "I figured you'd ask me that, so I looked it up. And the answer is neither. He just didn't show up for work one day. We still owe him back pay."

◆   ◆   ◆   ◆

That night, I was sitting at an out-of-the-way table in the Corner Restaurant in the Austin JW Marriott Hotel. I had checked into a top-floor suite and come directly down to the restaurant. I was tired and hungry and confused. Royce Rogers had gone underground, probably on a beach somewhere drinking a Mai Tai with a little umbrella sticking out of the glass. Why was I bothering to look for a man who very likely was impossible to find? Because, I concluded, I had been hired to do so by Howard Cox, and he deserved my best effort.

I ate my ample portion of shrimp and grits and thought about the man Hammer called Roy. Royce Rogers was a mystery, a kidnapper in a clown costume who had robbed a casino and spent years in prison. Everyone I talked to except his sister seemed surprised he would do such a thing. Even Gloria Davis seemed conflicted. I wondered if Royce could be a split personality. I had dealt with that on another case, but in all my interviews so far that possibility had never come up. I finally decided I would find out what I could tomorrow, and that if nothing significant turned up I would close the case and send Howard Cox a full report with my apology.

48

I was on campus in the Dean of Students Office at nine o'clock the next morning face to face with an attractive young clerk. Bobbie Summers was a fresh-faced brunette with an innocent smile and a not-so-innocent body.

"It must be exciting working with the FBI," she said.

"Sometimes," I said.

"Ever get shot at?"

"Sometimes."

"Strong, silent type," she said, batting her eyes.

"Sometimes."

She giggled.

Oh, to be in college again.

"Can you tell me if any professors are still here that had Royce Rogers and Glenn Evans in the same class?"

"I found three so far," she said. "Your assistant asked me to start looking. I made morning appointments for you with two of them that are free. I can make the other one for this afternoon, if you're going to be around."

"Thanks," I said. "Go ahead and do that. Who are the professors?"

She told me. None of them were the ones Buckley had interviewed.

"I can show you a good place to have lunch, if you have time," she said. She handed me a slip of paper. "My cell phone. Call me if you're free. I'm also free for dinner."

And what else? I wondered.

"Probably not," I said. "Tight schedule."

◆　◆　◆　◆

I spent most of my morning waiting outside the offices of the two professors Bobbie Summers had lined me up with. The waits were considerably longer than the interviews. Both went about the same, but I did get a couple of interesting pieces of information from Professor Mark Allen, my second interview. Toward the end, I asked, "Did you have Royce Rogers in any of your classes the following year?"

"Now that you mention it, I did," Professor Allen said. "The first day of class, I asked him about Glenn Evans, and he said no one had heard from him in months. He seemed upset about that."

Not the reaction I would have expected, had Royce known what happened to Glenn. Maybe Glenn's disappearance was just a coincidence. I didn't think so, but it was a possibility. Maybe Royce was just a good actor. The farther I got into this case, the more confusing it became.

"Anything else you can think of?"

He paused. "Well, I would see Royce and Glenn sometimes with a girl, a real looker."

"Tall blonde?"

"Tall, yes. Blonde, no. Dark hair. Looked like an athlete."

"Why do you remember her after all these years?"

Mark Allen smiled. "She was worth remembering."

◆　◆　◆　◆

Bobbie Summers set me up to interview professor number three right after lunch. That interview proved less enlightening than the first two.

I left campus wondering if this little side trip had been a waste of time. I turned in the SUV at the Hertz drop-off in the Austin airport and caught an afternoon flight to Tri-Cities with an hour layover in Atlanta. In the Delta lounge, I ordered a beer and called Gloria Davis's cell. She didn't answer, so I left a message for her to call me. I sat and sipped my beer and rehashed all I knew about Royce Rogers. Too many things did not make sense. I decided to go home and let this case sit on my desk for a week. If something didn't pop, I would close it.

I made another call. Howard Cox listened to my full report, including my decision to give things one more week.

"Sounds like you've done all you can, Don. I'll have to be satisfied in the knowledge that someday that bastard will probably burn in hell. You can close the case anytime."

"I'm still going to let it sit awhile," I said.

"Whatever you want to do is fine with me. But as of today, you're off the clock. Don't forget to send me a bill."

"No danger of that," I said. "My partner takes care of the billing."

◆　◆　◆　◆

That night, Mary and I sat at the kitchen bar eating pizza and drinking beer—Harp for me and Blue Moon for her.

"Man, this is good pizza," I said. "Maybe the best I've ever had."

"You're right," Mary said. "I'm going to have to be careful or I'll eat way too much."

"Where did this come from?"

"Johnson City."

"You went to Johnson City to get pizza?"

"No, silly. Bud Smith, a new patrolman who's from Johnson City, had to take a prisoner up there. He's always bragging about how good Greg's Pizza is, so he brought one back for me. I warmed it a few minutes before you came in."

"So, this patrolman Smith," I said. "He's no doubt trying to get in your pants by bribing you with pizza."

Mary smiled and took another bite. "Might work," she said.

"It is really good."

Mary laughed and changed the subject. "So you're going to close out the Royce Rogers case."

"Looks that way."

"I know you're not happy about it, but you can't solve them all. Solving cases is about catching breaks, and sometimes you cannot catch a break. It's the nature of the beast."

We finished the pizza and a couple more beers.

"Well, thank Patrolman Smith, and tell him for me he cannot get in your pants, but anytime he's in Johnson City he can pick up a pizza."

49

The next day, I called our local Nissan dealership and ordered a new Armada. I did not like the new Pathfinders. They drove like cars. The Armadas were still on a truck frame.

"What color?" Gina, the salesperson, asked.

"White."

She told me the options for the Armada. I said yes to most.

"Do you want that same package you had on the Pathfinder?" she asked. "You know, the Cincinnati package?" She was referring to the bulletproof glass package that had saved my life a few years back.

"Given my history, I think that would be wise."

She paused, then said, "I've got a white Armada on the lot that has everything you want. I'll send it off to Cincinnati tomorrow. I'm curious, Don. Did you ever find that Cincinnati option useful?"

"Twice," I said.

"Oh, dear," Gina said.

50

A week went by, and nothing happened on the Clown case. Royce Rogers apparently had pulled the perfect vanishing act.

Early that following Wednesday, I put the file in my back-cases drawer and left Gretchen a note to bill Howard Cox.

Then I called David Steele. "I'm closing the file on Royce Rogers," I said. "It's a big puzzle, and I'm missing too many pieces."

"You still think he did it?"

I thought about that for a moment. "Yes, but I'm not as sure as I once was. He is either, one, very clever at playing the 'I've been framed' game or, two, he's a split personality or, three, he's been framed. If forced, I'd bet on number one."

"Just so you know," David Steele said, "I added him to the wanted-for-questioning list. If he turns up, I'll be sure you get a crack at him."

"Thanks, Dave."

"Until next time, Youngblood," David Steele said. "Watch your six."

51

"I t's been awhile since you were in Little Switzerland," T. Elbert said as I came up the walkway on a cold, clear Thursday morning.

"Yes, it has," Roy said.

Roy knew I was coming but had said nothing about it.

"I saw you the night of the fire," I said to T. Elbert.

"You didn't see *me* the night of the fire," Roy said.

"Damn it, you guys," I said. "I've been a little busy."

T. Elbert grinned and drank some coffee. Roy took a bite of his bagel. I drank my coffee and sat quietly, trying to remember the last time I had been here. Over the years as my investigating business accelerated, I had spent less and less time on T. Elbert's front porch. *I was here a few days before Christmas.* I didn't share that thought, not wanting to get more grief from the two of them.

"That a new ride?" T. Elbert asked, referring to the Armada parked at the curb. Gina had put a rush on it with Cincinnati, and there it sat with bulletproof glass and reinforced sides. The upgrades wouldn't do much for my gas mileage, but I felt a hell of a lot safer.

"Just came in yesterday," I said. "The dealer delivered it to the condo right before dinner."

"Surprised you traded," T. Elbert said. "You loved that Pathfinder."

"A tree fell on it during the firestorm and exploded the gas tank. There wasn't much left."

"Damn," T. Elbert said.

"Good-looking replacement," Roy said.

"A little bigger and a better ride," I said. "So far, I'm happy with it."

We ate bagels and drank coffee and said nothing for a while.

T. Elbert broke the silence. "Fill us in on your two cases."

"Both closed," I said. "You-all know most of it."

"We want to know all of it," T. Elbert said. "Don't we, Roy?"

"Sure do," Roy said.

So I started to give the *Reader's Digest* version, but T. Elbert stopped me to ask questions so many times that it was useless to try and condense it.

When I got to the part about the tree falling on Levi Pickingill, T. Elbert said, "Struck down by the hand of God, I'd say. Right, Roy?"

"Works for me," Roy said.

"Works for me, too," I said.

We sat and thought about that for a moment. Then T. Elbert said, "You been back to your property?"

"A few times," I said. "We're rebuilding."

"Good for you," T. Elbert said.

"Listen, guys, I've got to run," I said, standing.

"Not so fast," T. Elbert said. "What about the clown thing?"

"The joke's on me," I said. "The clown has disappeared without a trace."

52

My new Armada was everything I had hoped for and more. I spent a big part of my days driving it out to the lake house to supervise the new construction. Tim, the builder, good-naturedly said on more than one occasion that I was being "a pain the ass." After about a week of my meddling, he said, "Don, find something else to do. If I need you, I'll call."

I stared at him, and he stared back. I mean, after all, I was paying for this. He didn't blink.

Finally, I said, "How about I come out every two or three days?"

Tim took a deep breath and said nothing. His eyes never left mine.

"Once a week?"

"For no longer than an hour," he said.

"Deal."

"Now, get out of here," he said. "I've got work to do."

◆   ◆   ◆   ◆

On my way to the office, I picked up coffee, a bagel, and a muffin from Dunkin' Donuts. I sat at my desk and devoured it all before my cell phone rang.

"Youngblood," I answered.

"Hold for the deputy director, please," a female voice said. She did not wait for a confirmation.

"You there?" David Steele said when he picked up.

"I'm here."

"I have some news you'll be interested in. When you closed the Clown case, I put a few flags in the system to alert me if anything turned up on Royce Rogers, Glenn Evans, or Jerry Altman."

"I'm listening."

"I got a hit this morning, so I made a call. I found out that New Mexico had some violent thunderstorms a few weeks back, and it seems the flash flooding uncovered some bones. Could have been death by natural causes, but maybe not, so the local authorities asked the state for a DNA test. Well, you know how long that takes."

"Forever," I said.

"Exactly. Anyway, they finally got a match."

David Steele was quiet while I processed what he had told me. He wouldn't call about just any match.

"Altman or Evans?"

"Evans," David Steele said.

"You thinking what I'm thinking?"

"I'm thinking that if your theory is right, there could be more bodies out there. I'll make this case official if you'll take the lead. You'll have to go solo. We can't spare anyone right now. Go have a look and tell me what you think. If you turn up anything, I'll send people."

"Where exactly was the body found, and by whom?"

"Some kids that were dirt-biking in the middle of nowhere spotted some bones in a gulch. Could have washed up there. The nearest significant city is about seventy-five miles."

"What city?"

"Santa Fe," David Steele said.

Santa Fe, I thought. Royce Rogers buried the bodies in his own backyard. He knew where to go. His bad luck was the only reason we had found Glenn Evans.

"On my way," I said.

"I'll set it up," David Steele said. "Call me when you're in the air."

I disconnected and immediately called Jim Doak. "Tell me the jet's available," I said.

"All day," Jim said. "What's up?"

"How soon can you be ready to go?"

"An hour, probably. Hour and a half tops. Where are we going?"

"Santa Fe."

"Better make that two hours," Jim said.

"I'll see you in two hours," I said.

I called Roy. "I'm using jet number one today, if that's okay. I've already talked to Jim."

"What's happening?" Roy said.

I told him.

"Good hunting," Roy said.

◆   ◆   ◆   ◆

"I'm in the air," I said to David Steele an hour and fifty minutes later. I had left Gretchen a note and rushed home. I changed into jeans, a button-down-collar flannel shirt, and boots. I packed for three days of cold weather. I called Mary on my way to Tri-Cities Airport and explained what was going on. She said it might be the break I was waiting for.

I wasn't sure how it was going to get me any closer to Royce Rogers, but it did advance my theory that he was killing his partners.

"How long before you're in?" David Steele asked.

"Two hours, maybe a little more."

"What airline?"

"Private. Fleet Industries jet."

"Nice to have that at your disposal," he said. "I'll have someone meet you when you land. I'll need a full report, since you're now on our payroll. If you need anything, let me know. It'll be nice if you can find this guy, Youngblood. You were right. This is a very bad guy."

I'm still a long way from finding him, I thought, but I said nothing.

◆   ◆   ◆   ◆

Jim Doak's landing was as smooth as the flight to Santa Fe.

"Good job, captain," I said as I exited the jet.

"Call me when you're ready to go back," he said. "I'll try to work you in."

As I came down the stairs, I noticed a county sheriff's SUV parked about thirty yards away. A young deputy sheriff leaned against the right front fender, sunglasses on, arms folded, blank expression on his face. The day was clear and cold but not unpleasant, thanks to calm winds. I unzipped my leather jacket a little.

Backpack slung over one shoulder, I wheeled a small suitcase over and stopped in front of him. "Am I in trouble, or are you my ride?"

He smiled. "Danny West," he said, extending a hand. "I'm you're ride. What do you want to do first?"

Officer West was young—my guess was early thirties. He appeared to be Native American. He was close to six feet tall and looked fit. He wore the uniform well.

"I'd like to see where the bones were found," I said.

"We can do that. Put your things in the back and hop in."

We drove west, going as fast as the roads would allow. There were few road signs; I guessed some of the roads were not even on the map.

"I'm guessing you're local," I said.

"I am."

"You seem to know these back roads pretty well."

"When you've been on the job as long as I have, you get to know them all," Danny West said. "I'll bet you know those East Tennessee back roads."

"You checked me out," I said.

"While I waited for you to land," he said. "You've made the news more than once."

"Lucky me."

"Yeah, I know what you mean. Make the news in our line of work and it's usually not good, although the press seems to like you."

"Until they don't," I said.

Danny West laughed. "Exactly."

"Tell me about the discovery of the bones. Did you get the call?"

"I did. A couple of kids from my tribe were out there with their dirt bikes and spotted the bones. They called it in, and I was closest, so I caught it. I called in our crime-scene guy, and we looked around and found some more large bones scattered over an area of maybe twenty square yards. After a while, we couldn't find anything else, so we packed up and went home."

"Understandable. You didn't know it would lead to anything."

We drove in silence as Danny West roared past the few vehicles on the road. The wind was picking up, and I watched as a tumbleweed bounced in front of us and exploded on our front bumper like a puff of smoke.

"So how do these bones connect to a missing person in Texas?"

"The deceased was a friend of a guy I'm chasing," I said. "His death may be connected to my case."

"Are you getting close to finding him?"

"Not that I can tell," I said.

◆　◆　◆　◆

A half-hour later, we turned off the state highway onto a dirt road. Five minutes after that, Danny West stopped the SUV. The wind had picked up, and sand was whipping about.

"You might want to wear those wrap-arounds you had on earlier," Danny West said.

I put on my sunglasses as we exited the SUV. The wind chill caused me to zip my jacket to the top and put on my leather gloves. Danny West seemed not to notice the cold. We walked about twenty feet and stopped. I noticed stakes driven into the sandy ground in no particular pattern. The farthest was maybe fifty feet from where we stood.

"I drove a stake every place we found a bone," Danny West said. "I took pictures before we bagged the bones."

"That's good work," I said. "Did you look anywhere else?"

"No need to. We thought we had enough. We went maybe another forty or fifty yards in all directions and didn't find anything else."

I nodded. Officer Danny West could not have known the FBI might show up looking for more bodies.

"Who decided the body might have washed up from somewhere else?"

"My grandfather," he said. "He used to be a lawman. He's good at solving puzzles. When I told him about the bones, he said that they were probably carried there by the flash flooding."

"Has he been out here?"

"No."

"Will he come and take a look if we ask?"

"He'll be honored to help."

53

Danny West called his grandfather, who promised to be at the site in thirty-nine minutes. I looked at my watch and noted the time. "Thirty-nine minutes?" I said.

"My grandfather is very precise."

We passed the time expanding the search area until we heard an approaching vehicle, an old pickup truck. I looked at my watch: thirty-nine minutes, give or take a few seconds. A small, wiry man emerged. He wore boots, jeans, a navy peacoat, a beat-up cowboy hat with a feather in the band, and a serious expression. He walked over and stopped in front of us.

"Agent Youngblood," Danny West said, "this is my grandfather, retired sheriff Daniel Looks to the West."

We shook hands.

"Thanks for coming," I said.

"Glad to," he said. "Boredom is a like an annoying friend that will not go away when he has worn out his welcome. Today, I leave him at home."

"I'm happy I can make your day more interesting," I said. "What I'd like to know is where you think the bones came from."

Daniel Looks to the West turned to his grandson. "Each stake represents a bone?"

"Yes," Danny West said. "Here is a layout of the bones—sizes and weights."

He handed his grandfather a folded sheet of paper. It rustled in the wind as the elder man opened it. After studying the sheet, he walked away. He circled the stakes while looking down at the paper. In a few minutes, he returned, folded the paper, and handed it back to his grandson.

"They came from there," he said, pointing to a small ravine that ran up into a canyon. "How far up, I cannot tell. It would depend on how much water came down. Let's go see what we can find."

We followed Daniel up the ravine. The footing was soft, and every now and then Daniel kicked at the sand to see if anything turned up. A few hundred yards in, he stopped abruptly. "You feel that?" he said to his grandson.

"Feel what, Grandfather?"

"Never mind," the older man said. "Let's scratch around this area and see if we can turn up anything."

Using our boots, we started kicking sand. The wind helped. Five minutes later, thirty yards from where I stood, Daniel Looks to the West dropped to his knees and gently began to brush sand from something he had found. I watched for a minute, then walked over and stared down into the empty eye sockets of a human skull. Daniel Looks to the West never looked up. He continued brushing sand from the skull until it was completely uncovered. He lifted it gently and examined it. There was a small hole in the back of the skull.

"Cause of death was a .22 caliber pistol," he said.

"Not a rifle?"

"No," he said. "Close work. Rim of the hole is dark with gunpowder."

"If you say so," I said.

He set the skull back into its hole. "We will leave it for the FBI crime-scene people. I'm sure you are going to call them in."

"Seems like a good idea," I said.

We turned and walked back toward our vehicles.

"There will be more," he said.

◆　◆　◆　◆

By the time Danny West drove me back into Santa Fe, it was getting dark. We stopped at a convenience store, where I bought snacks and a six-pack of Amber Bock.

"I'll buy you dinner if you're free," I said, getting back in his cruiser. "You can pick the place."

"I'm free," he said. "Where are you staying?"

"Residence Inn."

"I'll drop you and pick you up at seven. I want to get out of this uniform and take a shower."

◆   ◆   ◆   ◆

I checked in at the same Residence Inn where I had stayed when I came to interview Gloria Davis. I was upgraded to a two-bedroom suite, which would later prove useful. I settled in, opened a beer, and called David Steele.

"Agent Youngblood reporting in as ordered."

He laughed. "Nice to see your sense of humor is still intact, Youngblood. What have you got?"

"Good question," I said. "What I've got is a young third-generation deputy sheriff that was the first responder and is eager to help the FBI. Then there's his grandfather, a retired sheriff who has visions his grandson says should not be dismissed. I've got lots of places to bury bodies, and I've got a skull that may or may not be Glenn Evans, found by the grandfather while we were out at the crime scene scouting. Young deputy West thinks he can get DNA on the skull from the state lab faster than the feds, so I told him to have at it."

"Good thinking," David Steele said. "We're really backed up. What makes you think it's a crime scene?"

"Did I fail to mention the skull has a bullet hole in the back of it?"

"Yeah, I think I missed that part."

"I want a GPR machine and a tech that knows how to use it as soon as possible."

"How do you know about GPR?" David Steele said.

"I read. I figure the FBI has to have one or a dozen."

Ground-penetrating radar was used primarily to locate graves in old graveyards that did not have headstones. It was also used by law enforcement in locating burial sites of victims when evidence or information pinpointed a location.

"You think more bodies are out there?"

"The old man does."

"How about you?"

"I think Royce Rogers used this place as a dumping ground for murdered partners," I said. "The ultimate job termination. I guess that would qualify him as a serial killer."

"I think the closest GPR is in Dallas," David Steele said. "Let me make some calls. I'll get back to you."

As soon as I disconnected, I called Mary.

"You might want to record this," I said. "It's an obscene phone call."

"Oh, goodie," Mary said. "My favorite kind. What's the news from New Mexico?"

I filled her in on my trip. Mary liked details and sometimes asked questions and suggested things I hadn't thought of. She was quiet when I finished.

"I may be here awhile," I said.

"I was beginning to realize that," Mary said. "It doesn't make me happy."

"I know."

"Do what you've got to do and get your ass home, Cowboy."

◆   ◆   ◆   ◆

An hour later, showered and dressed in fresh clothes, I waited in the lobby for my ride. Danny was there promptly at seven.

Fifteen minutes later, we were at a local restaurant. Danny introduced me to the owner, Carl, and his son and daughter, who waited tables. The daughter, Carla, waited on us. We had a table in an alcove at the back that allowed us a view of the entire restaurant and the front door.

"Good location," I said. "Are you expecting trouble?"

He laughed. "No. I called ahead and asked Carl to hold it. This is my favorite table."

I ordered a beer. Danny West ordered a club soda with a slice of lime.

"You don't drink?"

"Only at home, and only when I'm in for the night," he said. "A long-standing family rule established by my grandfather and honored by my father and me. My grandfather's code is to lead by example."

The drinks arrived. Following Danny's recommendation, I ordered a medium-rare elk tenderloin, a baked potato, and a Caesar salad. I had never eaten elk. It turned out to be delicious.

"What's it like being a FBI agent?" Danny said.

"I'm not an FBI agent. I'm a private investigator licensed in Tennessee who sometimes consults for the FBI."

"Looks like you consult a lot, from what I read online."

"Somehow, I manage to get mixed up in cases the FBI is interested in, or I'm able to get them involved to assist my own investigations."

"I read about one case where you had to kill the perp. What was that like?"

I assumed he was referring to the Three Devils case. That one got more press than some of the others.

"I was trying to stop him from killing a girl he abducted," I said. "It was him or her and me."

I thought of the other three men I had killed. I had saved either myself or someone else, and I didn't lose sleep over any of them. I hoped Danny West wouldn't bring up the others. He didn't.

"I've never had to draw my weapon," he said.

"Try to keep it that way."

"I will."

"Enough about me," I said. "You married?"

"No," he said. "Steady lady friend. She's a lawyer and as busy as I am. We see each other two or three times a week. I'm happy with that arrangement, and she seems to be also."

Our food arrived, and the talking became minimal. I heard bits and pieces about the life of a deputy sheriff in New Mexico who worked for his father. Danny seemed to love it.

A half-hour later, I paid for the meal and Danny West drove me back to the Residence Inn. He insisted that I didn't need to rent a car, that he would be available to drive me back to the crime scene. He gave me his cell-phone number and told me to call or text him when I was ready to go. Since there was no way I would ever find my way back to the scene, I agreed.

◆ ◆ ◆ ◆

Back in my room, I opened a beer, booted my laptop, and went online. I had been ignoring T. Elbert, so I wrote him a long email. I checked the market and found nothing new or unusual. I looked at news headlines and sports. I was checking the college basketball standings when my cell phone rang.

"Two agents in an unmarked van with a GPR machine left Dallas an hour ago," David Steele said. "They'll spend the night in Amarillo, then drive in tomorrow morning. They'll meet you at the Residence Inn. I need you to arrange for their lodging."

"I'll take care of it first thing in the morning," I said.

"Let me know what you find out there."

"Yes, sir," I said. "Text me or email their names, please."

He laughed. "I'll do that, Agent Youngblood. That's all for now."

He was gone.

An hour later, I had a text giving me the last names and cell-phone numbers of the two agents, Wallace and Blackstone.

54

The self-serve breakfast was free, and I wasn't shy about taking advantage. No matter how much money you have in the bank, free is always good. I started with coffee, then toasted an English muffin. I piled my plate high with scrambled eggs and added bacon and potatoes. I knew I would need some extra calories if I was going to spend a cold afternoon in the desert. I finished the food on my plate, then made myself a waffle. I had another cup of coffee. Fifteen minutes later, I waddled to the front desk and made reservations for Agents Wallace and Blackstone. I then gathered my laptop and went back to my room. I placed the laptop in its usual spot on the desk and sat down to make some calls. The first was to Deputy Sheriff Danny West.

"Danny, it's Don," I said. "I won't need you until lunch or later. I've got a couple of agents coming in a van with GPR. I'll call you when they get here."

"That should be interesting," he said. "I've never seen one of those machines. Call me when you're ready, and I'll get to you as soon as I can."

I called Mary. She was on duty and couldn't talk long. "Too bad you can't see Lacy," she said. "Seems like she's just next door."

"Four hundred and seventy-one miles," I said.

"You checked already."

"I did."

"That's a good daddy," Mary said. "Got to go. Talk soon."

I sat and thought about Lacy. She was working toward a degree in law enforcement. In my estimation, a student trip to an FBI crime scene would be priceless. After all, I was the agent in charge of this field trip.

I dialed her cell phone.

She picked up immediately. "Don, is everything okay?"

"Everything's fine. I'm in Santa Fe working a crime scene with the FBI. I thought you might want to come and observe. It'd be one hell of a field trip."

"You're kidding," she said.

"I'm not."

"I'd love to, but I'd have to skip classes, and we lose points for missing."

"Talk to the head of your department," I said.

"The department head is Dean Wickman," Lacy said. "I'll schedule an appointment with him as soon as we hang up. I really hope I can do this."

"I think he might agree this trip would be worth it. Have him call me if there are any questions."

◆ ◆ ◆ ◆

When I'm bored, I try to touch base with friends I haven't talked to in awhile. So, in order, I called Bruiser Bracken, Scott Glass, and Sister Sarah Agnes Woods. The calls with Bruiser and Scott were fairly brief, they were both busy. The call with Sister Sarah Agnes was not. She was very interested in the Clown case and wanted to know every detail about Royce Rogers. So I told her all of what she had not already heard.

"What do you think?" I said when I finished.

"I'm perplexed," she said. "From everything you told me, it doesn't add up. I have a hard time believing the Royce Rogers you described is the clown kidnapper."

"The evidence is overwhelming. So, for the sake of argument, let's assume it's him. What am I dealing with, and how do I find him?"

"If he really is this clown kidnapper person, then you are either dealing with two different personalities or he is a pure sociopath, highly intelligent, cunning, and deceitful. He would not kill just to kill. He would kill because he perceives it to be the best course of action."

"Will he resurface?"

"Not until he thinks it's safe," she said.

My cell phone alerted me that a call was coming in, from the area code that encompassed Arizona State University.

"Sarah Agnes, I've got a call coming in I must take," I said. "Thanks for your insight. I'll call again soon." I didn't wait for a response. I clicked over to pick up the other call. "Donald Youngblood," I said.

"Mr. Youngblood," a male voice said, "this is Dean Wickman in the Law Enforcement Department at Arizona State. Your daughter has come to me with an interesting request. Can I have a few details?"

"Thanks for considering this, dean," I said. I was assuming dean was his title, not his first name. "First, it would be a highly confidential trip. Lacy could not report on this until the case was closed, and even then I'm not sure how much she could share. She would observe a crime scene being processed that would employ GRP, ground-penetrating radar."

"Yes, I'm familiar with GPR."

"Confidentially, we have identified one body from bones, more likely than not a murder victim, and we think there might be more. So Lacy would have a chance to observe the preservation of a grave site or two and to see how GPR works—the chance of a lifetime, I would think, if you're a law-enforcement student."

"Yes, I would have to agree," he said. "How long would she be gone?"

"I'll fly her in here this afternoon. She'll spend all day tomorrow at the site. I'll fly her back early the next morning. She'll miss a day and a half."

"Fine," he said. "You work it out with Lacy, and I'll deal with her professors. This is a wonderful opportunity. I'm sorry we can't send a whole class."

"Unfortunately, that's not possible," I said.

"No, I didn't think it was," he said.

◆　◆　◆　◆

I went online to book Lacy a flight from Phoenix to Santa Fe, a task not as easy as it sounds. I found one nonstop flight and a bunch of two-stop flights that took hours. I booked first class on the one direct flight and left the return open. I had just finished when my cell phone rang.

"Don, it's Danny. Going out to the crime scene will have to wait. There are high-wind warnings starting at noon, sustained forty-mile-an-hour winds with gusts in the sixties. We could literally freeze our asses off out there."

It was not a visual I cared to dwell on.

"What about tomorrow?"

"Tomorrow looks good," Danny said.

"Okay. Can you get me to the airport by 2:15 this afternoon? I'm meeting my daughter."

"Your daughter?"

I told him why.

"I like that," he said. "My grandfather would certainly approve. I'll be there around 1:45."

I said goodbye to Danny West and called Lacy. "You're on a 12:50 direct flight to Santa Fe," I said. "First class on American Airlines."

"Yes!" she yelled. "Thank you, thank you!"

"I'll see you at the airport," I said. "Get going."

I hung up, and then a thought hit me. High-wind warnings. I hoped I hadn't made a mistake. I called Lacy back.

"Something else?" she answered.

I told her about the high-wind warnings, and that I was concerned.

She laughed. "You're turning into an old woman. If that flight goes, I'll be on it. Relax, Dad."

She called me Dad when she thought I was being ridiculous. I felt better—a little.

I called Hertz and booked a rental car for our return trip to the Residence Inn. I was feeling guilty about taking Danny West away from more important duties.

A few minutes later, I dialed one of the cell-phone numbers David Steele had given me.

"Agent Blackstone," the voice said.

"Blackstone, this is Youngblood. No rush to get here. We are not going to the site today." I explained why.

"That's a good call, Agent Youngblood," he said. "GPR does not do well in extremely cold weather, and wind blowing sand around could really foul it up."

"Stop and have lunch," I said. "Take your time. I have to pick someone up at the airport. I won't be back until three or after."

"We'll see you when we see you," Agent Blackstone said.

◆   ◆   ◆   ◆

At 2:00, I was at the Hertz desk in Santa Fe Municipal Airport picking up the keys to my rental SUV. At 2:15, I was standing in front of security, staring at the arrival board. Lacy's flight was on time at 2:32. Five minutes later, it changed to 2:42. At 2:30, it changed to 2:50. I needed to find out what was going on. I circumvented security and was immediately confronted by a guard.

"Sir, you need to get in line and go through screening."

I flashed my FBI creds. "I need to meet the flight from Phoenix," I said. "I'm working a sensitive case."

"I need to get my supervisor," he said.

"Well, I don't have much time. Hurry, please."

Five minutes later, I was talking to a supervisor dressed in a police uniform and carrying a Glock .45. He introduced himself as Jake Slate. "They call me Slate," he said.

I couldn't help thinking of Kurt Russell's line from *Escape from New York*: "Call me Snake." "They call me Youngblood," I said, playing along.

"Donald Youngblood, yeah, I've heard of you," he said. "You cracked that serial killer case a few years ago."

For once, all that press might be doing me some good, I thought.

"That was quite a while ago," I said.

Slate had a shaved head that sat on a solid frame of around six feet. He probably weighed 220—another guy I'd want on my side in a fight. Over his shoulder, I noticed that Lacy's flight was now due at 2:55.

"Is the case you're working bigger than that one?"

"Very likely," I said. "And I need to meet that plane."

"You packing?"

"Yes."

He smiled. "Well, try not to shoot anybody unless you really have to."

"I promise."

"By the way, who are you meeting?"

I went with the truth. "My daughter."

"Got two of those myself," he said. "Let him through," he said to the guard.

Five minutes later, I was at the arrival gate. The board still read 2:55. I paced. My watch seemed to be mired in quicksand. At 2:55, Lacy's flight disappeared from the board.

I went to the desk agent near the door that arriving passengers would come through. "What happened to the Phoenix flight? It dropped off the arrival board."

"It's down," he said.

"What?" I said, ready to unravel.

"On the ground. It will be at the gate in five minutes."

I felt ridiculous. I blew out a breath and acted as cool as possible. "Yeah, right," I said. "Thanks."

It was more like ten minutes, but who was counting? The first few passengers through the door did not look happy. Then I saw Lacy, and she saw me and smiled. She came fast and gave me a big hug.

"Well, you were right about the wind," she said. "That was one rough flight."

55

The next morning, Lacy and I met Wallace and Blackstone in the Residence Inn dining room at seven o'clock for breakfast. Wallace was about five foot eight, stocky and had short sandy hair, brown eyes, and freckles. Blackstone was a handsome, dark-skinned man as tall as me with short black hair and hazel eyes that were somewhat unnerving. He had the potential to be a top-notch interrogator. They were both attentive to my beautiful blond daughter. Danny West showed up at seven-thirty and was equally enamored with Lacy.

We loaded up. Lacy and I rode with Deputy West, while Wallace and Blackstone followed us in their van. When we arrived at the scene, Wallace said, "I'm glad we had someone to follow. We sure as hell would never have found this place."

The day was cold, but the sun was on the rise. Danny West had promised a pleasant day in the mid-forties. Wallace and Blackstone unloaded. I did what any good special agent in charge would—stayed out of the way and let them do the work. Lacy was already taking notes. I had to be emphatic that she would take no pictures. Danny West left to handle some calls, promising to be back around lunchtime.

"We're going to stake it and string it so we don't cover the same ground twice," Wallace said.

"That's a lot of stakes and string," I said.

"Not really," Blackstone said. "We'll keep moving them out from the center as we go. We'll use the stake marking the location where the skull was found as ground zero."

They set about their business, first unloading the GPR. The frame for holding it looked like a big tricycle—two fat tires in the back and a small one in the front. The GPR attached to the frame a few inches from the ground, its flat surface facing down. A viewing screen spanned the handlebars. The operator pushed the frame in the direction of choice and watched the screen as the radar penetrated the ground.

Wallace took the first tour. I walked along beside him.

"Ever seen one of these things work?" he said.

"No."

"I'm looking for irregularities in the scan—color changes, soil changes, anything that breaks what looks like a pattern. Single bones can be hard. A full skeleton, not so much. A coffin is easy. If I see something suspicious, I can turn the radar to get a different view, look at it from all angles."

We walked slowly, and Wallace continued his tutorial, never taking his eyes off the screen. Blackstone was hammering stakes and stretching string.

"In the early days," Wallace said, "I was digging up everything. Now, I'm pretty good at it. Blackstone is just learning, but he's getting good fast."

Lacy came up beside me. "Can I watch?"

"If it's okay with Agent Wallace," I said.

"Okay with me," Wallace said.

A half-hour passed, and Wallace turned the GPR over to Blackstone and joined me back at the van. Lacy stayed with Blackstone.

"Pretty brisk out there," he said.

"Good skiing weather."

"Yeah, except we're not skiing."

"Too bad for us," I said.

◆   ◆   ◆   ◆

The morning passed slowly. Wallace and Blackstone continued to spell each other every half-hour. Lacy walked along with whoever was pushing the GPR and watching the screen. She seemed to be asking questions and taking notes.

Near lunchtime, I heard Wallace holler, "Youngblood! We got one."

Blackstone and I trotted over to where Wallace stood with Lacy. Moving the GPR around for different angles, Wallace looked at Blackstone. "See it?"

"Sure as hell do," Blackstone said. "Good work. I'll get some stakes and mark it off."

Wallace looked at me. "You need a crime-scene team," he said.

"I'll make a call."

I went to the van and called David Steele, feeling way over my head.

"The deputy director is in a meeting," I was informed by his assistant.

"Slip him a note and tell him Youngblood found another one. It's important," I said. "He'll know what it means."

"If I can," she said.

"It would be the safest thing for you to do."

A little threat never hurt anyone. I didn't wait for a response.

I went back to the group. Once the area was staked off, Wallace let Lacy string crime-scene tape. I thought it was nice of him to make her a part of it.

◆   ◆   ◆   ◆

Danny West showed up a few minutes after noon.

"We got one," I said when he got out of his cruiser.

"I figured you would. Grandfather is never wrong about these things. You want to grab some lunch?"

"Where?" I said. "Are we going to shoot a jackalope?" *An urban legend of a jackrabbit with antlers.*

He laughed. "I don't think they're any good to eat. There's a Subway about twenty minutes from here."

I turned in the direction of Lacy, Wallace, and Blackstone and released my infamous whistle. They all turned and looked my way. I mimed eating from a bowl, and they got the message. Wallace wheeled the GPR to the van, and he and Blackstone loaded it and locked the doors. We piled into the cruiser. I rode shotgun, and Lacy sat between Wallace and Blackstone. She didn't seem to mind, and neither did they.

We wound around the high desert until we came to a small town that had a gas station, a general store, and a Subway. The Subway was getting some business, so we waited in line to place our order. *The only game in town*, I thought.

We got our subs, chips, and drinks and found a booth for four. Danny West pulled a chair up to the end of the booth. Lacy sat inside, next to me. We ate and were quiet. Spending a cold morning on the high desert can burn some calories.

Blackstone broke the silence. "I bet we find another one before the end of the day."

"Maybe two," Wallace said.

"I think we'll find a lot more than two before we're through," I said.

They all turned and looked at me.

"You know something we don't?" Wallace said.

"I know a lot you don't."

"Care to share?"

"I just did," I said.

Lacy poked me in the ribs and gave me the cop stare she had learned from Mary. Translation: *Don't be a wiseass.*

"Okay," I said, looking at Lacy.

"I like this young lady," Wallace said to Blackstone.

I addressed Wallace and Blackstone. "I suspect this may be a dumping ground for a guy I'm chasing. And if you blab any of this, Deputy Director Steele will be looking for your heads."

"We can keep quiet until it's over," Wallace said. "Then we're going to brag like hell how we helped solve it."

"Be my guest," I said.

I looked at Lacy. "Not a word. Not even to Biker."

"Understood," she said.

I gave her a second look.

She smiled. "I promise."

So I told the group the whole story. When I finished, everyone was quiet.

"Putting all of that together," Wallace said, "that was really great work."

Danny West and Blackstone mumbled agreement.

"I'm really proud of you," Lacy said.

"Well," I said, trying to be cool, "there's still more work to do, so let's get to it."

◆　◆　◆　◆

Danny West dropped us back at the crime scene and went about being a deputy sheriff. By midafternoon, Blackstone had found another complete skeleton, maybe fifty yards from the one Wallace had found. They staked it out and kept on trucking. The days were short, and we would lose light soon. Danny West had not shown up as yet to guide us out of the maze, and I resisted the urge to call him.

Near sunset, Wallace found a third complete skeleton. I went to the van to call David Steele. Just before I got there, my phone rang.

"Youngblood," I answered.

"Sorry I couldn't call sooner," David Steele said. "There's some high-priority stuff going on. I hear you found a body."

"A skeletal image of a human body, if you want to be succinct," I said. "Actually three. Two more since I called you. We need crime-scene techs."

"I have a brand-new crime-scene bus on the way," he said. "Scott Glass is coming from Salt Lake City with two techs. They'll be there by midnight. John Banks has already booked them rooms, so you don't need to worry about that. No offense, but I want Scott to take the lead. We need an experienced agent on this thing."

"Fine with me. I understand completely." In fact, I was relieved. Being in charge was more than I had wanted in the first place.

"Damn good work, Youngblood," David Steele said. "Without you connecting the dots, we never would have put it all together."

"Thanks. But I'm not going to be happy until we find Royce Rogers. Something isn't quite right. It's a big puzzle, and we're still missing some key pieces."

"All you can do is keep working it. Sooner or later, you'll catch another break."

"I sure hope it's sooner," I said.

◆　　◆　　◆　　◆

Danny West arrived just before dark. He assured us the crime scene would be perfectly fine left unattended. On the way back, I called Mary and filled her in on our day. Then I turned the phone over to Lacy, and they talked for at least half an hour. By the time we made it to the Residence Inn, night had fully presented itself. Temperatures were falling, and it felt good to be inside. Lacy and I, both too tired to go out, had a light meal of meatball subs, chips, and salad in the Residence Inn dining room while Wallace and Blackstone went in search of steak. We ate slowly, talked little, and went back to the suite.

"Today was the best," she said. "I really appreciate it, and I learned a lot."

"You were a big help. The guys were really impressed. Scott and his crew will be in later tonight, so you'll be able to take a look at the crime-scene bus before you leave."

"That would be awesome." Lacy's cell phone rang. She looked at her screen. "It's Biker. I'll see you in the morning," she said. "Hey, there," she said to Biker as she started to shut her bedroom door.

"Hang on," I said. "Give me your phone."

With a puzzled look, she handed me her cell phone.

"Biker, how's it going?"

"Fine, Mr. Youngblood," he said tentatively.

"Listen, I'm going to let Lacy share her day with you, but you cannot talk about it to anyone else. Understood?"

"Yes, sir," he said. "Not a word."

I knew he wouldn't, and not telling him would have driven Lacy crazy. I handed the phone back to her. A huge smile lit up her face.

"Thank you," she said, turning through her bedroom door. "You are not going to believe my day," I heard her say as the door closed.

I went to my room, sat at the desk, and texted Mary, "Good night, my love!"

I waited. I knew she was still up, despite the two-hour time difference. "You had a long day," she texted back. "Get some rest. Sweet dreams!"

Fifteen minutes later, I was in bed. A minute or two after that, I was sound asleep.

Sometime later, Scott and his bus showed up.

56

The next morning, the group met at seven for breakfast in the Residence Inn dining room. Scott had not met Wallace and Blackstone, so I did the introductions. Then Scott introduced the crime-scene techs, Fine and Dumas. Fine was a young, innocent-looking blonde, maybe five-six, slender. She didn't look a day older than Lacy. Dumas was older. She was shorter than Fine and had dark features and eyes that blazed. As we talked, I sensed that she had been around for a while.

After breakfast, Scott took Lacy and me for a tour of the new crime-scene bus. It was equipped with some stuff I had never heard of. Describing it as state-of-the-art would be an understatement.

Back outside, Scott said, "Go home, Blood. You've done more than your share. We can take it from here."

"You'll keep me posted."

"Every day," he said.

"I hope to get out here in March and ski for a couple of weeks. We'll get caught up then."

"Looking forward to it," Scott said.

Danny West pulled up, and more introductions followed. After that, the convoy packed up and pulled out, Danny West in the lead with Scott riding shotgun, followed by the GPR van and the crime-scene bus. Seconds later, I noticed a nondescript white car parked across the street pulling out behind the convoy. I watched as the convoy turned right at the light and observed that the white car took the same turn.

I called Danny West's cell phone. "I think you have a tail. White car, male driver, no passengers."

"Yeah, I know," Danny West said. "A reporter. I saw him when I came in. He's not very clever. Guess the word is out. Somebody at the Residence Inn must have tipped him off that the FBI is in town. When we get out of town, I'll have our guys set up a road block and send him back."

"You can do that?"

"Sure can. Agent Glass thinks it's a great idea."

"He would," I said.

◆ ◆ ◆ ◆

Lacy and I packed up and an hour later were at the airport. I turned in the rental car, and we went to the Delta lounge. Spying an attractive brunette behind the service desk, I approached and said, "I need to get my daughter to Phoenix as soon as possible, any airline." I flashed my FBI creds, and the agent suddenly became motivated, fingers flashing over her keyboard.

"I have an American flight that leaves in half an hour," she said. "She'll have to hustle, but I'll make sure they don't leave without her. What's your daughter's name?"

"Lacy Youngblood," I said.

"ID?" the agent said to Lacy. Lacy produced her driver's license. More keyboard action, and then she handed Lacy a boarding pass. "I upgraded you to first class. Gate 22. Better get going."

"Thank you," Lacy said. She hugged me. "Thanks, Dad. Love you." She turned and was gone. I knew the *Dad* was for the ticket agent.

"Beautiful girl," the agent said.

"Thank you," I said, reaching for my wallet. "American Express okay?"

"Perfect," she said, taking my card.

I pocketed the receipt and said, "Now, what do you have for Tri-Cities Airport in Tennessee?"

The keyboard sang, and the agent slowly shook her head. "That's going to be a tough one," she said.

◆ ◆ ◆ ◆

I sat in a near-deserted part of the Delta lounge and called Roy Husky.

After a brief wait, he came on the phone. "I can't talk now, Gumshoe. If you need the jet, call Jim directly. In fact, anytime you need the jet, call Jim directly. It'll save us both time. Sorry, got to run."

He was gone before I even got a word in. *Big business.*

I called Jim Doak. When he answered, I said, "It's going to take me ten hours and two stops to get back to Tri-Cities. Please tell me you can come get me."

Jim laughed. "What did you do before I began flying you all over the country?"

"I can't remember."

"I'll be there in about four hours."

"You're a lifesaver," I said.

I got a second cup of coffee and a pastry and sat with my laptop to track Lacy. Her nonstop flight had just taken off and was estimated to land in an hour and thirty-one minutes. The weather for flying was perfect.

She had about a half-hour to go when someone said, "Agent Youngblood?"

I looked up at the security supervisor from two days before. "Jake Slate, right?"

"Good memory," he said. He was holding a full cup of coffee.

"Easy name to remember."

"Mind if I join you for a few minutes?"

"Sit," I said, putting my laptop aside.

Jake glanced at the screen. "Tracking you daughter?"

"How'd you know?"

"I saw her heading to her gate. She was in a big hurry."

"How'd you know she was my daughter?"

"I saw you walking out with her the other night."

"She should land in Phoenix in about a half-hour," I said.

"Arizona State?"

"You're pretty good," I said.

"I've got one at ASU and one at AU. Both on scholarship, thank God."

"How long have you been out of the military?"

He smiled. "You're pretty good yourself."

"I'd say Special Forces, Delta Force, or Army Rangers."

"Rangers," he said.

I thought back to the Crane case and the Southside Seven. I didn't go there. "Were you in Desert Storm?"

"I was," he said none too eagerly.

I waited. He didn't elaborate. We were quiet for a while as we drank coffee. I looked at my laptop screen. Lacy's flight was fifteen minutes out of Phoenix.

"I looked you up online after we met," he said. "It seems you've had an interesting life as a private investigator."

"That's an understatement."

"I saw you had to kill the perp in that serial-killer case."

Too many people have seen that, I thought. *That's all they want to talk about.*

"A young girl's life was at stake," I said. "He had a chance to kill me, but I got him first."

"How'd it go down?"

It was no secret, so I told him.

"Smart, that ankle holster," Slate said. "The bad guys never seem to think about the obvious. Was that your first kill?"

"Third."

"Never easy."

"Had to be done," I said.

"I hear you."

Slate's radio chirped. "Need you on Concourse A."

"On my way," he said. "Duty calls," Slate said as he stood. "It was a pleasure meeting you, Youngblood."

"You, too," I said. "Thank you for your service."

Jake Slate smiled. "Like you said, had to be done."

◆　◆　◆　◆

An hour later, I packed up my laptop and attached it to my small, wheeled suitcase. My journey would require significant walking. I headed for the main terminal exit and saw Jake Slate talking to one of his subordinates. I held up one finger, and he came over.

"Is there an easy way to get to the private aircraft terminal?"

"Sure," he said. "Follow me."

I followed him back past the Delta lounge toward the departure gates. At an empty gate, Slate punched a code into a keypad that allowed entry and led me down a jetway. At the end of the jetway, we went through a side door, down a short flight of portable stairs, and out on the tarmac. It felt good to be in the open air.

Slate looked around and spied an empty golf cart labeled *Airport Security*. "Let's go," he said.

I put my laptop and suitcase in a wire bin behind me and climbed in. We zipped across the runway, dodging jets and other traffic until we made it to the other side of the terminal, then turned right and went to the end, then around to the other side. At that point, I saw the familiar large hangar for private planes. A smaller terminal was attached. Slate headed straight for it.

When we got there, he pulled in front of an unmarked door and stopped. "One, four, four, two will get you through the door. Up the stairs and through another door and you're in the terminal," he said. "If you ever run into a situation where you need extra backup, keep me in mind. This job is pretty boring most of the time, and I can get time off."

"If that ever happens, it would be an honor to have you on my team," I said.

I got out and grabbed my gear. We shook hands.

"Safe travels, Youngblood," Slate said.

◆ ◆ ◆ ◆

When I came through the door to our condo, I heard soft music, accompanied by candlelight and the smell of something good cooking. I noticed a small bistro table set up in front of the living-room fireplace. A fire was in progress. Mary came out of the kitchen wearing ripped jeans, a white tank top off one shoulder, leather sandals, and a string of pearls. She rushed to me, and we embraced and kissed.

"I can't believe how much I missed you," she said.

"It's nice to be missed," I said. "You look sexy as hell."

She kissed me again, hard and deep. "Well?"

"Well, what?"

"Did you miss me?"

"It goes without saying."

"It does not," Mary said.

"I missed you."

"That's better."

"What's cooking?"

"Well, there's fettucine alfredo, makings for a Caesar salad, which you will toss, garlic toast, a good bottle of Chardonnay, and me for dessert."

"Can we skip the main course and go straight to dessert?"

"No," Mary said. "Remember, anticipation is 90 percent of satisfaction."

"Uh-huh," I mumbled. I had never believed that old wives' tale.

57

It felt good to be back in the office. I said hello to Ronda, who seemed always to beat me to the office, no matter how early I was. No problem. She was two offices away and never darkened my door. My inner sanctum was peaceful and quiet before Gretchen got in, and then phones started to ring. I sat quietly and read notes from Gretchen, mostly about investment clients. I found nothing of interest. In fact, after all this time, I was starting to get bored with Wall Street.

Shortly after ten, Gretchen was sitting in front of my desk with a pad full of writing. I resisted the urge to try to read it upside down.

"How was your trip?"

"Interesting," I said. I shared the highlights.

"That's some discovery—a serial killer's burial site."

"I didn't really find it. Mother Nature presented it to a couple of teenagers, who called it in to the local authorities. When it connected to the Clown case, more bodies became a real possibility."

"What's next?"

"I don't know," I said. "Wait and see what the DNA tells us."

"I don't know if you've noticed, but we've been getting a lot of business lately. Ronda is swamped."

"Why is that?"

"I ran a few ads in small-town papers within an hour's drive from here," Gretchen said. "We're getting a new case every other day. I'm going to get my license so I can help out with the small stuff."

"Really?"

"Don't act so surprised. Working for you, having Mary as a friend, and dating Buckley have given me a whole new edge. I just got my carry permit. Buckley speeded things up on that."

"I'm gone for four days and look what happens. Can you shoot?"

"I'm pretty good. You okay with this?"

"Sure," I said. "If anything juicy comes along, I'll still want it."

"You got it," Gretchen said. "I don't want to have to shoot anyone."

"Switching gears, I'm considering giving up my investment clients."

"Not surprising."

"You want to take them over?"

"No," she said without hesitation.

"That was fast."

"I like the direction I'm going in," Gretchen said. "You'll have to figure something else out on that one."

"I do have another idea," I said.

◆   ◆   ◆   ◆

After lunch, I went to see what kind of progress Tim the builder had made on the lake house. I was amazed at how far along he was.

"You're doing great," I said.

"I heard you were out of town," he said, "so I doubled my crew."

"Glad I could help. Any problems?"

"None. Guys are showing up to work, materials are on time, and the weather has been cool and clear. Right now, we're rockin' and rollin.'"

◆   ◆   ◆   ◆

Late afternoon, I was back in the office. I was hoping to get a call from Scott, but I realized his day was two hours behind mine. I hung around until five o'clock, then headed for the condo. Mary wasn't there, so I changed and took the dogs for a walk.

While we were out, Mary called. "I'll be about an hour," she said. "I'm catching up on some paperwork."

"Pick up dinner on your way home," I said. "Unless you want to go out."

"I'm beat. What do you want?"

"Surprise me."

"I can do that," Mary said.

I signed off, and the dogs and I headed back to the condo. Walking one dog is easy. Walking two dogs, not so much. The weather had turned cold, and Jake and Junior were frisky. Once inside the condo, they ran around, then settled down to eat.

Forty minutes after I fed them, Scott called.

"You haven't lost your touch for getting mixed up in strange cases," he said.

"How many more bodies have you found?"

"Four more, Blood. But three are really going to interest you."

"No games, Professor. Just tell me."

"Two are most likely women," Scott said.

"Women?" I thought about that. I hadn't seen that coming. Royce Rogers was really a cold-hearted son of a bitch. "I guess that's possible," I said. "What about the third one?"

"The third one hasn't been dead more than six months, according to my experts."

"What?"

"Six months. Officer West had the county medical examiner take a look, too. They all seem to agree: about six months."

"That doesn't fit. I wonder if it could be a random body."

"Doubtful," Scott said. "They all have a bullet hole in the back of the skull."

"Rush the DNA on that last one. Maybe it's Jerry Altman."

"I'm already doing that. I'll let you know as soon as I find out."

I ended my call with Scott and sat and thought about his news. Maybe Royce had pulled another kidnapping right after he got out of prison and then killed his partner. Maybe he had it all lined up. Maybe it would snow two feet tonight. I didn't know what to believe. Then I thought of something. The one-hour time difference meant he still might be in. I called his private number. He answered on the first ring.

"Dansk."

"Warden, it's Donald Youngblood. Working late tonight?"

"Normal day," he said. "I'm leaving soon. What can I do for you, Youngblood?"

"When you release a prisoner, does someone escort him all the way out?"

"Every time. We even wait until they're picked up."

"Do you know who escorted Royce Rogers out?"

"No," Dansk said, "but I can find out. What's this about?"

"I want to know who picked him up. Man or woman. Description, if possible."

"I'll call you Monday."

"Thanks, warden."

58

I got up at the crack of dawn the following Monday and went to Moto's Gym. Mary and I had spent the weekend with Maggie and Billy, just hanging out. Cherokee was a ghost town in the winter, and that was when I liked it most. Billy had been interested in my case and the Looks to the West family.

Moto was actually pleasant in comparison to his usual mood, probably because my membership was coming up for renewal. "Where are dogs?" he asked.

"Asleep."

"They smarter than you," Moto said, then laughed at his own joke.

I smiled and said nothing as I headed toward the ab machines. I went through my usual routine. The gym was almost empty, save for a couple of shapely young women on the treadmills. I gave them the perfunctory nod and went about my business.

◆　◆　◆　◆

An hour and a half later, I sat at my usual table in the Mountain Center Diner. It was weeks since I had seen Big Bob Wilson.

"So what's been occupying your time besides rebuilding the lake house?"

"Still chasing the clown," I said.

"Any luck?"

"No, but there have been some interesting developments."

"Such as?"

I told him the latest.

"You've been busy," he said. "What do you make of the body that's only six months old?"

"That one puzzles me. I'll know more when we get the DNA. I know Royce killed Ricky Carter. I just need to figure out if he killed the one that's only six months dead."

"Here's what I think," Big Bob said. "I think Royce had a job lined up the minute he got out of prison. He did the kidnapping and then killed his accomplice. The victim's father was probably so rich it wasn't worth his time to report it, which was what Royce counted on. Then he came to Tennessee with another accomplice and kidnapped Cindy Carter because he got the idea from Ricky. I don't think he would trust Ricky to kidnap his own daughter. So maybe there's another dead body in the lake or buried somewhere."

I stared at Big Bob. I had to admit that the tale he was spinning made sense. I said nothing. We continued to eat.

"Then Ricky showed up," Big Bob continued. "Maybe he heard about the kidnapping, or maybe he knew it was going to happen, but I'll bet he wanted a cut."

"So Royce killed him?" I said.

"Maybe. Or maybe Rasheed Reed heard Ricky was back, had him killed, dumped him in the lake, and hoped someone would find him. That would be good for business. Was the body weighed down?"

"Not that I know of," I said.

"Royce would have weighed it down, don't you think?"

"Maybe he didn't have time."

"Maybe," Big Bob said.

"Rasheed said he didn't kill Ricky," I said.

"And you believe him?"

"Yes."

"A drug dealer?"

"No reason for him to lie about it."

"No reason for him to tell the truth either," Big Bob said.

"Guess not," I said.

But I strongly suspected Rasheed Reed *was* telling the truth.

◆ ◆ ◆ ◆

I was in the office by eight-thirty. Alone. Ronda was working a case that required early-morning surveillance, Gretchen had said. Gretchen was showing up earlier since she had become a junior partner, but I still had some time by myself. It didn't take long for the phone to ring.

"Youngblood," I said.

"Warden Dansk here."

"You're at it early, warden."

"Always," he said. "I'm with Buddy Sims, the guard who escorted Rogers out the gate. He said a man picked up Rogers."

I sensed that Dansk wanted to be in control of this conversation, so I resisted the urge to ask to speak to Sims directly. The warden was hosting this little party.

"Did he recognize the driver?"

Dansk repeated the question to Sims. "He did," Dansk said. "It was Richard Card."

"Was anyone else in the car?"

Question repeated. "Could have been," Dansk said. "The windows were darkly tinted."

"Does he recall what Richard Card was driving?"

"What was Card driving?" A muffled reply. "A black Cadillac Escalade," Dansk said. "Looked new."

"Fancy ride for a guy who just got out of the slammer," I said.

"It is," Dansk said. "No doubt, not his."

"You wouldn't happen to have a security camera that captured the plate, would you?"

"Yes, but we keep footage only three months," he said. "Sorry."

I couldn't think of anything else to ask. "Thanks for your help, warden," I said.

"Anytime, Youngblood."

◆   ◆   ◆   ◆

I was at a standstill waiting on DNA. Normally, DNA tests could take up to a month, depending on what lab worked on them. A super-rush FBI

DNA result could be done in two or three days if the right pressure was applied. I was hoping Scott had the juice to get it done. I was tempted to go to David Steele, but Scott was the lead dog now, and I had to let him run with it.

I spent a good part of the day reviewing my list of financial clients. I handled most of them as favors for people I liked from the old days or for friends or friends of friends. Then there were those I had made a fortune from while working in New York. Now, for some unexplained reason, I couldn't wait to dump them all. I knew it was time.

Gretchen left at four-thirty, and the phones quit ringing. The office was quiet, and I sat and thought about the Clown case. So Ricky Carter had picked up Royce Rogers when he was released—not really surprising. From there, they had planned the Cindy Carter kidnapping, and Ricky ended up dead, and Royce was in the wind. Two things bothered me: where did Ricky get a new Cadillac Escalade and, more importantly, who was the six-months-dead body in the high desert of New Mexico? Could a third party have been involved—maybe our dead body? If we couldn't get a DNA match, there would be one more piece missing from an already confusing puzzle. I would either be rolling with a lead or at a dead stop.

With nothing more to do, I started shutting down the office. I had just logged off my desktop when the phone rang.

"We got the DNA results on the dead body you're interested in," Scott Glass said.

"That was fast, Professor. You must have pull somewhere."

"I think it's you who has the pull, Blood. The deputy director lit a fire under this one."

"For the record, I did not go behind your back."

"I know that," Scott said. "David Steele made that very clear."

"What have you got?"

"You're not going to like it."

"No match?"

"No match," Scott said. "We checked all the databases. But we still have more DNA test results coming, so maybe we'll match one of those and you'll get a lead."

"I'm not optimistic, Professor."

"Nor am I, Blood, nor am I."

"Was Jerry Altman in the system?"

"No, he wasn't," Scott said.

◆   ◆   ◆   ◆

Mary and I were having after-dinner drinks in front of the fireplace—Frangelico for her and Baileys Irish Cream for me. The weather was cold and damp, with a couple of inches of snow in the forecast, making the fire, the drinks, and my beautiful blond wife an idyllic scene to savor. I had no intention of moving from my spot on our loveseat for quite a while. We were casually discussing the Clown case.

"You may be right about a third player," Mary said. "Someone Royce needed for something, then got rid of."

"The question is who," I said.

"Probably someone he met in prison. Or maybe that Jerry Altman guy."

"Jerry Altman. That's not a bad thought, Wonder Woman." Sometimes, it's best not to say, *I already thought of that.*

"I am a cop," she said.

"And a damn fine-looking one," I said.

59

Early the next day, I had another thought. If the six-months-dead body in the desert wasn't Jerry Altman, was it possible Jerry was still alive? I sat at my desk and looked down on Main Street, which was clear despite the few inches of overnight snowfall. *Worth a shot*, I thought.

Remembering the time difference, I turned my attention to making a list of the clients I would call and another list of those who would receive letters.

Two hours later, I called John Banks. "I'll need a little of your time, if it's okay with Scott," I said.

"Is this about the Clown case?"

"It is."

"What do you need?" John said.

"There's a Jerry Altman in the file that's a missing person," I said. "Probably dead but maybe not. See if you can find any indication that he may still be alive. Try to track down whoever reported him missing. Maybe he's back on the grid and no one knows it."

"Will do," John said. "Probably won't be today."

"Yesterday will be fine," I said.

John hung up. No sense of humor.

◆ ◆ ◆ ◆

With nothing to do and no motivation to do it, I drove out to the building site. The lake house was almost framed—amazing what could be done with a doubled-up, motivated crew. I walked around and looked and said nothing. Tim the builder was busy giving orders and answering questions, and I knew in time he would get around to me. After I had a good look, I walked back to my Armada and leaned against the front fender, arms folded, a man with no particular place to go.

Tim finally got the idea that I wasn't going to leave until he acknowledged my presence, so he ambled over, friendly and casual.

"Your crew is really moving," I said.

"Well, they heard you were famous, and they're a mite star struck, so they're working their little asses off," Tim said.

"Very funny, Timothy."

He ignored me and rolled on. "Tell Mary to give me a call. I need to go over some of the inside stuff. We want to keep the wife happy, do we not?"

"We certainly do," I said. "I'll tell her."

◆　◆　◆　◆

I took the long route back to the office. The sky was a thick blanket of gray, the air was cold, and the landscape was dressed in white. The countryside always received more snowfall that the urban areas. The drive was peaceful, and I thought about maybe making a skiing run over to Beech Mountain or Sugar Mountain tomorrow to get my mind off the Clown case. The roads were nearly clear, but I had to be careful to mind the shady spots that could be deceptively slick.

An hour and fifteen minutes later, I parked my SUV in my space at the back of the Hamilton Building and climbed the back stairs to the second floor. I walked in and looked at Gretchen.

"John Banks called," she said. "He said to please have Agent Youngblood return his call."

I went to my desk, shutting the door behind me.

"Banks," John answered.

"Agent Youngblood returning your call."

John made no comment; he got right to it. "I did not find any trace of Jerry Altman. I did find the name of the woman who reported him missing. She lived in Galveston at the time, but now she's married and lives in Dallas. I'll email you the info."

"Good work, John. I'll await your email with great anticipation."

"You must be really bored," John said.

By the time I booted up my desktop, I had the email. Cynthia Smith was now Cynthia Mason, wife of Dr. James Mason. I thought about flying to Dallas, then rejected the idea as frivolous, since I now knew two agents in the Dallas office. I had both their numbers in my cell-phone directory. I dialed one of them.

"Wallace," he answered.

"Are you finished with the desert site?" I said.

"That you, Agent Youngblood?"

"I think that's former temporary agent Youngblood."

"Once in the club, always in the club," Wallace said. "You're one of us now, Youngblood."

"Nice to be wanted," I said. "What about the desert?"

"Yeah, we're done. Ten bodies in all. We stayed an extra day trying to find another one, then gave up and packed it in."

"How would you like to put away your GPR and do an interview for me right in your own backyard?"

"Love to," he said. "I don't get in the field much. It would be a welcome change."

I gave him the particulars.

"I'll call her tomorrow and set something up," he said. "I'll tell her I can come to her or she can come to the office. Don't want to jam her up with her husband over an ex-boyfriend."

"I like the way you think, Wallace," I said.

"I'll keep you posted, Youngblood. Thanks for asking."

◆　◆　◆　◆

Every now and then, I have an epiphany. Appearances were that we had hit a dead end involving the six-months-dead corpse in the New Mexican desert, but then again maybe not. I made another phone call.

"Cort Nelson," he answered.

"Mr. Nelson, this is Donald Youngblood, FBI. Remember me?"

"Yes, Agent Youngblood, I sure do. What can I do for you?"

I was getting tired of this Agent Youngblood stuff, but what was a guy to do?

"Do you keep a DNA file on your employees that work the Blue Dolphin?"

"Well, yes," he said. "How did you know?"

"I didn't. I was hoping you did."

"Working on an oil rig is dangerous," he said. "That's no secret. We could run into a situation where DNA is the only means to identify a body."

"I understand," I said. "Would you happen to have a DNA file on all the employees that worked on the rig at the same time as Royce Rogers?"

"Better than that. We have a DNA file on every employee that has ever worked on the Dolphin. I take it you'd like a copy of the file."

"That would be very helpful."

"I'll get with our medical staff and take care of that first thing in the morning," Cort Nelson said. "How do you want it? It'll be a big file."

"Someone from the FBI Salt Lake City office will contact you tomorrow. Thanks for doing this, Mr. Nelson."

"Always glad to help the FBI."

I hung up feeling rather proud of myself. I called Scott Glass. I told him what I had done and asked if he would have John contact Cort Nelson to arrange to get the file as fast as possible.

"That's a great idea, Blood," Scott said. "I hope we find what we're looking for."

"You and me both, Professor. Another thing. Have John share that file with Danny West. He's got the Santa Fe forensic lab working on a few of the remains."

"Sure thing, Blood," Scott said.

◆　◆　◆　◆

Before I left for the day, Agent Wallace called back.

"Mrs. Mason will be in my office at ten o'clock tomorrow morning," he said. "I told her it was in regard to Jerry Altman. I assured her it was routine, and that she was not in any trouble. I think you should be here. You're closest to the case and can do a more in-depth interview than I can."

"I'll see what I can do," I said. "If I work this out, can you have a car pick me up?"

"You bet your ass," Wallace said. "Agent Blackstone will be glad to do it."

"Sure he will. I'll text you the details."

60

The J. Gordon Shanklin Building at One Justice Way has been the home of the Dallas office of the FBI since November 2002. I sat in a fourth-floor interview room with Agent Wallace reviewing my Clown case file while waiting on Cynthia Mason.

The phone rang on a nearby desk, and Wallace got up and answered it. He looked over to me. "She's here," he said. "I'll go get her."

He was back in a minute or two with a tall, slender, ebony-haired women in her late thirties or early forties. She had blue eyes, a short haircut, and a square face that framed modest lips. After Wallace did the introductions, Cynthia Mason sat down.

"Coffee?" I asked.

"Coffee would be nice," she said. "Black."

Wallace rose and left the room without speaking.

"We are conducting an investigation in which Jerry Altman's name has come up," I said. "Since you reported him missing, we wanted to ask you a few questions. Depending on what you know, it could help our investigation."

"Investigation about what?"

"I'm not at liberty to say."

Wallace was back with coffee and set it in front of Cynthia Mason.

"Where did you meet Jerry Altman?" I said.

"At a bar in Galveston where I was bartending. I was working my way through nursing school."

"How long had you known him when you reported him missing?"

"A little over two years."

"What was your relationship?"

"We were going to be married," she said. "We lived together at my place most of the time, but he still kept an apartment."

"How long did you wait until you reported him missing?"

"A few days. I got a call from his foreman wanting to know where he was. He hadn't shown up for work that week, so I got scared and called the police. They never found a trace of him."

"Think he got cold feet and took off?" I said.

She half-smiled. "Maybe. I never thought Jerry was the marrying kind, and I was surprised when he asked. But he was fun and good looking, the sex was great, he made good money, and he liked to have a good time. I thought he wasn't a bad catch."

But you made a better catch, didn't you? I thought.

"Did you ever hear from him?"

"Never," Cynthia Mason said.

"Did he ever mention a guy by the name of Royce Rogers?"

"Not that I remember."

"Did he have a lot of money? Was he a big spender?"

She laughed at that one. "Jerry lived from paycheck to paycheck. He didn't mind spending what he had, but he wasn't rich or anything like that."

I looked at Wallace.

"Was he mixed up in anything that might have gotten him killed?" Wallace said.

She looked surprised at that question. "Not that I know of."

"So, if you had to guess," Wallace said, "why did he go missing?"

She took a few moments on that one. "If I had to guess, I would say that Jerry got tired working the rig, had second thoughts about getting married, and took off for parts unknown. I thought we were good, but I guess you don't ever know for sure."

"Think he could kill somebody?" Wallace asked.

"No, I don't. He was a schemer and sometimes a con artist, but he was not a killer."

Wallace glanced at me. I shrugged.

Cynthia looked at me and then Wallace, seemingly more relaxed. "Can I go now?"

"Thanks for coming in," I said, standing. "If you think of anything that might be helpful, give me a call." I handed her an FBI special consultant's card that David Steele had made for me. It was the first time I had used it. If Cynthia Mason was impressed, she didn't show it.

"I'll show you out," Wallace said.

◆   ◆   ◆   ◆

"She knows more than she's telling," Wallace said a few minutes later.

"How do you know?"

"She didn't volunteer much, just stuck to direct answers with a few qualifications and very little embellishment."

"She was being careful," I said. "She traded in an oil rig worker for a doctor. Maybe she killed Jerry."

"You think?" Wallace said.

"Probably not."

"I agree. If she hadn't reported him missing, he might never have been missed. He's the kind of guy who could move on and nobody noticed."

"Think she knows anything that could help us?" I said.

"Probably not."

"I don't think so either. But then again, I have a hard time telling when a woman is lying to me."

"Don't we all," Wallace said.

61

At midmorning the next day, I got a call from Danny West.

"I got the DNA file from Agent Glass that you had sent to the Salt Lake City office," he said.

"You got a hit?"

"We did. One of the skeletons was a match to Jerry Altman. Forensics dated the approximate time of death close to when he was reported missing."

"Does Scott know about this?"

"I told him a few minutes ago," Danny West said. "He said I could have the honor of telling you, since the Santa Fe lab made the match."

"Well, hell, there went my theory that Jerry might still be alive."

"Sorry about that," Danny West said. "Another thing. The local paper just ran a story about bodies in the desert. Someone tipped them off. The story did not have a lot of details, but it said the FBI had uncovered the burial ground of a possible serial killer. If Royce Rogers sees the paper or someone tells him about it, he'll know his dumping ground has been found."

I sat in silence. Royce Rogers was apparently the kind of guy who eliminated anyone who could be a source of information about his exploits and possibly his hiding places. I wondered if his sister was safe.

"Youngblood?" Danny West said.

"Sorry, just thinking. If I come back out there, can you pick me up?"

"Sure. When are you coming?"

"Later today, if I can arrange it," I said. "I'll be in touch."

◆   ◆   ◆   ◆

I did arrange it. In the late afternoon of the same day, Jim Doak again flew me to Santa Fe. Deputy Danny West picked me up at the same spot as before, leaning against the right front fender of his SUV, sunglasses on, arms folded, a blank expression on his face. Déjà vu.

"How can you see out of those things?" I said. "It's almost dark."

"Can't see a damn thing," he said. "But my girlfriend says they're cool."

I was hoping to spend only one night, but I had packed for two. I stowed my suitcase and laptop, and then we headed for the Residence Inn.

"What are you thinking?" Danny West said.

"I'm thinking that Gloria Davis, Royce's sister, might be a target if she knows where Royce is. Or she might know where he is and doesn't even realize she knows. I want to talk to her again."

62

Danny West came over the next morning, and we had breakfast in the Residence Inn dining room. The bank where Gloria Davis worked opened at eight-thirty. My plan was to let her get settled in, then show up at nine o'clock. A deputy sheriff in uniform might stir things up, although the first time I interviewed Gloria Davis I had the impression she was one cool customer who did not want to get involved in her brother's problems.

We pulled into the parking lot of the Loan Star Bank at nine sharp.

As I reached for the door handle to exit the cruiser, my cell phone rang. "Hang on a minute," I said to Danny West. "Youngblood," I said.

"I have news," Scott Glass said. "And it's, well, puzzling. And you're not going to like it."

"So tell me already."

"We identified the six-months-old body."

"How?"

"From the DNA file sent from Texas Oil."

"It was another Texas Oil employee?"

"Yes, it was."

"Who?"

"Royce Rogers."

I felt as if I had been tasered. I was having a hard time processing this information. My Clown case theory had just disintegrated. "Say that again."

"The six-months-old body we found in one of the New Mexico grave sites was Royce Rogers," Scott said slowly.

I sat there and stared straight through the cruiser's windshield into the high-plains desert and let my mind settle down. *Think*, I ordered myself. After a few moments, pieces started falling into place like the tumblers on a safe: *click, click, click.* And then I had it.

"Blood?"

"I'm here. Got to go, Professor." I looked at Danny West. "Call for backup."

"What?"

"It's her. Gloria Davis. They just identified Royce Rogers's body. It's got to be her. She's the killer." I got out of the car and headed for the bank.

Danny West followed me. "We don't need backup," he said. "We can handle it. She won't be expecting us."

I didn't want to waste time arguing. We went through the bank door into the lobby. I took a quick look around. Far in the back of the long, one-story building was a large office with a wall of glass that separated Gloria Davis from her subordinates. She sat behind a substantial desk. She looked up from what she was doing, and our eyes locked. She knew I knew. Her hand disappeared toward a desk drawer and came out with what looked like a Glock Ten. She opened fire. The glass shattered in a storm of tiny shards.

"Everybody down!" I screamed.

Danny West got off a couple of rounds and then was hit high in the chest opposite his heart. He went down, blood spreading on his khaki shirt. I stood still, took dead aim, and squeezed off a shot that should have killed her, but Gloria Davis must have moved at the exact moment the round left the chamber. She ducked behind her desk, came up, and got off three quick shots before I could again take aim. I felt a searing pain in my right side. It spun me to my right, and I went down on my right knee. Danny West was a few feet from me, and I reached out and pulled him behind a nearby counter as three more shots buzzed around us. I was bleeding as much as he was, but I knew my wound was not as serious as his. I poked my head up and fired three answering shots in the general direction of Gloria Davis.

"Call 911!" I yelled to no one in particular. "We need an ambulance and the police."

"I'll survive," Danny said through gritted teeth. "Go get the bitch."

I poked my head up in time to see Gloria Davis going through a door at the rear. I followed, my left hand around the wound in my right side, dripping blood as I went. I made it to the door and listened. I heard an engine start. I pushed through the door as a black Cadillac Escalade roared by, its tinted glass hiding the driver. It stopped by the sheriff's cruiser, and the driver shot both of the passenger-side tires. That was a fatal mistake. The Escalade raced out of the parking lot and took a left, heading west toward the high desert. I released my left side, put both hands on my Beretta, and took a second to check my sight line: clear. I tracked the vehicle from right to left, zeroed in on the driver's-side window, and led it by maybe a yard. I fired three quick shots. The window of the Escalade exploded, and then the SUV slowed, veered right, and crashed into a light pole. No movement came from inside. I had no strength left to go check the damage. I holstered my Beretta, grabbed my bleeding side, and staggered back into the bank as the ambulance and police arrived.

My memory after that was fragmented, as I went into shock, my adrenalin depleted. Chaos, police, stretchers, an ambulance ride, someone telling me I would be okay, an emergency room. I remember telling someone to call Scott Glass, Salt Lake City FBI. I remember someone saying, "You need rest. You've lost a lot of blood. I'm going to give you something to make you sleep."

I wanted to say, "Blood, that's my nickname," but it wouldn't come out. What came was a spiraling down into darkness.

63

I was out until dawn the next day, when I opened my eyes and saw Mary sitting in a chair next to my bed. This was a scene that had played before. A little voice in the back of my head said, *You have to stop doing this.*

"We have to stop meeting this way," I said in a low voice.

Mary opened her eyes and stared at me. "If I didn't love you so much, I'd beat the hell out of you," she said. "What were you thinking? Why didn't you call for backup?"

"I didn't think I was going to get into World War III," I said. The last thing I wanted to do was tell her that's what I had told Danny West to do.

"You could have been killed," Mary said. "You need to stop doing this."

Didn't I just say that?

"Are you going to stop being a cop?"

"If that's the only way to keep you alive, I will," Mary said.

This I hadn't heard before, and I knew she was scared. "Can we talk about this later?"

Mary smiled. "Sure. I'm sorry. I shouldn't have jumped on you so soon."

"You're welcome to jump me later."

Mary laughed. "Some things never change."

"Did you call Lacy?"

"Yes. She wanted to come, but I told her not to, and that you would be fine. You need to call her later."

"I will."

A shadow filled my doorway. "Mr. Youngblood, I need to have a word with you. Alone."

As he stepped into my hospital room, Mary stood. He was obviously Native American and a big man—I'd guess six-two, 250 pounds. A cop, no doubt.

"I'm staying," she said tersely.

"Ma'am—"

Mary cut him off. "I'm his wife and a police detective." She showed her badge. "If this is an interview, I want to hear it because I just got here and don't know any more than you do."

"Bobby Cloud, ma'am, Santa Fe Police, Detective Division." He handed Mary a card.

"Mary Youngblood, senior police detective, Mountain Center, Tennessee." She did not hand Bobby Cloud a card.

Bobby Cloud turned to me. "And you are Donald Youngblood, FBI special consultant?"

"Among other things," I said.

"Please tell me what transpired yesterday morning at the bank." He removed a tape recorder from his pocket. "Do you mind if I record this?"

"Yes, I mind," Mary said. "He's still groggy and might not get everything straight."

Bobby Cloud put the tape recorder back in his pocket, and I proceeded to recount in great detail the events of the last morning. He listened, taking notes.

When I finished, he looked at Mary. "Didn't sound all that groggy to me," he said.

"You never know," Mary said.

"I assume you know Gloria Davis is dead," he said.

"I figured," I said.

"Why did you think you had to kill her?"

I started to respond, but Mary beat me to it. "Because she was armed and dangerous and had just shot two officers of the law and probably murdered at least ten more people." Her words were like the *rat-a-tat-tat* of a machine gun.

Bobby Cloud flinched. The blond Wonder Woman was on the loose.

"There is a thing called reckless endangerment," he said, returning the salvo.

I saw the color rise in Mary's face. Bobby Cloud was walking into a shitstorm.

"Reckless endangerment would have been letting that bitch out in the general population," she said. "If that had happened and she had killed someone else, you'd be in here asking why he let her get away."

Mary was hot and getting hotter. I wondered if Bobby Cloud had enough sense to cut his losses. He was about to open his mouth when another figure darkened my doorway. As he was silhouetted against the light in the hall, I could not tell who it was. Then he opened his mouth, and there was no doubt.

"This interrogation is over."

"Who are you?" Bobby Cloud said.

"David Steele, deputy director of the FBI. Please leave."

I could tell Bobby Cloud was not happy to hear that directive from the former hard-ass Quantico instructor. His face hardened. "I'm leaving, but I'll be back," he said.

"Don't bother," David Steele said. "Agent Youngblood won't be here. This is an ongoing FBI serial killer investigation, and we don't need any interference from the Santa Fe Police."

Bobby Cloud mumbled something I couldn't make out, then turned and walked out of the room.

"Friendly," I said to David Steele.

He ignored the jab. "How are you feeling?"

"Not bad. The drugs are pretty good."

"I talked with your doctor. He'll release you tomorrow as long as your blood work looks good. Agent Wallace volunteered to come over from Dallas and scare away the local police."

"Mary could handle that," I said.

"I'm sure she could, but she has no authority here. I'm going back to Washington. Heal fast, Youngblood. I'll need a full report." He said goodbye to Mary, started out the door, stopped, and turned. "That was some unbelievable shooting, Youngblood. Wounded, going into shock, and you still took her down. Incredible."

He didn't wait for a reply. David Steele turned and disappeared into the hall.

◆　◆　◆　◆

After breakfast, Mary took me in a wheelchair to visit Danny West.

When she wheeled me into the room, Danny smiled and said, "Guess I should have called for backup."

"You damn well should have," Mary said.

"Yes, ma'am," he said meekly.

After that, things settled down. Mary went to get coffee, and Danny and I talked. He was looking for confirmation that he had handled himself okay, and I gave it to him. "You stood your ground, returned fire, and sent me away to finish it," I said. "Not bad for the first time drawing your weapon."

"Still, I'm sorry I didn't make that call," he said. "I could have gotten us both killed."

"She's dead, we're alive. Let it go."

"Thanks, Youngblood," Danny West said.

◆   ◆   ◆   ◆

In the afternoon, Mary intercepted a number of phone calls inquiring about my condition. The only one I took was from Big Bob.

"He's going to be okay," I heard Mary say. She pointed at the phone, and I nodded. She handed the cell phone to me.

"You okay?" he said.

"A little out of it, but they tell me I'm going to live."

"Well, nice work out there. You took a bad one off the board."

"Thanks. We'll get together soon and have breakfast. I'll tell you all about it."

"Deal," he said. "Get some rest."

◆   ◆   ◆   ◆

We watched the evening news out of Albuquerque. One of the hooks leading into the report was, "The shootout in Santa Fe."

"Catchy," Mary said.

"Yeah," I said, "if you weren't the shooter."

"Or the shootee."

A few minutes later, the serious-looking news anchor said, "Early yesterday morning, a Santa Fe deputy sheriff and a special agent for the FBI exchanged gunfire in a local bank with a suspected serial killer." A picture of the bank surrounded by crime-scene tape filled the TV screen. "The suspect, bank vice president Gloria Davis, was shot and killed while trying to escape." Gloria Davis's picture appeared. "Both the deputy and the FBI agent, whose names have not been released, were wounded in the exchange. Both are expected to fully recover. We will bring you more details as they emerge."

"Well, at least they didn't mention my name," I said.

"I wouldn't get too giddy about that," Mary said. "They'll get around to you sooner or later."

◆   ◆   ◆   ◆

Wallace came later to make sure the locals didn't try to kidnap me. He filled me in on the latest as the FBI tore Gloria Davis's life apart. Mary slipped away, promising to bring dinner when she returned.

"Gloria Davis had her bags packed," Wallace said. "Looked like she was leaving today."

"Did you check flights?"

"Nothing under her name," he said. "She probably had a phony passport, but we didn't find it."

"What else?'

"She was at the University of Texas at the same time as Royce and Glenn Evans. She had a master's in finance. Our guys found her picture. She was a brunette then."

"That fits," I said.

Wallace paused for effect. "Then she joined the army. Outstanding record, including a marksmanship award. She was a borderline sociopath, according to her psych eval."

"All that fits, too."

"You hit her twice. One in the neck, the other in the temple. The third bullet was in the front windshield post on the passenger side. Wish I could shoot like that."

I said nothing.

"Don't feel bad, Youngblood. You probably saved more lives."

We strayed away from the case and swapped stories. Fulfilling her promise, Mary smuggled in medium-rare filet mignons with fries and salads, and we had dinner in my room. I assumed Mary had scared the nurses away because we never saw one until much later.

64

The next morning, the doctor, reluctantly and with stern instructions, declared me fit to leave. I said goodbye to Danny West and Agent Wallace. Mary wheeled me to the front door. She helped me into a waiting limo, and we rolled away toward Santa Fe Municipal Airport and the sanctuary of a Fleet Industries jet. The Santa Fe Police were not waiting for me on the tarmac. I guessed they considered the case closed.

When we were in the air, I called Jimmy Durham.

"You made the news," he said. "How bad were you hit?"

"Not bad," I said. "Through and through. No vital organs were touched but it nick a rib. I'm sore, although the meds are holding back the real pain pretty good. I'm glad she wasn't using hollow points."

"Did she kill the guy we pulled from the lake?"

"We're assuming she did, so you can close the books on that one."

◆　◆　◆　◆

I spent two days convalescing at the condo and on the third day carefully made my way to T. Elbert's front porch. I was still sore. I could feel the wound and the bruised rib anytime I moved, so I moved as little as possible. Touching it and the areas around it was like touching a boil. I had quit the pain meds the day before, which made the soreness worse but my mind clearer. I moved slowly up the walkway while T. Elbert and Roy waited. They were expecting me.

"Need help?" Roy said.

"Better not," I said. "You might do more harm than good."

I managed to get myself seated. Roy handed me a cup of Dunkin' Donuts coffee. I sipped: hot. Then he handed me a sesame seed bagel with cream cheese, cut in four pieces. I wanted to say, *I should get shot more often*, but that would have sounded weird, so all I said was, "Thanks."

"How are you feeling?" T. Elbert said.

"Okay. Sore."

"Feel like telling us about what went down?" he said.

"Sure. I need to get it straight in my own mind." So I filled them in on everything that had happened since we last met. "I didn't know it was Gloria Davis until Scott called right before the shootout. Then the pieces fell into place. She was the clown all along, and she did the casino job and for some reason framed Royce for it. She planted the money and the clown costume, hoping he would get linked to the kidnappings. I should have researched her background, but I didn't suspect her. I focused on Royce from the get-go. Turns out she spent two years in the army after college and was an expert marksman. Her psych eval had her listed as borderline sociopathic. Had I read all of that early on, I might have focused on her."

"Do you think Royce ever figured it out?" T. Elbert said.

"I think he figured it out in prison. I'm sure he wondered where the clown costume came from. I'm sure he was questioned about it later, if anyone made the connection. I need to find that out."

"You need to forget it," T. Elbert said. "It's over."

I looked at Roy, who had said nothing, content to let T. Elbert extract the info. "He's right, Gumshoe," he finally said. "Let it go. Case closed. Game over."

"I think somehow Gloria Davis made contact with Ricky Carter," I continued. "Probably while he was in prison. She got close to him when he got out. She probably told Ricky she knew where the money was, and that they had to get rid of Royce. Ricky was greedy and stupid, a bad combination. So Ricky picked up Royce when he was released and set him up to be killed. I'll bet Gloria Davis killed him the same day Ricky picked him up. Then Ricky convinced Gloria to kidnap Cindy, or maybe she convinced him. He paid for that little misadventure with his life."

I drank some coffee and took a rest from storytelling.

"I have to call David Steele," I said. "The FBI is continuing to tear Gloria Davis's life apart as we speak. I'll know more once I talk to Steely Dave."

◆   ◆   ◆   ◆

Somehow, I mustered the strength to go to the office, although it seemed like it took me an hour to climb the back stairs. Gretchen and Ronda fussed over me.

"You shouldn't be in," Gretchen said.

"No, you shouldn't," Ronda said, "although both of us want to know what happened out there."

"Tomorrow," I said. "I can tell that story only once a day, and I've already told it to Roy and T. Elbert."

They seemed satisfied, so I went to my office and closed the door. I phoned David Steele and left a message for him to call when convenient, which was code for *Not urgent*. I spent the morning formulating emails to most of my financial clients. The ones who I was really close to, I would call.

In the early afternoon, I called Bentley Williams. He was on the phone. I left my name and number. He called back in five minutes.

"How are things, Bentley?"

"Things are terrific, Mr. Youngblood. Lola and I are getting married."

"What's the family have to say about that?"

"Well, I haven't been disowned yet," Bentley said. "They're trying hard not to like Lola and losing the battle. It's fun to watch. I think she cast a spell on them."

I wondered if Bentley knew Lola was a self-proclaimed white witch. *None of my business*. I said nothing.

"I have an offer, if it's something that interests you," I said. "I'm getting out of the financial consultant business, and I'd like you to take over my accounts if you want them. I can send you a list, and you can decide after you see it."

"I don't need to see a list," Bentley said. "I already know some of them, and I'd be honored to take over for you. I'm sure Mr. Shoney will be thrilled."

"I'll send you the list so you can touch base with all of them," I said. "I've laid the groundwork. They'll be expecting to hear from you. Wait a couple of days. You'll get the same deal I had. Ten percent of the profits and 5 percent of the losses."

"Sweet," Bentley said. "You send the list, and I'll get started later this week."

"Keep in touch, Bentley. Say hello to Lola for me, and let me know the wedding date."

"You'll be at the top of my list," Bentley said.

◆　◆　◆　◆

By four o'clock, I was crashing. Then my cell phone rang.

"How are you feeling?" David Steele asked.

"Not bad. A little sore. Everything considered, I was lucky."

"I understand Agent Wallace told you most of the story. We're tearing Gloria Davis's computer apart, but she had strong encryption, so it may take a while. There's evidence of a foreign account with well over a million dollars in it, but so far we don't know where or the account number."

"Well, if you figure it out, you should steal it."

"We wouldn't do a thing like that," David Steele said.

"Then let the CIA steal it."

"Let the CIA find its own windfall," he said, then abruptly changed the subject. "Listen, Don, you did great work on this."

Whenever David Steele called me Don rather than Youngblood, my antennae went up. "What do you want, Dave?"

"I want you to hear me out without jumping to a conclusion."

"Sure," I said. I knew what was coming.

"I want you as a full-time consultant. You'd be a special agent assigned to me, working some high-profile cases and maybe some secretive ones also. I know you're bored when you don't have a big case to chew on. This way, you'll always have something going without having to wait months for something to pop up. Think about it."

Actually, I had been thinking about it. But that was my little secret.

"The only way I would agree would be if Mary was part of the deal," I said.

"Does she want to be part of the deal?"

"Don't know," I said. "But I'll have to offer it to keep the peace."

"Not a problem," David Steele said. "I'd love to have both of you."

"We could work cases together?"

"Absolutely."

"And get time off when we need it?"

"Of course."

"I'll need some time to think it over and talk with Mary."

"Don't take too long," he said. "I've got something really juicy that you'd love working on."

"Of course you do," I said.

Epilogue

A few days passed and I was healing nicely, so we packed up the Armada, handed the dogs off to Billy, and drove to our Singer Island condo. The weather was perfect, and I spent time in our cabana on the beach. During that time, I made some phones calls. Warden Hal Dansk was one of them.

"Damn, Youngblood," he said. "I heard about you on the news. Who was that broad you shot?"

"Royce Rogers's sister. Royce was telling the truth all along. He was framed."

"Well, I'll be damned. His sister."

The warden thanked me for calling and then was gone, a man on the move with no time for idleness.

I called Sister Sarah Agnes and gave her a G-rated version of the Clown case. She promised to pray for me. Never hurts having a nun on your side.

I had a long conversation with Scott Glass about the case, his love life, his house, the job, and skiing. I told him skiing would have to wait until next year. I was in just good enough shape to lie on the beach.

My final call was to Danny West.

"I'm back at work," he said. "Desk duty. Still sore. Doing some physical therapy. I'll be back on the road in a few weeks. How about you?"

"Doing fine," I said. "Sorry I almost got you killed."

"I almost got myself killed," he said.

"Yeah, but I dragged you into it."

"And I'm glad you did. I can brag to the grandkids that I worked with the famous Donald Youngblood."

"I hope you find more to brag about than that," I said.

◆   ◆   ◆   ◆

We were at the Bonefish Grill just north of Singer Island discussing whether or not we wanted to become special consultants for the FBI. We had been kicking it around ever since David Steele made the offer. We had an annoying waitress who wanted to talk. Right now, she was off getting two orders of Bang Bang Shrimp and allowing us to continue our conversation.

"It does sound exciting," Mary said. "But you're not used to having a real boss."

"David Steele is okay. We understand each other. If he's too hard to work for, then we quit."

"You and I working together," Mary said. "Think we can do that without killing each other?"

"You bet," I said.

The waitress was back with the appetizers and more conversation. Mary started coughing. The waitress was undeterred. "You okay, honey?" she asked. "I think there's something going around. My sister had—"

"Actually," Mary said, "I think some bread would help."

"Sure, honey. I'll get you some bread." The waitress was off for the kitchen.

"If she doesn't stop annoying me, I'm going to embarrass the hell out of her," Mary said.

"How?"

She told me.

I laughed. "That would do it."

Luckily for our waitress, she found another table to annoy—two older couples who seemed more than willing to talk. We spent the rest of our meal in relative peace.

◆   ◆   ◆   ◆

"So what do we tell David Steele?" I said as we walked the beach at sunset.

Mary stopped and looked out at the ocean, her arm around my waist. "Right now," she said, "David Steele is the farthest thing from my mind." Then she turned and kissed me.

The End

Author's Note

On November 28, 2016, wildfires, supported by dry conditions, an inordinate amount of ground fuel and hurricane force winds, swept through Sevier County, Tennessee. The fires destroyed an estimated 2400 homes and businesses and claimed a documented 14 lives. That figure will forever be up for debate. The fires were uncontrollable, burning hotter than a crematorium. Luckily, my wife, Tessa, and I were out of town visiting friends for the Thanksgiving holidays.

Because the City of Gatlinburg was locked down, it was days before we knew if we had a house or not. As you have probably guessed from this story, the news was not good. Our home of 23 plus years was totally destroyed along with all our possessions. Unlike Donald Youngblood, we chose not to rebuild. We have relocated and are slowly recovering, furnishing a new home and getting acquainted with a new community, new friends and a new routine.

I was asked numerous times if I was going to write about the fire. I thought not. Then one of the characters in this book decided to make the fire part of the story and I had no choice. Some of the fire sequence is based on true events, first-hand accounts from people who went through it. Their stories were terrifying.

This book is late because I did not write a word for four months. It wasn't writer's block. It was a feeling of being untethered, disconnected, and uncertain about the future. Once the decision was made about where to live I was able to get back to the task at hand. One keystroke and the story awoke like a hibernating bear. I am continually surprised by how my books refuse not to be written. When I think they're going nowhere they take me by the hand and lead me in the right direction. They write themselves, basically, using my fingers to tap out the story on my laptop keyboard, allowing me at times to interject a thought here and there. I am amazed and humbled by the process.

I've started book eight. I'm anxious to see where it takes Don and the gang.

A final thought: To all those volunteers who fight the flames, give aid and comfort, food and shelter; I salute you. Your tireless service is invaluable, inspirational and lifesaving. May God bless you all.

Visit Donald Youngblood and friends @
www.donaldyoungbloodmysteries.com

Write the author @ DYBloodmysteries@aol.com

Visit **Donald Youngblood Mysteries** on Facebook

Acknowledgments

My thanks to:

Buie Hancock, master potter and owner of **Buie Pottery** who has given Donald Youngblood and friends a spotlight in the Gatlinburg community. Visit **Buie Pottery** when you are in town.

Steve Kirk, editor supreme, who litters the cutting room floor with words unnecessary for a tight, fast read. Steve, now teaching, still found time to work his magic. Six books and counting. Great job, as always, Steve!

Todd Lape, Lape Designs, for text and jacket design. Another great jacket image; intriguing and mysterious.

Ron Lawhead, web master, for attending my web site @ www.donaldyoungbloodmysteries.com

Mary Sanchez, my publicist, who continues to work tirelessly to introduce Donald Youngblood to the masses.

My wife, Tessa, proofreader extraordinaire, who catches mistakes, makes suggestions and always makes my books better.

And finally:

To all those Donald Youngblood fans who support the work and encourage me never to quit. I thank you. Without you this series would not continue.